RED
DOG

ALSO BY JASON MILLER

Down Don't Bother Me

RED DOG

A SLIM IN LITTLE EGYPT MYSTERY

JASON MILLER

HARPER

NEW YORK · LONDON · TORONTO · SYDNEY

HARPER

HarperCollins books may be purchased for educational, business, or sales promotional use. For information, please email the Special Markets Department at SPsales@harpercollins.com.

FIRST HARPER PAPERBACK EDITION PUBLISHED 2016.

Designed by Jamie Lynn Kerner

Library of Congress Cataloging-in-Publication Data has been applied for.

ISBN 978-0-06-244906-1 (pbk.)

16 17 18 19 20   RRD   10 9 8 7 6 5 4 3 2 1

This one's for Momma.

Heaven goes by favor. If it went by merit you would stay out and your dog would go in.

—MARK TWAIN

Red dog: a byproduct of coal mining, similar to coal ash; also, a dog that is red.

PART ONE
SCRATCH LINES

0.

Little Egypt. The Shawnee. A place near the Simpson Barrens. As I tear through tangled berms of yellow rocket and rape mustard and on up the hill, I can feel them on my heels. The killers. A pair of them. My heart is rattling like a jazz drum, and my mouth is full of blood. I'm not in full control of my legs, and they get out from under me. Funny how that can happen. Less funny if you fall.

I fall. I try to hug the world, but the world doesn't want my hugs. Instead, it tips me asshole over teakettle and backward I tumble, through the mosquito stabs of the pitch-pine needles and finally, painfully, into the toothy grin of a sandstone brace. I'm imagining what Anci would say when the cell purrs in my pocket.

Once. Twice. Silent.

Maybe he's given up or maybe the signal's dropped out again. I'm not sure. I'm not sure it matters. It won't be long now. They're in the rocket, in the rape mustard, shredding the flowers, coming on fast. There's blood on my hands. In my mouth. I spit gobs of it against the trunk of a pignut hickory, the deep rivulets of the bark.

It won't be long now, I think again, and in that same instant a wild-animal cry issues forth and a crash as the high grass bows *down as though in reverence or fear at their approach and through it they come in a blur.*

    The killers.

    The dogs.

    My death.

1.

It was Scrabble night at Indian Vale, and my daughter, Anci, and I had the tiles out. We had a yellow pad and a fistful of pencils to scratch down our scores. Anci's column was filled with numbers. Mine were more like imaginary numbers. We had that Ben and Jerry's ice cream with the real cookie dough in it, though, and that took away some of the sting. We also had those orange sodas Anci favors and a dictionary as big as the engine battery for an Abrams tank. We were living the high life. Anci was, anyway. She beat me three out of four matches, and it felt like she threw our last match out of pity. Afterward, she said, "Just so you know, I threw our last match out of pity," but maybe there's more than one way to interpret a comment like that.

It was a hot summer night in Little Egypt. Goddamn, it was hot. A suffocating vegetative haze hung in the air. The cricks had sucked themselves empty, and every blade of grass between our little valley and the LaRue-Pine Hills had been cooked down to fried nettles as sharp as carpenter's nails. Even the springtime migration of snakes and other slithering critters toward the Scatters, with its cool layers of spatterdock and Sputnik-clumps of buttonbush, had been poorly attended. Anci and I were at the kitchen table, sweating in sleeveless T-shirts. Two weeks earlier, the house's ancient air-conditioning unit had expired in a belch of lavender smoke, and there hadn't been money lying around to repair or replace it.

Despite our heat rashes, life of late had been relatively calm. I'd done some easy jobs, and there hadn't been any murders. No one had tried to shoot me with guns or kidnap my daughter or throw the pair of us off a bridge. It was a good stretch. Somewhere in there, a guy from Olney hired me to retrieve some stolen chickens. He loved those chickens like they were kin, and I took the job and managed to recover the birds without fuss, or anyway without much of it. Along the way, one of them pecked me on the thumb. This was one of these salmon faverolles they got in the exotic bird game, a snooty specimen with a floppy comb like a slouch hat and eyes full of contempt. He didn't like you, and he didn't mind if you knew it. I guess as chickens go he was pretty tough. Anyway, that's about as exciting as things had gotten lately.

Anci drummed her fingers on the game box.

"Wanna go again?"

"I don't know. Frankly, I'm not too happy with this losing business. One or two ain't so bad, maybe, but after a while it starts to feel like a pattern."

"Shame Peggy's not around, then," Anci said. It was, too. Peggy was back home north helping her sister sort through another car crash of a divorce. Crash number five,

I think it was. The entire family was like that, a hotbed of marital disquietude, and it was this, likely more than anything else, that explained why Peggy and I had yet to get hitched.

Anci interrupted my thoughts. "I know she gives you words, she thinks I'm not looking."

"Maybe she's just whispering sweet nothings in my ears. You ever consider that?"

"Twenty-point sweet nothings."

"Says you. Besides, isn't tonight *The Bachelor*?"

"That's Thursday. And I thought you hated it."

"I do," I said. And I did. "But anything's better than being kicked around your own kitchen by a thirteen-year-old and her fancy vocabulary."

She rolled her eyes and started setting out tiles. We were going again. We were about to start when someone knocked on our door.

Anci checked the time on her phone.

"Kinda late for company," she said.

We live in a lonely country place, my daughter and I. Lonely might be understating it some. You get more bustle in an oil painting. We got a den of foxes, though, and the occasional bobcat. In the springtime, we had kittens even, with their plumes of dappled fur and sidereal eyes. Every so often, a flock of wild turkey will pass near the house, bathing in the dirt and fallen leaves, how they do, and raising their throaty ruckus. What we don't get much are human visitors, especially during nighttime hours.

I said, "Wait here."

She never wanted to wait. She followed me to the door, and we both looked through the porthole. In the driveway was a swamp-colored Chevy with a kind of homemade yurt anchored to its flatbed with mismatched bungee cord and jute, and standing shoulder to shoulder on my front porch were two men. They wore dark wool suits of the quality you might find on deep discount at JCPenney or the Walmart, and these suits were further darkened by sweat patches on the underarms and thighs. The white shirts beneath their jackets had gone nearly transparent with perspiration, revealing dark curls of chest hair underneath, and on their feet were patent leather shoes, polished to brilliance. The older man was in the neighborhood of sixty or sixty-five. He wasn't much taller than five four and was basically a beer belly on legs. We get that a lot around here. The younger one was so skinny he could have been a skeleton in a biology classroom.

I opened the door and stepped out and closed it behind me. Anci stayed inside, but I knew she'd be near the door, so I kept my back to it to form another bit of barrier. The old man must have noticed this small caution because he grinned shyly through the fuzz on his chin and said, "Blessed be," and like a conjurer's trick produced a handkerchief to mop at his brow and jowls. "Is this not a hot night?"

"Hot as hammered hell, as my momma used to say."

"I ain't ever heard that one," he said. He passed his handkerchief to the boy, who took it and rubbed it around his face too. I worried they'd hand it to me next, and I worried over what I'd do if they did. "Mind if I use it sometime? Season such as this, man is wont to say such things."

"Feel free."

He was appreciative and nodded his head some to show it. He retrieved the sweaty hanky from his boy and replaced it in a pocket, much to my relief.

"You Slim?"

That's me. I'm Slim. The younger fella frowned. He didn't like wasting time on such things maybe. Now I got a better look at him, he showed himself to be even stranger than I first thought. He was in his late twenties, probably, but it was a rough late twenties. The years had not been kind. In fact, they'd been downright mean. His hair was thin blond, balding a little anywhere you looked, and his skin was pitted and discolored as though with small bruises. He might literally have been beat with the ugly stick. His gaze was flat and his eyes irregularly shaped, his lips stretched as though tugged from either side by fishhooks, which gave his jaw an off-center appearance, like the top part of his skull had been set down carelessly atop it. He wasn't going to be on any magazine covers.

The old man said, "I'm Sheldon Cleaves. This is my boy, A. Evan. Sorry about the hour. Wonder if we might come in for a sit. Got bidness with you. Private investigator bidness. You're in that line, ain't you?"

I was and I said so. The sign in my front yard said so, too: SLIM: REDNECK INVESTIGATIONS. "But any new cases get run past my manager," I hastened to add.

I decided they looked harmless enough. Anyway, nothing I couldn't handle. They weren't armed that I could see. Their suit jackets were too snug to disguise holster bulges, the jacket tails too long to make pistols in the back of their trousers anything close to practical. There was a soft, friendly purr in the old man's voice that put you quickly at your ease, and on a windy day you'd want to tie a string around the boy to keep him from gusting away. I waved them on and they followed me into the house, where we found Anci waiting with a book in her lap. She smiled at Sheldon and frowned at A. Evan. I bet he got those frowns all the time and anywhere he went.

"Back to your reading?" I said. "How's the story?"

Anci turned her attention from our guests and gave it back to her book.

"It's okay," she said, closing it with a thump. "Though I confess I find Holmes's style mildly frustrating. He spends half his time showing off his . . . what was that word again?"

There was a vocabulary list on the end table, and I picked it up and looked at it. The list was a corker, full of archaic and weird vocabulary the teacher thought her advanced class might enjoy. I read aloud, "*Ratiocination.*"

"That's the one. I can't keep it in my brain, some reason. Maybe I'm not the Scrabble champ I pretend to be. Anyway, Holmes spends half his time showing off that whatdoyoucallit and the other half fiddling around while the dead people pile up. Ask me, he ought to turn Watson and his pistol loose more often, get some quicker results."

"Well, that is one way of looking at it," I said. "But I don't suggest you write that down comes time to do your paper."

The schools all had summer reading programs now, and

the one Anci was in was a survey of classic mystery stories: Poe, Doyle, Sayers, and Collins. Much to her dismay, there wasn't any Crumley, Box, or Barr, her favorites. She went so far as to give her teacher a paperback copy of *Bordersnakes*, trying to grease the skids a little I guess, result of which I ended up in the district office getting a talking-to from a school counselor.

Sheldon was suddenly interested. He and A. Evan had squeezed themselves together, again shoulder-to-shoulder, on the love seat, but he was looking at Anci.

"Which Holmes is it?" he asked.

"*The Hound of the Baskervilles*."

"That's a good one."

I said, "I liked it."

A. Evan said, "I ain't much of a reader."

Anci ignored us. "That's not bad enough, the world's brilliantest detective sends his assistant into a ruckus—and with a haunted dog, no less—and doesn't even bother to tell him what the caper is. It's unethical."

"Are you reviewing the story or Holmes's professional conduct?" I said.

"Heck, what's the difference? Look at it like this: I wager if you were in the market for a consulting detective, and he told you he was going to solve the crime from his easy chair, you'd fire him on the spot, no matter how many fancy brain tricks he pulled out of his pipe."

"I guess so," I said, "but I'm not sure that books always have to be entirely realistic.

"I know that, man," Anci said. "I've read the stories

about the boy wizards and the virgin vampires, and I didn't come crying to you about them. But this is different. This is mystery solving, and it ought to have a higher standard."

Sheldon cleared his throat a little in a polite way.

"Speaking of which."

"Sorry about that," I said. "We do carry on sometimes. You should have seen us during *Murder on the Orient Express*. We fought like geese."

"Poirot should have hanged them all," Anci said, still fit to be tied over it.

"Like to see about hiring you on for some work," Sheldon went on, determinedly, because that was the only way it was going to happen. "A man in your line ever search for any missing persons?"

Before I could reply with anything, Anci said, "Depends. Who's missing?"

"Family. Shelby Ann Cleaves. She's . . . She's our little one."

"Oh, my. I'm so sorry. How little?" I said.

Sheldon paused to swap fretful faces with A. Evan. Some faces are new to fret and some reveal a lifetime of it, and these faces did the latter. A lifetime of fret and then some.

Sheldon said, "Two."

A. Evan added, "Two and a quarter."

I paused. Something like that is always a sock in the eye. I remembered what'd happened a year or so ago with my own daughter and I shivered as I always did and always would. It's a nightmare wrapped in your darkest fears of helplessness and thrown off a cliff. Then they dynamite the cliff. I looked around in my mind for words. Finally, I said, "Sir, I hate to hear it. Truly I do. But missing children, that's really a job for the police."

Anci said, "How long?"

"Couple weeks. The pear blossoms were just coming on pretty. White and pink how they do. So mid-May or thereabouts."

I said, "I'm sorry to say this, but a couple weeks is a long time."

Anci said, "What have the cops done about it?"

Sheldon had given up on me and was now talking directly to Anci.

"What if I told you they weren't interested in our troubles?"

"What if I told you I wasn't surprised?"

I was surprised, but I didn't have a chance to say so. A. Evan reached something across to Anci. A smartphone open to its photo app.

"Forward only, please," he warned, and winked. "Some sights a little one just ain't fit to see."

Anci scowled at him, but she swiped the screen forward. I had to look over her shoulder. She had taken over the agency and was now fully in charge. She'd probably want to put her name on my sign. Maybe even take my name off.

Anci flipped through the photos. She handed the phone back to A. Evan. She looked at me. I looked at her. We both looked at the Cleaveses.

I said, "Why, Mr. and Mr. Cleaves, that is a dog."

Sheldon said, "Yes, sir. A dog. More specifically, our

dog. Purebred pit and likely the sweetest thing you will ever meet."

"But . . . a missing pet . . . I'm not sure I'd be worth your money, sir."

This was truer than I realized. A. Evan wasn't done handing things. He dug around in his pockets some. I didn't want anything that had been in his pockets, but he was determined. He brought out a fistful of something and tossed it to Anci. Maybe seventy bucks. Maybe not even. Anyway, not enough to fix the air conditioner unless the only problem was that it was unplugged.

"Sixty-five," Sheldon said, settling the question. "We got a piece out Union City way. A thousand acres or so. Grain sorghum plus soybeans and a patch set aside for truck farming. Town people like that these days, getting their vegetables that way, but times have been kinda lean of late, and this season unforgiving."

"I really don't know what I'd do," I said. "Have you posted flyers? Reward sometimes does the trick."

"Did. Paper flyers and reward cash both. Nothing useful come of it."

I said, "She could be anywhere."

"No, sir. Man claims to know her whereabouts. Man on the phone, I mean."

It was starting to make sense.

"Did this man mention his name?"

Sheldon shook his head. "Refused to."

Anci tossed back the money.

"He doesn't have the dog," said Anci and me both.

"But he described her. Described the hurt on her leg."

I said, "No. He got you to mention it somehow and used a trick to make you think he'd come up with it himself as proof."

Anci said, "It's a swindle, sir."

"That it is," I said. "Someone spots your ad, knows you're desperate. I know it's tough to swallow, but there's always someone out there willing to take advantage of folks in a pickle. And this one's a rural classic. This particular someone phones to say he's seen your dog and knows where she is, but there's a hitch. This kind of deal, there's always a hitch. Let me guess, he doesn't have Shelby Ann personally, right? I mean, he doesn't have her in his possession, but he knows who does?"

They nodded.

"It's his boss? Or his wife's boss? Anyway, I'm guessing work's involved somehow. He needs to remain anonymous, and the situation is real delicate and has to be handled carefully. And by carefully, I mean with money."

Sheldon's cheeks reddened.

"Has he asked you to Western Union him anything? He probably called it a finder's fee or some such."

"That he did, and that we did," Sheldon admitted. "Said he'd require a thousand dollars. Times are lean, though. We could only swing five hundred, and even that was a stretch."

"He doesn't have the dog," I said again, but couldn't help thinking of the measly sixty-five they'd offered me. I put that in my Happy Box. "This is a scam gets run out here sometimes. I'm sorry to be the one to tell you."

A. Evan said, "We know him."

"Know who?"

Sheldon said, "Man who's supposed to have her. Fella on the phone slipped up a little one time and said his name. Reach. Dennis Reach. He runs a little place out our way. Roadhouse name of Classic Country."

"That might have been a trick, too," I said, uncertainly. "Let me ask you, how do you know this Reach?"

Sheldon said, "Like I say, club's not too far from our place. We might have wandered in there once or twice with a thirst. Reach likes to tend bar, time to time, and he's known to spin a tale."

"Any idea why he might be wrapped up in something as low-down as dognapping?"

Sheldon shrugged. "Club's full most nights, so it's not likely he needs any kind of ransom."

"Would you say he's an enemy?" I said, because that seemed most obvious.

"I wouldn't say I know him well enough to call him that, but I'm pretty sure that if I did I would."

"Have you asked him?"

"No, sir." Sheldon again. "I do that, I'm liable to shoot the rascal. We was kinda hoping you'd do it for us. Ask him, I mean. Not shoot him."

I nodded and looked at Anci again. I said, "You're sure this one passes muster?"

"Sounds harmless enough," she said. "But are we really taking dogs for clients now?"

"What can I say? Times are *rough*."

She said, "Someone really ought to keep you away from jokes."

"We'll do it," I said to Sheldon. "Anyway, I'll run out there. See what there is to see."

"Well, I figured you would. But thank you."

"Figured how?"

"You know a feller name of Lew Mandamus?"

"Sure, I know Lew," I said.

"He's the one aimed us at you. Said you have a soft spot for critters."

"I'll have to find some way to thank him."

"Don't know what to say," Sheldon said. "We was . . . we was desperate."

He wiped at something in his eye with a finger. A. Evan farted. I scratched down the names and numbers. Reach's address was near the Classic Country Showroom, a residence behind the bar. We shook hands all around. A. Evan's was like a refrigerated chicken's foot. His fingers were long and bony, the skin cold and slightly moist, despite the temperature both outside and in. I wiped my palm on my pants and thought I was being sly about it, but the skinny little shit noticed and smiled meanly at me and winked again. Then he followed his old man out of the house to the Chevy flatbed and in another moment they'd vanished down the dark throat of Shake-a-Rag Road.

I said, "Well, that is something you don't see every day."

"Or smell," Anci said. "Did you get a whiff of A. Evan? It's like he bathes in hog guts."

"It's called *personal* hygiene for a reason. And what was

with you back there? You might have got us involved in a missing-kid case. I'd rather chew barbwire."

"I would, too," she said. "But I could tell by looking at them it wasn't a kid. You look at folks, you get a sense of them. I confess I didn't think of a dog, though. My money was on 'car.'"

"A car? Named Shelby Ann?"

"Could be. Some people name their cars. And stop being so damn sensitive all the time."

"And for sixty-five dollars, too."

Anci rolled her eyes. "Oh, I *know*. Usually, you get kicked in the head for free. Why not try it for money this time? Besides, this is your chance to do a good deed, pile up some karma."

"You can't eat karma, darlin'."

"No, but it can eat you."

2.

IT WAS EARLY THE FOLLOWING AFTERNOON THAT WE SET OUT to solve the case of the missing puppy. Anci said she'd come up with a snappier title later on, record everything that happened in her notebook. I said that was fine. She also said if she was going to play Watson to my Holmes maybe she should have a pistol, like how the good doctor does. I told her to focus instead on her notebook and detective work. Guns were for the adult people, I explained, responsible folks with calm nerves and sound judgment. The two of us shared a laugh over that one.

The Cleaves had mentioned Lew Mandamus as their original contact, so that seemed a good enough place to start this business. Plus, I needed Lew's help, I was going to do this thing correctly and with at least a wink at personal safety. After lunch, we snugged into our helmets, climbed on my motorcycle, and rode out of Little Egypt into northern Kentucky, a trip of an hour and a half or thereabouts. The Mandamus residence was south and west of Tolu township, past the bright ripples of Bennett Lake and some long stretches of browning pastureland. This was a good size cut, alluvial tillage inherited from Lew's father, a one-time Pinkerton's agent who'd come to the area on a job and decided to stay but then basically needed two thousand acres of buffer between himself and the heads he'd busted during his days as strikebreaker. The property edged its way along the bend of the Ohio River, girded farther south by dense woodland spreading up gentle slopes and to the north by more floodplain and some marshland sucked dry by the heat. When Lew had come back to this place following a long stretch in Korea, he'd buried his father and the memories of his wickedness and with his new wife settled the land, which he named Shinshi. A mythical place of spirits.

Anyway, we pulled up the dirt car path and stopped. The electric fence and gate were new, taller than the previous model and glinting molten silver under the hard sunlight, but my old combination code still worked and I buzzed us in.

I switched off the Triumph and put down the stand, and Anci and I pulled off our sweaty helmets and walked the few hundred yards up to the old farmhouse. You had to walk, otherwise it was like navigating an obstacle course. Shinshi was full of spirits, and the spirits did their best to be underfoot. There were cats and dogs and geese. There were some yardbirds and some raccoons. Anci calls them maskies. Around back, there was a big pond and a herd of ducks lounging around a fingering stream nearly choked with canary grass. Lew owned the pond on paper, but the ducks owned it in fact. Everywhere you looked there were critters, because that's what Shinshi was: a rural preserve and recovery center for wayward, injured, and unwanted animals.

Anci and I went up to the white farmhouse and knocked but nobody answered so we walked around a little more until we found Eun Hee on all fours in a tangled vegetable patch. She was plucking at a clump of Jimsonweed and muttering swears when the thorns got her even through her heavy work gloves. When she saw us, she sat back on her shins and smiled and said, "Well, I'll be. He's alive."

Eun Hee was in her mid-sixties, a pretty woman with deep brown eyes and eyebrows shot through with white threads like spun silk. Probably her hair would have been white too, but chemo had taken it, and so now she wore a dew rag to protect her smooth scalp from sunburn. She said, "We were starting to think the wolves had got you, Slim."

"Not yet, anyway," I said. She stood up off her knees and we shared hugs all around. "And I thought it was supposed to be the Indians."

She chuckled.

"Political circumstances required us to find a more sensitive replacement."

"Except now you're on the wolves' case."

"Life's just full of trouble, isn't it?"

"For example, I see that you've got some new security."

Eun Hee nodded. "Sadly, we had no choice. Had some break-ins a couple weeks back. Up at the sheds, I mean. At first we thought it was bored kids doing what they do, but . . ."

"But?"

"Well, I don't know really. Just a feeling, I guess. An itch. Maybe bored kids but maybe something else. Anyway, Lew decided it was time to tighten things up some."

"Any idea what were they after? Whoever they were?"

"Not the animals, anyway. You can get those anywhere. But there's some equipment back there, and some copper wiring from that outbuilding we pulled down last spring. It's not much, but you know how it is nowadays. You leave a basketball sitting out, there'll be someone along forthwith to steal the air." She pulled off her gloves and rubbed a hand through Anci's hair and said, "You're growing fast, angel."

"It's a project."

Eun Hee looked at me.

"I don't guess this has escaped your notice, but she'll be dating soon."

"Heaven protect the suitors."

"From her or from you?"

"No comment. Lew around?"

"Number six," she said, "with an abuse case," and pointed a frown in the direction of one of a small clusters of shelters, a pole barn up a brushy path a few hundred yards on.

"Bad?"

"You could say bad. You could say terrible. You could also say just another day at the ranch. All three are correct."

"I honestly don't see how you do it."

"Sometimes I don't, either." She shook her head a little about it, the world and its people and their ways. "We made a decision a long time ago about the kind of life we wanted to lead and I'm proud we stuck it out, but I admit there are days it don't exactly put whipped cream on my apple pie, you'll pardon the expression."

I pardoned the expression. I like apple pie just fine. Whipped cream, too. I said, "You think Lew will mind I go up and see him?"

"Not at all, Slim." She wrapped Anci in her arms from behind and kissed the top of her hair and said, "But this young one stays here with me."

I nodded. I pounded fists with Anci and left them and walked up the way. The path turned east slightly and then up a grade toward a long line of black elm and yellow poplar that in the summer scorcher had gone as still as bas relief. A duck waddled across my path and gave me a snotty look, but thankfully that was as ugly as things got. Honest to God, I don't know what it is. Me and birds. The duck kept walking, and I kept walking. I went to the big shed and slid open the door and stepped inside.

The floor was thick with fresh straw and the air heavy with its smell. The walls were fitted with shelves atop jig-sawed brackets and lined with metal boxes of various sizes. It was quiet in there, as quiet as a chapel, but for the sound of many small breaths. And there in the dim light was Lew Mandamus. He stooped over one of the boxes, a silver carrier with the name *Maggie* written in black felt on a strip of masking tape.

"Pose for your portrait, Slim," he said, finger to his lips.

I froze. Lew returned his attention to the cage. The little metal door was open, and there was a cat inside. Maggie, I guess. Lew had something between his bare fingers. A piece of meat, something like that. The cat had retreated to the back of the box.

At first, she wouldn't move. Or couldn't. I couldn't tell which. Lew was talking softly, and the critter was twitching her nose and hissing a little. Growling some in her throat. She tried to get up, but something had been done to her back legs. Lew's hand inched farther into the box, and the cat growled some more and then came forward just enough to take the treat from Lew's fingers, and Lew said something gentle to her and closed and latched the box.

He turned to me and smiled an unhappy smile that reminded me a little of Eun Hee's frown and said, "We can chat outside, son."

We went out and Lew shut and bolted the door behind us and lit a smoke.

I said, "Rough day?"

Lew Mandamus was maybe seventy. He was wiry and tall with long arms and a long face and probably the same close-cropped hair he'd worn during his days in army intelligence. For twenty-five years, he'd run the Ballard County Animal Cruelty Task Force, which meager state funding relegated to little more than a couple of desks and a box of paperclips. Everything that happened at Shinshi was freelance.

"I've had better. Good to see you, Slim. We'd started to think the Indians had got you."

"Eun Hee says wolves."

"She's got a dose of that political correctness maybe."

"What's the story on the deli in there?"

"Would you believe it's taken me a month to get her to do that? To show that kind of trust? I can't use gloves with her. Gloves scare her. The first few times she dang near took off a finger."

"Tough life," I said.

"Believe it or not, she's a house cat. Never been wild. Family owned her relocated out west somewhere, but their boy goes to school in the area. One reason or another, they gave the cat to him. Not sure why. Doesn't matter. What matters is that cats don't like being moved, even across town to a new house. This cat wanted to show her disapproval of the new situation so she pissed on the kid's bed."

"He beat her."

"That he did. Badly. Then he poured gasoline on her and set her on fire."

I said, "Say, where is this young fella now?"

Lew cocked one of his bushy eyebrows.

". . . Why?"

"Well, because I'm going to kick his ass until he begs me to stop. Then, when I'm tired of kicking or my leg falls off, I'm going to pay someone to kick it for me. Big fella probably. Somebody with a leg like a redwood."

"Can't help you. Much as I'd like to."

"Somebody like that, probably end up hurting a person."

"Not fully outside the realm," Lew said. "Try telling that to the poll-sniffers in our state legislature, though. Way the law is written, the kid basically got let go with a small fine and a pat on the fanny."

"That sucks."

"It throws sucks off a barstool and steps on its neck, but that's what it is. At least for now. What brings you this way, Slim? You dropping off?"

"Actually, I wanted to talk to you about the Cleaveses."

"The who?"

"Sheldon and A. Evan Cleaves. They paid me a visit last night, said you'd given them my name."

Lew sighed.

"Oh, Christ. Those two. They come to you dressed like a father and son mortician team?"

"So you do know them? I almost thought they'd made it up."

"I know them. But not well. You might say no one knows 'em well. I met them through the agency a ways back. They ask you to locate their missing animal?"

"Yep."

"Something to do with a fella name of Dennis Reach?"

"Yep."

He said, "He doesn't have the dog."

"Nope."

"It's a swindle gets run out here sometimes. Country places."

"I know."

"How much you into them for?"

"Think of a number. It's less than that," I said.

He thought about it a moment, sucking his long front teeth, then nodded.

"You want to borrow one of the trucks?"

"I was hoping you'd offer."

"I'll get the key," he said. "But it'll cost you."

"Name it."

"A few hours with your little girl. It'll make my Eun Hee happy."

I said, "She was kind of wanting to tag along, but I bet she'll go for it."

"Good. She's a good girl."

"Yes, she is."

"Another thing."

"Name that, too."

"The dog, you'll bring her to me first?"

"He doesn't have the dog."

"I know," Lew said. "They never have the dog. It's what the whole deal is about. If he does have her, though."

"For a checkup?"

"Something like that. You can count on her not being fixed or vaccinated. That wouldn't exactly be the Cleaveses' style. The last thing we need is a surplus of stray pits roaming our neighborhoods. We had a boy attacked up here not long ago, in Tolu. Thing tore through him like a buzz saw. Kid lost an arm."

"I'll see what I can do," I said.

"I'll owe you one," he said, and then the two of us walked together back down the property.

The day got hotter. I don't know how it managed it, but it did. We were having that global warming, probably. Someday—and someday soon—the earth would bake for good, the waterways empty, the glaciers collapse beneath the weight of our error. I reflected on that sometimes, as I reflected on the part I'd played in it all during my time as a coal miner and more generally as a person who liked cheap electricity. I guess you could say I was ashamed. I liked to think others would be ashamed, too—those fools in government and public life who denied anything was amiss—but cash money beat shame every time, and by a span, too.

I stopped thinking about the end of the world and followed Lew into a detached four-bay garage, whereupon we laid eyes on part of the problem: a pair of oversized Dodge gas-guzzlers. There were dog crates welded in their beds, though both were basically big enough to transport circus elephants. I refrained from comment. My own truck wasn't exactly a Matchbox car. Forgive us, America. We rural folk have stupidly large vehicles in our blood.

"I ain't seen that black one before," I said.

Lew nodded.

"I've reached that age when the people in your life start dying off, leave you things. Money."

For a moment, both of us were thinking about the woman in the farmhouse up the hill. Neither of us looked at each other. Then Lew shrugged. He took a key ring off a pegboard on the wall and gave it to me. He unlatched a container crate in the corner and scrounged up some equipment: a pair of heavy leather gloves and a telescoping metal rod fixed with a retractable noose.

"One more thing," he said. "I've got some pretty good tranquilizers in my kit. You want them?"

"No, thanks. I'm plenty relaxed."

"Ever been dog-bit, son? I mean, really bit? Pit's bite tops out in the neighborhood of two hundred thirty-eight PSI. How much you weigh?"

"You know what, I think I'll take those tranqs."

After a while, I had my kit together, and Lew and I went back to the house, where I found Anci sitting on an air-conditioning vent with a zoology book propped on her bare knees.

She said, "Eun Hee wants me to stay and visit."

"Lew does, too."

"There's a fox out here, man. An actual fox."

"We got foxes at home."

"Those are stand-off foxes, though. Snooty foxes. This one, you can pet."

Eun Hee came into the room with a tray of sandwiches and cookies and a couple of those bottled orange sodas that seem to follow Anci around. I don't know how she does it. It's like she phones ahead.

Eun Hee said, "He was caught in a trap. Someone found him and freed him and called the county. The county called Lew."

I turned to Anci.

"I thought you were going to keep me from getting eaten by a dog."

"That was before I knew there were foxes involved."

That was fair enough and I said so. Secretly, I was happy she'd decided to stay on her own and save us the argument. I hung around long enough to eat a sandwich and a couple of cookies. I even saw the fox, which wasn't much more than a kit, in a pen behind the house.

"I already named him Dave," Anci said. "So don't bother."

"Dave's a fine name for a fox," I said.

"Agree in full."

I kissed my daughter. I said good-bye to Lew and Eun Hee and Dave, and pretty soon I was on the bridge back into Illinois.

EAST ALONG 146 IS THE IRON FURNACE AND JUST PAST THAT is Union City, not far from where I figured the Cleaveses' little farmstead was situated. It's mostly fields of soy or corn out that way, and a coal mine or two, though these days the coal works are as often as not abandoned. By the time I arrived at Loves Corner and the Classic Country Show-room, it was nearly seven o'clock—still daylight, but now with dusk's purple threads showing themselves above the low foothills somewhere far away to the west.

It was Sunday, and the place was closed. I parked in the dirt lot and climbed down from Lew's truck. I folded the leather gloves and tranqs into my back pocket and retrieved the rod and noose from the bed of the truck and walked up. Some grackle birds burst from the high grass at the edge of the lot and squawked at me a little before fluttering off into purpling sky. I told them where they could put their squawks. I was on important business and had sixty-five honest dollars to earn. I walked up to the club to pick a lock.

They were good ones, Reach's locks—commercial

Grade 2 with the cylindrical levers that made them a pain in the ass to crack. When I finally popped the door I found the inside of the club empty and quiet. There wasn't anything more threatening to the Classic Country than one of those fancy El Toro mechanical bulls looming in a corner and an elevated dance platform I managed to trip over in the dark. I searched the rest of the place. There were tables and stools and a small stage with spotlights for the band and lots of TV screens for sports-watching and such. There didn't seem to be a dog anywhere. The floors smelled of cleaner, and the bathrooms were fully stocked and their counters slick, so I figured I'd missed the janitor by no more than a half hour. In the back was a fry kitchen and a walk-in cooler for beers and burger patties and that sort of thing. If Reach kept a business office somewhere, it wasn't on-site.

Well, then, I thought, maybe it was in his house, which was up a path a ways behind the club. This was one of these underground builds that were a fad for a few seconds in the energy-anxious days of the mid-seventies, and in the failing light I almost missed it: a bit of window and siding squeezing itself from under a grass-covered hummock as though the landscape was devouring it, but slowly, because it almost couldn't bear the taste. There was some tall grass and the crook of a solitary oak. There was a bit of boardwalk, too, a DIY project that'd never been finished or sealed and now buckled under the weight of neglect. A beat-up red Trans Am hunkered nearby on bent rims. There was a lamp in the front window, and the lamp was on so I went up. If Reach really was holding Shelby Ann

Cleaves hostage, I'd do the noble thing, punch him in the brain and take her back. And if he wasn't, I figured we'd share a laugh over it all. Shake hands. Part buddies. In my heart, I'm an optimist.

I knocked on the door but no one answered. I turned the knob and found it unlocked and pushed my way inside. I called Reach's name—quietlike, so not to startle him—but no one answered. One of those giant high-def TVs was on and turned up loud with some sports program. Despite the time of day, there were breakfast smells issuing from the next room over, and a ruckus, another noisy TV set, maybe, or a radio, so I made my way in that direction through the sparsely furnished space and past a large fireplace that took up nearly an entire wall. Beside the fireplace was a tool rack and in the tool rack with the poker and brush and pan was a machete. Thing like that catches the eye. I'd paused a moment out of curiosity to pick it up and look at it when suddenly a bullet tore the air just above my left shoulder.

The bullet had come from a gun, and the gun was in the hand of a man standing in what I took to be the doorway to the kitchen. Dennis Reach, by the Cleaveses' description. He was maybe six two, and he had dark curly hair and a chest you'd have trouble squeezing into a rain barrel. His face was wide and red-cheeked and full of murder, and he was wearing one of those short-short bathrobes from which his butt hung like a hairy bell and that otherwise left tragically little to the imagination. He was holding a nickel-plated pistol. .45 auto, I guess it was. He showed me his gun barrel again.

I decided against getting shot. I came in low and crossed the short distance between us as the gun fired, once more missing high. Way he was holding his piece, he was always going to miss high. Unless you were a giraffe, you were probably pretty safe around him. I raised up hard and hit Reach in the chin with an uppercut and followed it with an elbow strike to the face. He took two steps back and dropped the pistol, but he was faster than he looked, and he leapt forward suddenly with a lunge-kick that sent me flying backward onto a coffee table. I came to my senses and rolled to the floor before he stomped me in half like a communion wafer. The table wasn't so lucky.

He said, "Why, you little pecker. That was my table. Tables are expensive. Now I'm really going to kick your ass." He bent down and picked up the .45 and aimed it at me, more carefully this time, and said, "Good night, asshole."

The gun fired a third time, but I was already moving. Moving like a wild dog. I went down below his knees and I could feel the hot kiss of his gunshot above my shoulder blades. Not especially high this time, but higher than me. I picked up the fireplace machete from where it'd fallen on the carpet and brought it up smoothly and swiftly in an arc between us.

Well, I meant to hit the gun mostly but my aim was just slightly off and then so was Dennis Reach's left thumb. Part of it, anyway. The top part. It flew across the room and hit the screen of the big TV, where it left a red blot before dropping to the floor with a thud. We both stood there a moment, blinking at it. Then Reach looked at me. I looked at Reach. I punched Reach in the brain, and he pitched backward onto a nearby armchair and held the remainder of his hand like he meant to keep that from flying away, too.

"Sweet fancy Moses," he said. "You chopped off my thumb."

"Didn't mean to," I said. I picked up the Colt and stuffed it in my jeans. I went and found the thumb and picked that up, too, but I didn't put it in my jeans. The machete was as sharp as it looked. The digit was cut in a neat line above the joint. I didn't look at it long enough to paint a picture. I said, "You're Dennis Reach, I guess?"

"That's me. Little less of me than before, but me."

"Okay, Mr. Reach, let's turn off your breakfast before it burns."

"Burns more, you mean."

"Have it your way."

In the kitchen, I opened the freezer and dropped the thumb into a box of ice cubes. I moved a pan of steak and eggs off the stovetop and put a lid on it to trap in some of the smoke. I tossed some blackened toast into the sink. Reach grunted as though to say he'd been right about breakfast. He wrapped his hurt in a dish towel. There was a bottle of Dickel on the counter. I looked a question at him and he nodded so I poured him a shot.

He said, "You cut off my thumb. You might as well drink my whiskey, too."

"I'll pass. How's the hand?"

"You'd think it'd hurt, losing a finger, but it don't hardly at all."

"It will," I said. "You're all adrenaline now, but that'll wear off pretty soon."

"I guess," he said. "What do you want? You already got my thumb, and I don't keep anything valuable around here to speak of."

"You might have asked me before, instead of trying to turn me into a sprinkler."

"You surprised me," he said. "Standing in my living room like that."

"I'd heard tell about that robe of yours. Wanted to ask where you bought it."

"Plus, you were holding my machete. Or did you bring your own?"

"It was yours."

"You were holding my machete, and I thought you meant to do me harm."

I nodded. It all made sense.

I said, "Fortunately, you just happened to be cooking breakfast at seven o'clock at night with a forty-five auto close at hand. Like regular, churchgoing folk will."

"I work funny hours. Live in a funny world."

"Kinda gives new meaning to the idea of getting shells in your eggs, though, don't it?"

He shook that off. He didn't want jokes.

I was curious about something, so I asked, "Why do you keep a machete in here? Near the fireplace?"

"Snakes in the woodpile," he replied. "I use it on them sometimes. Should have been worried about snakes in my living room. Buddy, what do you want with me?"

I took out my phone and showed Reach the picture of Shelby Ann that A. Evan had texted me. She was sitting in some tufts of high grass and smiling up at the camera with her tongue lolling from her mouth and the sun on her red fur.

Reach took a long time to answer. He opened his mouth and closed it. He licked his lips and cleared his throat. Then cleared it again. Finally, he said, "You wanted me to get you a puppy, all you had to do was ask."

"You're fun, Reach. I like you." I dragged over a stool and took a load off. I was trying to put on casual airs, but my casual airs were running through the town square screaming, "*Someone actually has the goddamn dog!*" I tell you, I couldn't believe it, but there it was, and I felt like I'd won some kind of crime fighter's lottery. I said, "By the way, the sooner you get to the hospital, the sooner you can get that digit sewed back on."

"Don't know anything about it. You, the dog, none of it."

"How much time you figure before you lose it for good? An hour? Hour and a half?" Really, he had more like fifteen or sixteen hours—fingers are tougher than you think—but I counted on him not knowing that.

He said, "I'm sure it'll be fine. In fact, I'm confident about it. I got that Obamacare now. I think they do thumbs."

"But what if they don't? Think about it for a minute, will you? You've spent your entire life as a two-thumbs-up-his-ass kind of guy. How are you going to get along with just the one?"

"What was it you said you wanted again?"

I threw up my hands. "Jesus, Mary, and Jolene. There's no stubborn like country stubborn."

"Wish I could help you. Really I do."

"Buddy, your partner gave up your name," I said. "Slipped and gave you up on the phone. That's the help for you these days."

That got through. Reach shook his head and looked at the nub of his thumb through the folds of the bloody towel and muttered, "He really did that?"

"How do you think I found you? Drew your name out of a bedpan?"

"Wesley, you dumb bastard."

"Where is she?"

He looked at me sharply, face begging for sympathy. "They owe me money, you know? Really they do."

"They owe me money, too. Also, really. Where's the dog?"

"First Carol Ray fucks me over and now this," he said. "We were doing this the fair way, you'd have to get in line behind her."

I looked at my watch and sighed like high school theater.

"Oh, to hell with it then," he said, and gave it up, the information I wanted. The address wasn't more than a few miles up the road. Reach liked his dognapping convenient. The addressee, according to Reach, was a Classic Country bar-back, name of Wesley Tremble.

"Dangerous?" I said.

"As a Jell-O mold."

I thanked him, and I meant it. I was grateful. I told him

to stand up, and he did so without fuss. I led him to the sink and made him sit. I wrapped his injured hand in the towel and tied it off. Not too tight but tight enough it would staunch the bleeding and not slip off. Then I handcuffed him by his good hand to the pipe under the faucet.

He said, "You can't leave me here like this. Bleeding. Missing a finger. It ain't humane."

"Said the dognapper."

He shook his head. "You're fixated on that. Dwelling on it. Put it aside for a moment. I got to get to an ER."

"You will. I'm even going to drive you. But first I need you to wait here for me." Moments like this one you reflect on later, question, regret even. If I were a praying person, maybe I'd do that. Ask forgiveness. Or mercy. But I didn't do any of it—pray, question, or regret—at the time. At the time, I wanted to get to Tremble and the dog as quickly as possible. Taking Reach with me was out of the question, and leaving him able to access a phone was even more so. It turns out I was making a mistake, a tire fire of a mistake, but I didn't know it yet. I said, "You want one for the road?"

He did. I served him a generous pour, four fingers, which seemed appropriate, given the circumstances. I still had his gun in my waistband. I didn't want his gun, and I didn't want him having it. I had my own gun, and—to be honest—I don't like the wicked things, anyway. More guns meant more trouble, so it was always best to keep their numbers to a minimum, if possible. I walked to the back door and opened it and tossed the Colt as hard as I could over my head, onto the grassy overburden that served as the house's roof.

"I'll be back in twenty," I said.

"Ten's better."

"Fifteen, then," I said. "Life is a series of compromises."

"This is like one albino telling another albino he's got a pale dick."

And that's where I left him at 7:30 P.M. on a quiet Sunday evening at Loves Corner. When I set off to find Wesley Tremble, the one-thumbed, dog-thieving owner of the Classic Country Showroom was slumped against the cabinets in his porno robe like an old drunk left out in the sun to blister and rot. But I'll be danged if he looked like any country music song I'd ever heard.

More like a dirge.

3.

ON MY WAY TO CONFRONT THE TREACHEROUS BAR-BACK, I phoned Anci to tell her a little of what had happened. I smooth-talked past that business about Reach's thumb, on account of not wanting to give her nightmares, and I didn't tell her about his robe for the same reason. A father has to think of such things. She was just as surprised as me about the dog, though.

"I already had it written down in my notebook as a hustle," she said. "Guess I got ahead of myself."

"I guess we both did."

"So why'd he take the dog?" she said. "It don't make no sense. Even if the Cleaveses really do owe him a debt. There are better ways to get your money back, some of them even legal."

"I don't know," I said. "People don't always think things through as much as you might imagine. So maybe it's that. General foolishness. I can ask him more about it later, comes to running him to the hospital."

"Do that. Meantime, I got editing to do."

I left her to her editing. I drove back west on 146 and

then south a few miles before I found the address near the
Brown Barrens nature preserve. This was a tiny nothing of
a frame house on a pea-gravel lane up a hill and beneath the
district's water tower, which the county had painted yellow
and decorated with a giant smiley face. I didn't know what
there was to smile about or who to smile at. There wasn't
much out that way, except Tremble's house and a sprawling
timberland and, far away to the south, some turkey buzzards
circling a bald knob of hilltop like a black halo. There was a
late-model Honda in the drive with one of those "Coexist"
bumper stickers you see time to time and a big silverber-
ry drooping pitifully in the yard like it was waiting for an
armed passerby to put it out of its misery. There wasn't a
dog anywhere that I could see. I tucked Lew's thick gloves
in my back pocket again along with a pair of the tranquilizer
sticks and got down from the truck and walked up to the
front door. I knocked a couple of times and waited until it
opened with a frigid exhale from the air-conditioning inside. A young woman in a nightshirt was behind the screen.

She said, "Hot enough?"

It was hot enough, but she didn't let me answer. She
pushed open the door and turned and padded back into the
house without bothering to ask my sign or what I did for
dollars. I followed.

"He's in bed sleeping," she said over her shoulder. "Surprise, surprise."

She was in her early twenties with one of those ragged
haircuts looks like a drunk person done it. Her freckled nose
was pierced silver, her hazel eyes so bored they might have

belonged to a clothes mannequin. Her cheeks held a scattering of freckles, too, in case her nose wanted more, and her right ear had one of them big holes in it the kids did then. Gauges, I think they're called. Her bare arms and legs were covered in tattoos.

The rest of the place was plenty interesting, too. There was a sofa and a TV on a big painted console and a couple of posters on the walls, and there was a forest of pot plants growing everywhere there was space to put them. I tell you, it was a sight. They were on the floor and on the little divider wall between the living room and kitchenette. They were on top of the TV set and stereo and on the arms of the sofa. An ancient turntable had been switched on, and one of them was spinning in slow circles on that. The ceiling was fitted with maybe a half dozen banks of CFLs nestled inside metal hoods and suspended from silver chains. Their light and their buzzing sound filled what was left of the space to fill.

"This is something else," I said.

"What is?" she said.

"Nothing. What time's he usually wake up?"

"Wes? Depends."

"On?"

"His aura, mostly."

That was sensible enough. Guy had a bad enough aura, he might not want to get out of the sheets. He might want to lie down in a culvert ditch or a lonely patch of red clover, or walk screaming into a forest. There were any number of possibilities.

I said, "Can you wake him?"

She nodded, but instead of waking him she flopped down on the sofa and said, "I don't know you," which seemed like something she should have thought of before, but I was too polite to say so. She picked up a one-hitter and tamped down the bowl with a blackened thumb and touched fire to it with a lighter on a cord around her neck. "Don't remember your face none, neither. What's your name?"

"Slim."

"Funny name."

"I never stop laughing about it."

"I'm Star-Child," she said. She handed me the pipe. I turned it around in my hand and gave it right back.

She said, "It's quality shit, ain't it?"

"Seriously?"

"What?"

"Nothing," I said. My head hurt. "That your real name? Star-Child, I mean?"

"No. Duh. Actually it's Tiffany. Tiffany Scruggs."

"Believe it or not, it's better than Star-Child. You live here with Wes?"

"I live here with Wes," she said. She didn't look excessively thrilled about it. "I'll go get him up. Might take a minute, aura he's having. While I'm gone, you decide how much you want. And be precise about it."

"I promise to be precise."

"I'm serious now. Wes hates any kind of dickering."

"I promise not to dicker."

She looked at me and my promises a moment longer

and then nodded at the three of us and tottered out of the room, grabbing the doorframe a little as she rounded the corner. I got up from my seat and made a quick search of the space. There was some secondhand furniture and a pile of video games and some CDs of bands I'd never heard of and a guitar on a stand. I went into the kitchen and opened the utility room door and checked the pantry for dog food cans but found only canned SpaghettiOs and some sudden memories of my own wayward youth. I went to the window above the sink and parted the blinds and took a peek at the backyard. There was more dead grass and some patches of bare earth where even the dead grass didn't want to live anymore and a crooked apple tree without any apples on it. There was an outbuilding, too, a yellow tin and fiberglass shed under not so much as a stipple of shade. In that weather, basically a sweatbox.

"Surely not," I said to myself.

But also maybe so. Maybe even surely so. Nobody ever went broke overestimating the cruelty of people. Just heartbroke. I pushed open the sliding door and stepped out of the kitchen and into the heat. I crossed the lawn and unchained the shed and opened it, and there she was in a ball on the dirt floor. A red dog. And not just any red dog. A sixty-five-dollar red dog.

"Excuse me, ma'am, you wouldn't happen to be Shelby Ann Cleaves, would you?"

She was too weak to use her voice maybe. She lifted her bony head to look at me through clouded eyes, and the knob of her docked tail twitched. I don't guess she'd have lasted much longer. It was as hot as a coal stove in there, and there wasn't any food that I could see. Her water dish was as dry as the inside of a mummy, and she'd done her business all over the floor. The smell of it made my eyes water. I don't imagine Shelby Ann was any too happy about it, either. I squatted down and scratched the red fur behind her ears, she licked my hand, and we became friends. I had half a water bottle in my truck, so I went back and got that now and brought it to the shed to fill up her bowl. She lapped it down immediately and looked up at me with sad eyes for more, hopeful but not expectant.

I said, "Wait here just one more minute, darlin'. I'm gonna go shove my foot up someone's ass."

I stormed out of the shed. I left the door open and walked quickly across the yard and into the house again. There was a boy in the kitchen now, a skinny thing in tighty-whities and nothing else with a pistol in his hand. He pointed it at my head.

I didn't let him pull the trigger. I grabbed his arm and twisted until the gun dropped from his hand. I kneed him in the gut, causing him to bend over, and I hammered the back of his head so that his face bounced off the kitchen counter and he fell to the floor. He tried to rear up and turn again toward me but I pulled out the tranquilizer needles and stuck them in his ass. Both of them. He moaned and struggled around a little for a moment and then fell still. I took the stickpins out of his butt and just then Star-Child came into the room with the corner of her T-shirt in her mouth.

I said, "Just FYI, your boyfriend's a dick."

"Is he dead? Is that poison?"

"No. Just some sleep stuff. He's like to be out for a while."

"Oh."

"Try not to sound so disappointed," I said, and she looked at me and then quickly at her feet and blushed. I softened my voice. "You don't have to stay here, you know? And not just here-here. Here in this kind of life, I mean. There's all kinds of things you can do instead."

"Like what?"

"I don't know. Law school?"

"Drugs are more honest."

I said, "Okay. That's a point for you. How about business classes, then? Or computers? Or anything other than this mess."

"It ain't that easy for everybody."

She was right about that, anyway. I thought about my sixty-five-dollar fee and rang up the hospital bills I'd narrowly avoided so far. Sixty-five dollars wouldn't even cover the hospital parking. I looked at the boy snoozing on the floor and worried about a sore back.

I said, "Help me with him, will you?"

She agreed to help. Probably she was feeling guilt over plotting to murder me. She took Wesley's bare feet and together we carried him through the house and into a room down the hall where we dumped him unceremoniously on the bed. After that I collected the firearms and bullets, Wesley's piece and a shotgun I found in the bathroom near the fixture.

"Why on earth would he keep a thing like that in there?" I asked her.

"Some people can't ever relax."

She said there weren't any more firearms in the house, and I believed her. I took it all to the shed and deposited it in a handy wheelbarrow. Then I unclasped Shelby Ann's collar and leash and carried her to the truck. She probably could have walked, but I elected not to risk it. Locking her in the dog box didn't seem right, not after what'd been done to her, so I buckled her up in the front seat next to me.

"For safety," I told her, and climbed behind the wheel.

I pulled out of the drive and turned south and then east past the tinderbox that the preserve was turning itself into. Along the way, I stopped at a convenience store and bought a can of dog chow, some more bottled water, and some disposable bowls. I turned the radio on low and the AC up as high as it'd go. An old Don Williams number came on— "If Hollywood Don't Need You," a favorite—and I ended up singing along with it a little while Shelby Ann downed her meal and three dishes of the water. She was filthy and undernourished, but near as I could tell she didn't actually appear to be physically injured. Beneath her leather collar was a shaved rectangle with a tiny row of XXXs stitched into her skin, but the incision had healed some time ago and the stitches were clean. After a while, I started the truck and we moved on.

It was a little before nine when we returned to the Classic Country Showroom, and the dark was finally coming on for real.

"I'll be back in a minute," I said to Shelby Ann. You talked to enough crazy people in your life, talking to a dog didn't seem like much to throw on the pile. "I only ask that you not judge me by the company I bring."

I left her in the cab with the engine running and the air conditioner on and walked up to Reach's house and went inside. I called out, but he didn't answer. The light was on in the kitchen, which I didn't remember from before, it still being daylight and all when I'd left. That gave me pause. Pause and anxiety. For a moment, I worried Reach had somehow slipped his cuff and set up a machete ambush, but the machete was back with the fireplace tools where I'd returned it following our scrape.

"Reach?" I said. Nothing. I made for the kitchen. I was starting to worry.

I shouldn't have worried. He was still on the floor in his robe and still cuffed to the pipe under the sink. But that was all he was, all he'd ever be. Someone had shot him in the face at close range, blown his head all over the walls and kitchen cabinets. Blood filled the little holes in the mesh of the window screens, the keyhole in the handcuffs. The ones I'd slapped on him. I couldn't even look at the chasm in his face, that grotesque second mouth, or in the one in the back of his head, much larger.

So I stood not looking at them for a moment, hoping I'd be able to control the shaking in my hands long enough to call the cops. Somehow, I managed it, but as soon as they arrived in a squealing herd of prowlers, I sort of wished I hadn't. Maybe they'd been without a murder for too long. Or maybe they were just inexperienced in such things. Probably that last thing. You imagine there wasn't much in the way of murders out there. The cops were so excited by it all, they walked all over the forensics and arrested the first thing in sight, as though on impulse.

"Christ Almighty," one of them said, a kid in a thin mustache. "This guy's insides are out. And I bet you've got a perfectly reasonable explanation, right?"

He dangled his cuffs in front of me like a silver noose.

"Damn it all," I said. "I was going to take him to the hospital."

"Well, you can take him, but I don't know it will do any good."

The other deputies tittered their appreciation. Mustache ate it up.

"Nice guys finish last, son," he said, though he was almost young enough to be mine.

"At least they finish."

The deputy agreed. But he slapped the cuffs on me anyway.

4.

I'VE BEEN IN WORSE JAILS, AND IT MUST HAVE BEEN THE OFF-season, because my lone cellmate was a former ventilation boss who'd gone after his unfaithful wife with a Weed-whacker. He must have been pushing eighty, and he moved with the painful resolve of someone who'd worked underground too long. His breaths were the rasping snorts of camel snores—or what I imagined camel snores to be—but somehow he'd chased the old woman out of their ancestral home and down a half mile of deer path and into a dry streambed, where the whacker finally and mercifully sputtered itself empty of fuel. I told him to think about forgiving his wife and getting himself a good lawyer. He asked me if I knew one, and I just laughed and laughed until he flipped over on his bunk to face the wall.

After another little forever, a deputy with a face like mashed turnips brought me a telephone on a wooden stool. I asked him to dial it for me, told him my dialing finger had been hurt by the mean cop with the mustache. He chuckled about that some then showed me his own finger—not his dialing finger—before going back to watching the tube or strangling his chicken or whatever deputies did when the boss wasn't around and the professional criminals were taking a personal day.

I put in a call to my own lawyer, but the worthless shit wasn't in, so I left a message and then phoned Anci, first sucking a few deep breaths to brace for what I knew was coming.

"You're kidding?" she said, when I'd given her the rundown.

"I wish," I said. "But this time even the extenuating circumstances have extenuating circumstances."

"Uh-huh. That's what you said last time. Remember the thing with the chickens?"

"I thought we agreed not to talk about the thing with the chickens."

"You agreed. I don't remember agreeing."

"I remember it different maybe."

"You get hit in the head a lot. Forget things. What happened to the dog?"

"Technically, she's evidence in a homicide, but the county doesn't have a shelter, so they called the Cleaves. I understand they've already been by to pick her up."

"At least someone's happy, then," she said.

"I'm guessing that someone ain't you."

"No. No it is not. This a hold-and-release kind of deal?"

"I sure hope so."

Anci said, "See you in seventy-two, then," and hung up on me.

The warm support of children is one of the great comforts in a parent's life. Seriously, you can ask them.

After a few hours, I was cuffed again and led into interrogation. It was a small room, smaller than my cell even, and they'd crammed in too big a table and too many chairs. There were cops in there, too. Uniform officers, I mean. Their presence didn't have any purpose that I could detect. They weren't sweating me or taking notes about the case or bouncing me around for fun. They were just bored and waiting for the show to begin.

After a while, one of them looked at me with gathered eyebrows and said, "You really kill that guy? Reach?"

"No."

"I can't fathom why you'd do something like that," he said, shaking his head. "It's just mean."

"I didn't do it."

"I used to go out there sometimes," he continued. "Classic Country. Pretty nice place."

"I guess."

"Seriously, it was. Food was pretty good, too. He did that catfish sandwich I liked. One with that sauce. What do you call it?"

"Tartar?"

"That's the stuff. Tartar. I like it. And there were things to play, too. Games. Darts in the back room. That kind of thing."

"He got one of them mechanical bulls," I said, and the cop nodded.

"Got it and liked to show it off on account of he could afford such a gadget, but it was unplugged. Too many insurance claims. You put a bull and a bunch of drunks in the same room like that, you're always going to get insurance claims. It's one of them inevitables. I guess old Reach finally come to his senses about it." He paused a moment, reflective, and then said, "It was a good place for dancing, though. That's for sure."

Well, that perked up some ears. The other cops laughed and joked at him a little for liking to boogie, big old tough county lawman like that, and he got sore about it. He turned away from me and his remembrance of lights fantastic to share words with his brother officers. He explained that his wife liked to dance and that as her life partner he had a responsibility to make her happy by doing some of the things she enjoyed. Those other cops, he bet their wives liked to cut a rug sometimes, too, even if they never said so out loud, but they never got dancing. They were neglected. Someday maybe a real dancin' man would come along, and then their wives might go dancing with him instead, and the error of their ways would be laid bare but too late. He got pretty hot about it, but it was a nice enough speech, and in the end the other cops were shamed and fell silent. I hadn't laughed at him, but I felt ashamed, too. I thought I might take Peggy dancing more often, she got back from her sister's. I didn't want no dancin' man to come along, and I said so, and the deputy looked at me and nodded, and I nodded at him, grateful for his wisdom, and then the door opened and the sheriff came in.

He said, "You ain't called a lawyer?"

"Tried to, but he wasn't around," I said. "He's one of these characters always takes off on you."

"You'll pardon me saying so, that don't sound like much of a lawyer."

"He's inside the budget, though," I said.

The sheriff was satisfied. He didn't want me having a lawyer, anyway—good, bad, or indifferent. He waved a hand, and the other cops filed out of the room. He pulled out a chair and sat opposite. He put a recorder on the table between us and switched it on and said the date and time and his name and mine. My real name. He added that I was commonly called Slim around those parts, result of some time spent in the coal mines. I told the recorder that this was so. The sheriff told me to shut up.

He was on the young side for his office—early fifties, I guess—with a handsome black face and the beginnings of silver at his temples. His name tag said R.L. Lindley, but I didn't need to read any name tag. Everybody in those parts had heard of R.L. Lindley, him being Little Egypt's only black county sheriff and all, but we'd never been formally introduced.

He said, "I hope you don't mind we skip the usual back-and-forth, son. Keep this direct."

"I guess I don't mind."

"Fine. Now, why don't you start by telling me—directlike, mind you—why I shouldn't drop your trouble-making ass down the deepest, darkest hole I can find."

"The more I think about it, though, too much direct-ness can be dull."

"That your answer?"

"Be patient," I said. "That's only *one* of my answers. Got plenty of others. You might even eventually like one."

"No offense, but I kinda doubt that," he said. "You know what? I'm in a generous mood tonight, some reason. I'm going to do something I ain't never do. Give you a second chance here. Let you start fresh. How about that?"

I nodded at his agreeableness. "Okay. Thanks. What if we start fresh with the fact that I didn't do anything."

"Just an innocent bystander, that right?"

"Innocent as a napping puppy," I said and told my story. Parts of it, anyway. I left out that I'd been the one to cuff Reach to the drain, that I'd cut off his thumb, everything about Wesley Tremble, and the fact that Dennis was angrier at someone called Carol Ray than he was at me. Call me crazy, but when you deal with rural cops it's best to keep your cards in your sleeves and a chain on your wallet. Plus, there was the little matter of me wanting first crack at whoever had killed Dennis Reach. So what was left wasn't much, and a lot of it was lies or lies of omission. A cheese grater has fewer holes.

"So you're just a guy looking for a dog? That what you're saying?"

"Yep."

"For sixty bucks?"

"Sixty-five," I said.

"Sixty-five." He nodded. He mulled it over some and then finally said, "Okay, then, way I see it is this. And feel free to stop me if you disagree."

"I'll stop you."

"Way I see it is this. Either you're a liar and a killer, or else you are some kind of major-league chump. I'll let you tell me which."

"What if I want to call myself something else?"

He shrugged.

"Stick a feather in your ass, call yourself a Tyrolean hat, all I care. You still got to choose one of mine. You got a reputation in this part of the world, Slim. That business last year—Luster and Galligan and that mess—they say you were right there in the middle of it, and they ain't even ever accounted for all the bodies. Plenty of stuff since then, too. This thing recently with the chickens."

"I don't like to talk about the thing with the chickens."

Lindley ignored me. He said, "I don't even know what to say about that kind of a thing. Grown person behaving that way. I kind of wondered when you might bring your act into my county. Kind of wondered what I'd do when you did, too."

"So what's your decision?"

He thought a little about that, consternation in his face. You could tell he wasn't about to offer me five dollars and a yellow balloon. Finally, he said, "I got to think you're on the hook for this. Whether or not I can charge you for it to-day, you're on the hook. People have a habit of disappearing around you, Slim. Dying, too. And too many parts of your story plain old don't add up."

He banged the table with his hand. Right on cue, a pair of deputies came back in and plucked me from my chair.

"Do me a favor, would you?" I said before they led me out.

Lindley looked at me with smiling eyes. He said, "Oh, gee, I was hoping you'd ask."

"Come on, man."

"Sitting here this whole time thinking, why hasn't Slim asked me to do him a favor? I wish he would. And now you have. Makes my night."

"Okay, please."

"Well, since you sprinkled a little sugar on top . . ."

"Call Ben Wince."

"Your sheriff buddy over there to Randolph? He'll vouch for you, that it?"

"I like to think he would, yes." But for all I know Lindley wasn't listening. Some jokes weren't worth more than one laugh.

I never found out if he did my favor. They kept me seventy-two hours then kicked me loose when I didn't cry on their shoulders and sign a confession. They couldn't tie me to the murder weapon, maybe, but possibly there was something else.

Even my cut-rate lawyer didn't know. Maybe I should say *especially* my cut-rate lawyer didn't know. You never met a person who didn't know so many things with so much conviction. This was a kid from Red Bud, a farm boy who'd got his law degree at a college they advertise on television and who reminded you of nothing so much as a mobbed-up version of Huckleberry Finn. He had ragged red hair and an odd birthmark on his left cheek and a slight overbite.

He struggled pitiably with courtroom Latin. The rest of his personal style he appeared to have gleaned from B-grade gangster flicks: double-breasted pinstriped suits from the Walmart, a black Lincoln Continental he must have inherited from a dead relative, and, in his imitation snakeskin briefcase, a Colt .357 Python. A volcano of a gun I liked to think he had never fired and hoped he never would. When he materialized near the end of my third day of incarceration, sporting a brand-new set of black eyes from a vacation to West Memphis, Arkansas, the cops acted like he wasn't worth wasting a Kleenex on.

"The police are hiding something," he said, and the desk sergeant winked at the two of us and cracked a theatrical grin as he handed over the manila envelope with my name on the front and my life inside, but the kid didn't get it. He never got a joke, that I know of, not even his own.

Lew's truck was impounded in the car yard across town, so I got a lift from the kid, handed my ticket to a fat lady in a climate-controlled metal box, and in ten minutes was on the road back toward Tolu and the Mandamus compound. My head was full of worries, though, the dark arithmetic of murder, and I knew I wasn't going to be able to just set it all down and walk away. Whoever had shot Dennis Reach hated him so much that they'd killed him like an animal on a leash. I wanted to know who and I wanted to know why and I wanted, if possible, to atone in some small way for putting that leash on him in the first place. Halfway to Harrisburg, I dialed the Randolph County sheriff's office on my cell.

"What is it, Slim? I'm eating my supper," Ben Wince said.

"Filling station burrito?"

"No."

"Filling station corn dog?"

"Strike two."

"Something from a filling station, though?"

"Between you and me, it's one of these frozen diet dinners."

"Lean Cuisine?"

"Healthy Choice. Chicken Florentine. Supposed to only have two hundred ninety calories, but I'd be shocked if it had even that many. I've seen bigger food in a dollhouse. Is there a point to this call? Or are you just filling time with your favorite hobby?"

"I guess you heard about my troubles."

"Everybody has."

"Do me a favor, would you? Find out why the Jackson County sheriff let me go."

"Don't have to find out. Already know. They didn't have evidence to hold you, they let you go. That's how these things work."

"No, they don't."

"I know."

"Anything else?"

"Well, in this case here, it's enough. Dennis Reach was shot at close range with a Colt rifle. AR-15 model. Dang things seem to be everywhere these days, don't they? I guess there really is no such thing as bad publicity. Anyway, your man Reach was shot with one of them nasty things. He must have turned his head at the last second, because the shell glanced off his right cheekbone and tunneled through the nasal cavity before blowing his brainpan all over the dirty dishes. Otherwise, it would have taken his head clean off. How's that for TMI?"

"What?"

"It means too much information. It's a thing the kids say. Like when you give them too much information about a subject, they say TMI."

I said, "I know. I know what it means. What I'm wondering is why are you saying it."

"New girl in the office. Guess I picked it up from her."

"Might also pick up that grown women don't like being called girls anymore. That's another thing the kids say."

"It's a bad habit," he admitted. "Anyway, this thing. Your thing. The gun."

"I was hoping we'd get back to that eventually."

He grunted at me and my attitude. "Funny thing, Jackson County found it floating in the shit-pond behind the house. The lagoon, that is. I reckon they let a new guy go in after that one."

"Registered?"

"Nope. Not stolen, neither. Least as far as we can tell. Fact, it's as clean as a beaver. Probably a gun-show gun. Loophole gun."

"A dead end, then."

"Appears so, anyway. I suppose it'd be stupid to ask if there's anything personal in this with you?"

I said, "Nothing personal, except that I spent three days in lockup for a murder I didn't do."

"I'm guessing Peggy's none too thrilled about it, either."

"Don't know about it yet. She's visiting her sister in Kankakee. Anci's pretty upset, though."

"I guess that would sting some. Anci more than the time in lockup. Unofficially, I can't blame you for being sore about it."

"What about officially?"

"Different story. And Lindley will play it official all the way down the line."

"He thinks I'm good for it," I said.

"He's leaning in that direction, anyway, and you can hardly blame him, story you're telling. Slim, I like you. You're a pain in my ass sometimes, but I like you, and I got to tell you, you're putting your pecker in a hornet's nest with this thing. Dennis Reach was what you'd call flush with enemies. There were three pretty nasty divorces and some lawsuits against former business partners that led to death threats and the whole nine. Little shit had his fingers in so many people's eyes I'm guessing he carried insurance against pitchfork mobs. Tell the truth, I think Lindley was surprised it took this long for one of them to do something about it."

"Yeah, but which 'it'?"

"Good question," he said. "But not really yours to answer. Now get yourself on home. Make things right with Anci. Get her some of that orange soda she likes. Maybe some pizza. She like pizza?"

"All kids like pizza."

"Okay, then. Soda. Pizza. Get it done. That's an order."

I didn't have time to question the chain of command. He hung up.

And looking back now, I know that's what I should have done. I should have collected Anci and the bottled sodas and some pizza. I like pizza pretty good my own self, so there was that, too. I should have made some kind of reparations to Lew and Eun Hee Mandamus and then gone on home to hide under my bed until the police cleared the case. Hindsight may not be 20/20, exactly, but it sure seems a lot clearer now. Right then, though, I was mad enough to chew nails and spit out staples. Somehow or other, I'd played a part in Dennis Reach's murder. I didn't know what part and I didn't know how. I didn't know why he'd been killed, and I didn't know what or whether that red dog had to do with any of it. And I didn't think I wanted those questions haunting the inside of my head for the rest of my life. Plus, there was the small matter of avoiding an indictment for capital murder.

I made a U-turn and drove Lew Mandamus's truck back toward Loves Corner.

WES TREMBLE, THE SKINNY WEED DEALER, DIDN'T TRY TO shoot me in the head this time. That was a relief. He was wearing more than tighty-whities this time, too. That was an even bigger relief. He opened the door and smiled a sour smile as though to say my reappearance was something he'd expected. He took my arm and led me into his house and

shut the door behind us and locked it. He turned the bolt
and put the chain on. The curtains were closed, but he
closed them again.

"Look at you out there," he said. "Standing there. It's
like you're trying to get seen."

"Seen? Seen by who? There ain't anybody around."

Just then, he wouldn't have taken a bishop's word for
it. Living where he did, he probably could have heard cops
coming ten miles up the road, but as far as he was concerned
they might as well have been hiding in his pants.

"There was a silver pickup out there a while ago. Last
night, too. It's been watching the house."

"A silver pickup? Any idea who it might belong to?"

He shrugged but didn't answer. "I remember you," he
said instead. "You're the one stuck me in the butt."

"You're the one wanted to shoot me in the head."

He wanted to forget that part of it, I guess. He shook it
off and said, "What was that stuff? In the needles, I mean."

"Diazepam, I think. Valium. They use it as an animal
sedative sometimes."

"Well, it worked pretty good, whatever it was. I kinda
wish I had some more."

"Me, too. For you, I mean. You're making me a little
anxious."

He didn't want to be rude, and he didn't want to make
a guest anxious. He might try to put another hole in your
head, but he still had those kinds of house manners. He sat
down stiffly on an ottoman and grabbed his knees. I sat on
the couch.

He said, "You aren't the police. What are you, like a rent-a-cop or something?"

"Mall police," I said. "But our powers extend way outside the malls now."

"Malls have taken over everything," he said, and frowned at the regrettable state of it.

"Maybe remember that next time you decide to play tough with us."

"I will."

"Good. Now I got a question or two for you I hope you won't mind answering."

"I guess I don't mind."

"Thanks," I said. "By the way, where's Tiffany?"

He looked confused.

"Star-Child."

"Oh. Her." Like it was ages ago. "She's cleared out. You know. After what happened."

"I guess I'm not surprised."

"The guns and stuff. And then the po-po. She ain't into any of that."

"Maybe she'll come back when it blows over."

He didn't have an answer for that. Maybe she'd come back, maybe she wouldn't. He said, "It's not my fault." He wrapped his arms around his skinny chest. They almost went twice. "I wasn't even there. When Dennis took the dog, I mean."

"So the cops have been to see you? The non-mall cops, I mean?"

"Not here," he said. "Not yet. But they grilled everyone

at the Classic Country, asked if we knew anything. I told them I didn't know anything. Did you tell them about the dog?"

"I didn't have any choice but to explain the dog," I said, "but I didn't mention your part in it all. I told them Reach had nabbed her and left it at that."

"I hope they believed you."

"They don't believe anything yet, which is most of the reason I'm here. I got busted for the whole thing."

"It wasn't my idea," he said. "Dennis needed a place to keep her for a few days. I agreed to watch her. I shouldn't have."

"Probably not."

He said, "I'm sorry about the water dish, too. I've never been able to take care of a plant, much less a pet."

"Seriously?"

"Seriously, what?"

"There's a jungle of plants in here, man. And they all look pretty healthy to me."

He waved a hand at it all.

"That's different. That's business."

I shook that off. "So Dennis gave you the dog to look after?"

"Yeah. He said he was dogsitting but that he couldn't breathe on account of his allergies, something like that. I knew he was up to something, though. You could always tell when Dennis thought he had someone's shit in a sack."

"But then after a couple days you figured you'd make a few bucks off her, extort her owners a little?"

He almost looked ashamed.

"I guess I did. I saw a flyer for the dog up there near Belco and it mentioned a reward. Another thing about Dennis is he doesn't pay very well."

"Didn't pay very well," I corrected.

"That neither."

"Did Reach tell you why he snatched her in the first place?"

"He never even really admitted that he'd stolen her. Folks around the club had it that her owner was supposed to owe him money or something. Maybe that has something to do with it."

"I don't guess you ever met anyone named Cleaves, did you?"

"Cleaves? Not to my recollection, no."

"Who's Carol Ray?" I asked.

"Dennis's ex. Wife number three, memory serves."

"You have any idea where I can find her?"

"I think she lives somewhere near Freeman Spur. Look out, though."

"Tough?"

"Like all Dennis's women. He liked them that way, I guess."

"Ask me, he liked things tough all around."

Wesley said, "Lots of folks do, you look around a little."

I said I guessed that was right. I thanked him for his time and stood to go. I walked to the door and paused a moment and finally turned and said, "Son, you really should get these things out of here. Your crop. If the sheriffs ever stop by for a chat, you'll need to get reincarnated to serve out the jolt they'll drop on you."

"I know," he said, and swung his head away with something like emotion in his eyes. "It's just I'm having a hard time saying good-bye."

IT WAS AFTER TEN THIRTY WHEN I FINALLY REACHED THE Mandamus compound, and the night was still and heavy with humidity. Bats fluttered here and there in the cool sodium light of the security lamps, snapping insects from the air. Lew was making a last round with the animals in the pole barn. He raised a hand when he saw me but didn't call out and then quickly disappeared up the hill and into the dark. I circled the house and found Eun Hee sipping bourbon and soda from a rocks glass on the back porch. Anci was already asleep.

Eun Hee said, "You raised that one right, Slim. She's an angel."

"Thanks," I said. "But soon as I wake her, that angel is going to give me the Nine Hells."

"She surely will, but that's family."

"Mad?"

"She was at first. Mad as a hornet. But mostly she was upset. Worried. You won't let her come see you?"

"In jail? No, I won't. One thing, I don't think it's good for her to see me like that. Another, she'd take a picture of me with her phone, and it'd be on our Christmas card until the day I die and probably after."

"Likely for the best, then. You all right?"

"I've had better times. Mostly I'm sorry for adding to your woes."

She said, "Don't be silly. And don't feel sorry for me, Slim. I'm doing well enough these days."

"You're tough," I said, because I didn't know what else to say. You never know what to say in situations like that, and when you settle on something, whatever it is, you come out sounding like a dummy.

"I'm tough enough," Eun Hee said. "But something gets everybody eventually, Slim. At least I know what mine's going to be."

"Does it bother you?"

"I don't know. Sometimes, I guess. But listen, when whatever happens happens, and I spend my last days here or in hospice or wherever Lew and I decide is best, at least I'll have stared down my death. It hasn't blinked but I haven't, either, and one day we'll meet head-on in the middle of the tracks like a pair of trains. I'm not afraid, Slim. Never have been before and I'm not now."

"Maybe I will have that drink."

She poured me a short one and gave it to me and smiled and patted my hand.

She said, "I've worried you."

"It's not that, exactly. It's just I've seen maybe more than my fair share of death, and I'll tell you, I don't like it."

"Me, neither. But I'm not gone yet."

We toasted not being gone yet and drank our drinks. Afterward Eun Hee offered to put on a pot of coffee, maybe scratch together some late supper, but I was exhausted from my stay in Jackson County and my parley with Wesley Tremble, so I offered up some more thanks and a little money for Anci's food and lodging, but was refused.

"I think you might be taking a baby fox home, though," she said.

"God, I hope you're kidding."

She was kidding about the fox but not about Anci being steamed. The ride home, she read me the riot act up one side and down the other. *Man,* she was mad. After a while, though, she ran out of gas and sat quietly, watching out her window, remembering maybe that it'd been her idea to the take the Cleaveses' business in the first place.

Finally, she said, "At least you didn't get shot."

"Just shot at. So there's that."

"But the guy who took the dog did."

"That's right."

"Dead."

"As leg warmers," I said.

"What?"

"It was a fashion thing. Leg warmers. A long time ago."

"How long?"

"I don't know. Thirty years or more."

"Yeah, maybe update that one."

"Okay, fine. I'll update that one. Meantime, this thing with Reach, I don't like it, and I'm going to keep not liking it until I do something about it."

"Oh, monkey hell.

At last, we arrived home. Indian Vale. The house my

father had built that had become mine and that one day
would be my daughter's, if she chose to stay in the area. She
wouldn't, though. Why should she? The young people here
moved somewhere else as fast as they could, and the old
folks withered away and died. The factories vanished and
the mines and mills sank into the ground, and in their places were erected fast food joints and furniture rental places
and pawnshops. Sometimes I hear places like where I live
called "Real America," and I know it rankles some folks—
city folks, mostly—something awful, and I wish I could tell
them it's only done out of politeness. That it's only people
saying nice things about the dying.

It was dark that night, and the moon was off doing other stuff, I guess. Even with the stars out, it's hard to find
your way around our little valley, so I nearly tripped over
the porch steps getting to the front door. I have a penlight
on the end of my keychain, and I used it to try to find the
keyhole but even with that it was like looking for spilled ink
inside a coal scuttle.

"No hurry," Anci said behind me. "We can sleep standing up, like horses."

"Keep your spurs on, will you?"

Finally, I got it. Unlocking was achieved. I put the key
in the lock and turned the knob and heard Anci suck a
breath all at once. My heart jumped.

"Motherfucker," she said.

I wheeled around. And there, leaning casually against a
porch post in the country dark, was A. Evan Cleaves, still in

that stupid black suit, his face aglow in the sudden spark of a cigarette lighter.

He said, "Didn't know when you'd come home."

"I didn't, either," I said. I put down my fighting hands. "You waited long?"

"Not long. A day or two."

Oh, shit-fire.

He said, "Thanks for finding the dog. They called us from the sheriff's office. Let us come collect her. Dad teared up pretty good over it."

"It wasn't anything," I said. "I heard you'd been to get her."

"And we heard you spent some time in the slammer."

I said, "Three days, but that goes along with the job. You don't happen to know anyone name of Carol Ray, do you?"

The boy stared at me with his needlepoint eyes.

"No. Thanks again." He stepped forward, stuffed an envelope in my hand. A big manila envelope that had been folded over and taped into a smaller shape. He showed his weird smile to Anci. Then he loped off the side of the porch, into the lawn, and out of sight. I looked around, but couldn't see the flatbed truck or the yurt or anything. Not so much as a skateboard. For all I knew, he'd walked the twenty miles from Union City.

I turned to Anci. "You okay?"

"I think I peed myself."

"I think I did, too. We better check the place out."

And so we did, but the locks were intact and there weren't any scrapes on the doors to show they'd been forced. The windows were in place and the latches latched. Anci inspected her room while I peeked in at my office and the rest of the house. Nothing seemed out of place. No one had riled the cats. The plants needed watered but it was hard to blame A. Evan for that. I blamed him for it anyway. When we'd finished our reconnoiter, the two of us regrouped in the kitchen.

Anci said, "Hopefully that's the last time we'll see him."

"Hopefully. It nearly was anyway. I almost beat the shit out of him."

"Might've ended up in jail again."

"That'd be a record."

"Oh, I'm sure it'd hold up, too. What's in the envelope?"

I'd almost forgot the envelope. It was in the back of my trousers, where I'd stuffed it, but my mind was elsewhere. I opened it and looked inside. I showed the inside to Anci: thick stacks of hundred-dollar bills.

5.

I FINISHED COUNTING. I PUT THE LAST CRISP BILL DOWN ON the kitchen table and neatened the stack and patted it with my hand. I said, "Goddamn. A hundred thousand bucks."

Anci whistled and said, "I want to say goddamn, too. Can I say goddamn?"

"You already did. Twice. Also, you're punished."

Anci whistled again and picked up some of the bills. "What do you think it means?"

"Truck farm business must have picked up some. Either that or sorghum prices are doing better than I thought possible."

"Probably it's that. The sorghum thing."

"Probably."

"Say, what is sorghum, anyway?"

"It's a crop. Like a kind of grass. They make molasses out of it, some other stuff. Beer sometimes. Why?"

"Just hard to imagine them growing anything. The Cleaveses. Burying stuff, I can imagine. Cutting it down. Burning it. Growing it, not so much."

"I guess I have trouble believing it, too."

"Upshot is, we can finally get the air-conditioning fixed. Maybe even get a brand-new one. And none too soon, either. Can't fit no more box fans in my bedroom."

I nodded. "I know it ain't exactly been a hayride around here lately, and I appreciate your patience . . ."

"But?"

"How do you know there's a 'but' coming?"

"You're smooth-talking me up for one. A person can tell. That bit about the patience and how you're proud of me and my maturity and how I'm turning into a grown lady and all."

"I actually didn't say a lot of that stuff. The maturity stuff and the grown lady stuff. You tossed those on the pile yourself."

Anci wanted to ignore this. She said, "Think you're being slick, but—guess what?—you ain't. Might as well have it painted on your face. I know you, you rascal."

"Okay, *but* maybe we ought to hold off for a just bit longer, make sure this money isn't tied up in anything nefarious."

"It came from that Cleaves boy, didn't it?"

"Handed it to me himself."

"It's tied up in something nefarious," she said.

I dropped the envelope into the safe in my office back of the house and then Anci and I watched a movie for a while—something happy, *Singin' in the Rain*—until we were laughing hard at Donald O'Connor and the unsettling memory of A. Evan Cleaves began to fade and we felt ready for our beds.

★ ★ ★

It rained a little the next morning, thin pelts of rain. That should have been a relief, but in the end it was one of those summer showers only seems to make things worse. The paved roads smoldered and the air grew thick with a suffocating humidity. The rainwater pooled in black mirrors on the baked earth, and as soon as the clouds pushed off the sun came out again and drank it all greedily back down.

"It's like we're being punished," Anci said.

I said, "We're being punished," and went inside to scratch together some breakfast: chunks of fresh apple and melon and some berries so we wouldn't have to use the stove. Anci found some cold biscuits in the fridge. We filled our coffee with fistfuls of ice.

We were cleaning up our plates and mugs and things when my cell rang. It was Susan, a cranky woman but a fairly decent business manager (Anci says assistant manager) and occasional operative. Susan had been on the periphery of that mess with Galligan and Luster and the Becketts a while back—my first official case—and when it was all over and put back in the hatbox she'd agreed to do a little work for me and my fledgling agency. Mostly she kept our books and prevented me being arrested by the IRS, but she was good at other kinds of work, too, computer work and using the Google and that kind of thing.

She said, "I found her, Slim."

"Reach's ex? Carol Ray?"

"No. Vivien Leigh. I found Vivien Leigh."

"There's no reason to be snoos about it," I said. "Carol Ray then. Where is she?"

"Freeman Spur. Like your drug dealer boy told you." She gave me the address and even described the house, which she'd seen on Google Street View. She said, "Kid wasn't kidding about the tough part, either. She's got priors."

"Oh?"

"Citation for disorderly conduct. Five years ago."

"Doesn't sound like much."

"I didn't think so, either, at first, anyway," she said. "Dug a little deeper. Turns out the disorderly conduct involved setting Dennis Reach's car on fire."

"Oh."

"With Dennis Reach inside," she said.

"I want to say 'oh' again but it'd be the third time."

"I noticed that. Before you ask, nothing much came of it, besides that disorderly. Reach must have been real popular with law enforcement over there in Jackson County because they basically let Carol Ray walk with a slap on the fanny and a promise to be a good girl. She had a gun, too. A *pistola* in the glove box of her car but no carry permit, so they took the gun, but again, no charges."

"If there's one gun around, there are probably others."

"That's usually how it works. Maybe even an AR-15."

"I'll be careful," I said.

"Good," she said, and paused, thinking. Then she said, "Maybe go ahead and mail my check this morning, though."

GUNS AND CARRY PERMITS AND CAR FIRES ASIDE, I DIDN'T have any reason to think Carol Ray was a danger to anyone outside her late ex-husband. There were more guns in southern Illinois glove boxes than gloves or ice scrapers or haphazardly refolded road maps, and if you were going to start worrying about folks carrying firearms without the proper permits you were probably going to stop going outdoors altogether.

Late morning, Anci and I rode my motorcycle north and east to the village of Freeman Spur. We found the address Susan had given us in a little neighborhood on Mount Moriah Avenue, a Craftsman new-build surrounded by some pleasant-looking Amur maples and juniper bushes. We parked next to an ivory Porsche 911 and climbed off and pulled off our helmets. Anci looked at the car and hummed approvingly.

"Will you look at that lovely thing," she said. "Maybe that's what we should do with our new dognapping money."

"Yesterday you said you wanted an air conditioner. Said your bedroom is full of box fans. Remember that?"

"That was yesterday. As of this morning, this is today."

I said, "Tomorrow you'll see a spotted horse and want that."

"Now that you mention it."

We went up to the house and knocked and waited and waited, but nobody answered.

Anci wrinkled her nose. "Car's here, so she must have another. Maybe even something nicer."

"Maybe it's that spotted horse."

"Another foolproof deduction," she said. "Why not run into town for another cup of coffee, swing back in a bit?"

We were about to ride away when a sandy-haired boy appeared from next door and ran over to us, waving sunburned arms.

He said, "That's a cool bike."

"Thanks."

"Pretty sad lope, though. I've heard louder thoughts."

"Not-so thanks," I said. "You think you know something about bikes, do you?"

"I know a thing or three," he said. "Example, I know you unscrew that baffling, you'll get a better lope."

"I like my lope just fine."

"Whatever. I get a ride on that?"

"No."

He looked at me regretfully a moment. Finally, he decided he didn't want a ride on the bike with the pitiful exhaust note anyway and shrugged and said, "You after Carol Ray?"

"I might be. You her boy?"

"I'm *a* boy," he said. Unnecessarily, I thought. He looked at Anci and smiled with every tooth in his head and then looked back at me. "But not hers. I take messages for her sometimes."

"Okay."

"Service for which I get five dollars."

Reluctantly, I took out my wallet. The boy licked his lips and craned his neck to look inside the billfold. I had a ten but no fives.

"You got change?"

"Sure don't."

He took the ten.

He said, "Carol Ray ain't here."

"I think I want my money back."

"She's over to Shotguns & Shakes."

"That a place?"

"Last I looked. Got a parking lot and a sign. Carol Ray works there."

"Do you know the address?"

He said, "Do you know how to Google?" and smiled again at Anci before slipping away to await the appearance of his next mark.

Behind me, Anci said, "What a wonderful boy."

In fact, I thought he was a bad boy, a terrible boy, but I refrained from saying so. I was still in that time of life where I wasn't sure how to react when she said such things. Boy-related things, I guess I mean. Other parents had cautioned me that, to some extent, anyway, I'd have to let Anci make her own choices and—yea, verily—even her own mistakes. Mainly, they said, it was important that I not overreact, but I confess that part of me wanted to walk quietly into the sea whenever the subject came up.

Anyway, we rode into town and grabbed that coffee. Anci had more ice in hers. Mine was straight up. I wanted a pastry, too, but I'd given most of my cash to that little con artist, so I settled for frowns. Then the two of us looked up Shotguns & Shakes on Google and discovered where and what it was.

Anci said, "You got to be kidding me."

"It's the world we've made for ourselves," I replied.

Shotguns & Shakes—a combination burger joint/shooting range with an emphasis on getting firearms into the hands of little ones—was south and east of us a little in the abandoned strip fields and farmland near Moake Crossing and the retail sprawl that had built up around the I-57 exchange. There was a restaurant with some picnic tables and playground-type equipment outside and in the field beyond a hot zone of funnel traps and an impact berm maybe thirteen or fourteen feet high situated just north of the complex and facing the old Tombstone Lakes. The restaurant was busy with an early lunch crowd kitted out in Realtree and Mossy Oak and Carhartt, but we managed to snag a harried-looking food server and some directions.

"Range B," he said, and pointed. "Grab some cans before you go out."

We grabbed the aforementioned ear protection and walked around outside in the booming air. Everywhere was the crack of gunfire: small arms, long guns, something that sounded like a bazooka. A five-year-old ran past us carrying what appeared to be an Uzi, laughing manically.

"Where do you think her parents are?" Anci asked.

"In Kevlar, if they've got any sense."

After a while, we found four men and one woman firing shotguns on a trap range near the edge of the complex. The men were regulation upper-middle-class rural sportsmen—jowl-cheeked and gutty—but the woman was a surprise. Carol Ray was twenty years younger than I imagined she'd be. She was tall and willow-thin, with expensively cut blond hair and an adorably crooked mouth. She had pale blue eyes and a nose turned up just slightly at the end. She looked like she belonged on the cover of a magazine, and I wanted to buy that magazine and sleep with it under my pillow. She was dressed in a light hunting vest and amber eye shields and was holding a Super Black Eagle shotgun with the camo finish and pistol grip. When she saw us standing there, she waved a hand and left the group of men and came over.

She said, "We're almost finished here, in case y'all want to bring your kits up."

"We don't mean to interrupt your shooting class."

"Not a class," she replied with a bright laugh. "Just fun. We shoot at these traps and swap dollars. Mostly the boys there do the swapping, if I can take the risk of bragging. Please don't tell my accountant, though."

"We promise," I said, and introduced the two of us. "You're Carol Ray? We don't want to get you in trouble at work here."

"That's me. Carol Ray. And you can't get me in trouble. I own this place."

WE WENT BACK INSIDE WHERE THE SUN WASN'T TRYING TO melt our faces and got some complimentary sodas before Carol Ray led us toward her office at the back of the main building. As we were heading in, a man was coming out. He was tall and powerfully built with dark hair and one of those walrus mustaches stakes a claim to most of your face. He had gray eyes and the slightly yellowed fingers of a cigarette smoker and was rocking a leather holster loose on the hip of his denim jeans. In the holster was an ivory handled revolver, a replica of the Colt 1873 single-action maybe.

Carol Ray stepped an intimate distance toward this person and said quietly, "See you later?"

"See what I can do," he replied, and smooched her awkwardly on the cheek. He looked at me once or twice with a frown, and then he and his fancy pistol and kisses were gone.

Carol Ray sighed a little and shook her head, watching after him. Then she gathered herself and turned to us and with a grin said, "I hope y'all like conditioned air."

"We like it good enough," Anci said. "When we get it, that is. The one at home is broke."

"You poor thing."

She opened the door, and we went in. The office was like a meat locker and our chairbacks and cushions radiated with the cold. We sat around Carol Ray's desk. There was a computer, along with enormous paper ledgers and, sitting in an open safe, piles of cash. On the wall was mounted an antique long gun, a Henry Hammond Sporting Deluxe, probably made during the end of the 1860s. Behind the desk was a big picture window filled with the empty field next door and vibrating with the sound of the firearm reports.

Carol Ray said, "Just out of curiosity, you always take your daughter along with you on private detective business?"

Anci said, "No, but sometimes I take him."

I smiled at her. To Carol Ray, I said, "We're after information about Dennis Reach. Anything you'd be willing to share might end up being useful."

"I'll do my best. You were working for him?"

"No, but I probably was the one ran into him last," I said. "Besides his killer, I mean. I ended up spending three nights in the Jackson County lockup for it. I'm guessing the police have talked to you already."

"They certainly have," she said. "Made me rehearse my alibi a half dozen or so times. Maybe more. Honestly, I lost count. Finally, they were satisfied. I do have an alibi, you know?"

"Okay."

"You don't want to hear it?"

I said, "Only if you want to rehearse it again."

She laughed again and touched my hand lightly and said, "You're adorable," but then she didn't rehearse her alibi for me. Instead, she said, "There was that sheriff and a cadaverous-looking person with him. Ammons, I think they called him. A state cop. I don't remember the sheriff's name."

"That'd be R.L. Lindley."

"That's him. A serious person. But not as serious as Ammons. Have you met him?"

"Not Ammons, no."

She said again, "Very serious. And you say they arrested you for it? Killing Dennis?"

"I was held for it briefly, but not charged. They think I'm tangled up in it somehow and wanted to know what I know. Trouble is, I didn't have much to tell them. Still don't. I was only hired in the first place to retrieve a dog that Mr. Reach had kidnapped."

A confused look crossed her face. "I misheard you, hon. It sounded like you said Dennis kidnapped a dog."

"That's right."

"Dog's not slang for something I don't know about, is it?"

"I don't know. It might be. But in this case I mean a *woof woof* kinda dog."

I showed her the picture. "Name's Shelby Ann Cleaves. She belongs to a pair of Union City sorghum farmers of the same name."

"That's amazing."

"We thought so," I said. "I'm guessing you didn't know anything about it, or the dog."

"Dennis and I aren't exactly in the same phone tree these days. Do you know why he did it? Took the dog?"

"He was . . . he died first, I regret to say. Frankly, I was hoping you might help to fill in a few of the blanks for us."

She was still thinking about the dog, though. You could tell. Finally, she blew out a breath and shook her head some and said, "Well, Dennis and I were married back in 2010. Divorced not much later. A few months, I guess it was. It was one of those marriages. You know the kind. Quick as knife, twice as nasty. Dennis gave up wives after that. I guess I spoiled it for him. Marriage. I know he spoiled it for me. Well, him and the next two husbands. You married, Slim?"

"Not at present, no. What happened?"

"I don't know. The usual things, I guess. It was a poor pairing. Like when the earthquake met San Francisco. Dennis hired me to keep the books at the Classic Country. I was twenty-two years old and didn't know anything about nothing. Dennis . . . Well, Dennis was just a bad man." She paused to sip some of her cola. "And that's not even to mention his so-called friends."

"Friends?

"Hard to imagine, ain't it?"

"A little."

"Well, he called them work friends, but really they weren't much more than a gang of hard-core bikers, losers, fellow White Dragons."

Hello.

"Wait, Reach was a white supremacist?"

"He was. For many years. His daddy was, too, and his older brother, and I think they got him mixed up in it. And this was a person with ambition, too. Wanted to be First Dragon or whatever they call it of that chapter of his. He let them use the CC as their clubhouse, even when he wasn't there. And, let me tell you, that led to some awkward circumstances. One night I dropped in up after close and walked right into a coke buy gone bad."

"Fund-raising drive?"

"The Dragons don't sell T-shirts and sugar cookies, Slim," she said. "It took me ten minutes to talk a guy with one hand out of shooting me in the face, and another day and a half to find a new place to live, as far away from Dennis Reach as possible."

"Any notion that they did him in?" I said.

"One of them, maybe. It's possible. Or one of his other exes. But they live in other states. Maybe that boy of his, Jessie. I'm just surprised it took as long as it did."

I said, "You're not the only one. He seemed to think you'd ripped him off."

"He said that? Mentioned me to you, I mean?"

"He did," I said. "He was under some duress at the time, though, and maybe not the happiest camper in the world. I wouldn't put too much stock in any of it."

"You could never put much stock in anything Dennis said to you. That was the kind of person he was in life. Ambitious but mean and lazy and just a bit too stupid for his own good. A person can be happy-stupid or stupid-stupid, and Dennis was the latter. He'd take money from anyone, but even with that he was an expensive hobby. You've heard of throwing good money down a hole?"

"Sure."

"Dennis Reach was the hole."

"Someone told me a story you set his car on fire with him inside it. Anything to that?"

She said, "Really it was just some hay bales in the bed of his pickup. Car caught fire a little, I guess. Not much. Car won't burn like hay. Found that out. Anyway, just my little way of serving divorce notice."

"And yet no jail time?"

"I didn't know better, I'd think you were nettling me some."

I shrugged. "Maybe some. Sorry. Vocational force of habit. But really, no jail time?"

She laughed a little at me and my persistent nettling. "Turns out the judge I drew handled Dennis's earlier divorces. Knew the man. Knew what he was like. Knew what he'd drive a woman to do. Nothing like a bad man to introduce you to desperation. You got the sense the judge wouldn't have minded setting Dennis Reach's car on fire his own self."

We thanked her for her time. We shook hands again and I said we might be in touch, anything came up to be in touch over. Carol Ray said that would be fine and gave me her phone number. Then she said she was pleased to meet Anci, who was a polite young lady and sure enough would come to big things in the world. Anci beamed a smile at her and thanked her for her kind words, and then the two of us went out into the hallway and closed the door behind us and Anci said, "She did it."

"YOU THINK?"

We'd gone outside before continuing our talk, account of me not wanting Carol Ray to hear a thirteen-year-old accuse her of first-degree murder. Anci climbed on the Triumph behind me. A fat man I knew from town was walking to his truck with a shotgun in one arm and an infant in the other, an image that probably ought to be stitched on some kind of flag for rural places.

Anci said, "Now, don't be jealous I figured it out before you."

"I'll try."

"Probably all the detective reading I've been doing lately."

"Oh, probably."

"She had a motive, one. Reach said she owed him a

debt. Maybe she couldn't pay. Or maybe just didn't want to. Plus, not sure if you noticed, but it appears to me like there's a firearm or two around here."

"But these are registered-type guns," I pointed out. "Paperwork guns. One the killer left behind wasn't."

"Fine, I'll give you that one. But I bet if she wanted to get her hands on a gun like that, she'd know how to do it."

I guessed she would, at that, though I hesitated to say so. It was still too early in the game to accuse anyone of murder.

Anci had a play date around that time—she punched my arm when I called it that—so we rode into the next little town over where I dropped her off at a friend's. This friend's daddy, an employee with the state, I believe, was in the yard tending his dead grass and shrubs, and when he saw me he waved and gave me the peculiar look state employees give to private eyes on motorcycles. I thought for perhaps the millionth time of the life I was leading and the life that I was giving to my daughter thereby, one of mayhem and murder and the occasional kidnapped dog. I wondered whether it was worth it or whether I ought to do something sensible like take my civil service exam and deliver mail or fill potholes on county roads. I waved back at the disapproving man and told Anci I'd be back around to pick her up. She said that was fine. She said not to accuse Miss Shotguns & Shakes of murder yet, on account of she wanted to be there to see it when I did, as I surely and inevitably would, her being the culprit and all. I promised I wouldn't, then backpedaled out of the driveway and rode away, happy to have some alone-time to contemplate what my next move should be, who I should talk to. When you're dealing with rifle decapitations, you generally want to lock down as many of the facts as possible. R.L. Lindley surely would.

Right then, though, I wanted to lock down lunch. All that running around and interrogating had left me with a hunger. I found a pizza place I liked near midtown and got off my bike and went inside. It was crowded with lunch business, and I had to fight my way to the counter, where I found myself standing beside an off-duty cop I'd known as a boy way back in grade school.

When he noticed me standing there, he scowled and said, "Keepin' yourself out of trouble, dill weed?"

I said, "Well, Bill, I ain't beating up meth dealers for payoffs, but I scrape by."

That got him. He stared back at me with dark little weasel eyes, hate flaring his nostrils. I smiled at him and patted him on the shoulder in a friendly way. I ordered two slices of pepperoni and an orange soda. That's how full of life I was feeling. I was so full of optimism, in fact, that I decided to diddle around with our heavily armed local hate group. I knew a person I could talk to, maybe get some answers. I figured if I could get some sense that Reach had been offed by his racist pals, I could aim the Jackson County sheriff in that direction and walk away clean from the whole mess.

I was proud of myself and my plan and eager to put it into action. I finished my lunch and went out again. I got on my bike and rode north on Park Avenue and then through the intersection at West Madison, where the cop from the pizza joint was waiting for me in the cross street. He pulled in behind the bike and turned on his globes. I stopped on the shoulder and put down my stand and watched him walk up to me, already writing a ticket in his little book.

"Taillight's out, Slim," he said.

"It's not."

"Taillight's out, Slim," he said.

"We can both see that it's not."

"Taillight's out, Slim," he said.

"Just give me the goddamn ticket."

He gave me the goddamn ticket.

He said, "Hey, you really kill that club owner?"

"No."

"Heard you blew his brains all over his kitchen. Ruined his breakfast, too. Sheriff's report says steak and eggs."

"I didn't do it. I didn't do either of it."

"Wish I could burn you for it."

I said, "Let me ask you something, Bill, what did I ever do to you?"

"You personally? Nothing specific."

"Then what?"

"Private snoop ruined my marriage."

"By ruined, I assume you mean caught you in the hay with another lady?"

"I said ruined."

"Okay. Fine. Ruined. But it wasn't me."

"Nope."

"I got to go," I said.

He tipped his hat and started back to his prowler.

I called after him, "And don't you break my tail—"

He broke it. His nightstick swung hard from his hip. Shards of red plastic clattered to the street.

Sonofabitch.

A WHILE LATER I FOUND THE NEIGHBORHOOD I WAS LOOKING for. I stopped in at the little P&R near the old Catholic church and picked up a bottle of wine and some of that good bread they got and then I rounded another corner south and there it was: the same house on the same lot under the same tall silver maples. There was a Lincoln in the drive with the curb feelers and whitewalls and everything and a garden in the side lot with freshly turned earth and plenty of tomato and pepper and basil plants sprouting under green wire cages and fine netting. Just like I remembered it, just like it'd been when I was a boy and hanging around there probably because my own old man wasn't worth two shits and a cough.

I found them in the backyard, shooting a pellet gun at a line of coffee cans on some old concrete blocks. Dad's old friend and union buddy Cheezie Bruzetti was eighty-two years old and walker-bound but still strong in the arms and chest with a full head of curly white hair. His son Paul was in his fifties, fat, and bald, and he looked as defenseless next to his invalid father as a depilated squirrel. When they saw me, Cheezie smiled and Paul frowned, Cheezie because he was one of my dearest friends and Paul because I was intruding but also because he was an unlikable little shit given to frowns and sour moods.

The old man said, "Slim, come shoot cans with us."

He kissed me on the cheek. Paul rolled his eyes. I took the pellet rifle, cocked it. The cans were maybe twenty yards away. Not far. I sighted and fired and missed. Paul smirked.

Cheezie said, "CO_2 cartridge probably needs replaced. Try again, and remember that the pellets drop a little near the end."

I sighted again and remembered about the pellets, then fired and shot the cans down, one after another. They make such a nice sound when you hit them. Satisfying. I handed the rifle to Paul, who snatched it from my hand with a grunt. I'd spoiled his smirk.

Cheezie said, "Your daddy could shoot like that. You're his son all right."

"I guess."

"You been to visit him recently?"

"Not recently, no," I said. We'd talked once a year ago or thereabouts, my dad and me, but Cheezie had been there and knew all about it. "We don't visit much these days, Cheezie."

In response, the old man shrugged and smiled a little and said, "Family," but you could tell he didn't understand, not really.

"Let's go one more time around with these pellets," Cheezie said. "I'm feeling lucky."

I went and set up the cans. As I was doing so, I happened to spot another can, an extra can, in the tufts of grass behind the wall of blocks. Somebody had filled it with concrete. A cheater. Paul, probably. It was either a good way to win a bet against a superior shooter or a bad way to get a pellet in your ass if the superior shooter had more than a few brains in his head. I left it alone. I went back across the lawn and waited my turn with the gun.

Cheezie went first. He hit the first couple of cans and grazed a third but missed the rest.

"Not so lucky after all," he said, and handed the gun to Paul while I set up the cans again. "My eyes ain't what they used to be. And by 'used to be,' I mean yesterday."

I came back from setting, and Paul took his turn. He knocked the cans down, quickly and neatly, with center shots. He smirked again at me and handed across the gun. The stock was sweaty from his fat little palms.

"I'll get them this time," he said, and jogged across the lawn. I watched him set up the cans. The last can was the concrete can. You could tell all the way from that distance. Paul jogged back over, wearing self-satisfaction like a Sunday hat.

"Let's see what you can do," he said.

I sighted again and fired, remembering about the weak Co2. I knocked them all down until I came to the last can. Then I hesitated.

Cheezie said, "He hits that last one, he wins the day."

Paul nodded and grinned his thin-lipped grin. No one likes a cheater and no one likes a thin-lipped sort, and Paul Bruzetti was both. A thin-lipped cheater. Nature's mistake.

I squinted down the rifle barrel at the concrete can. Even with a full gas cartridge, there was no way to knock it over. I began to squeeze the trigger. At the last moment,

I turned the gun and shot Paul point-blank in the ass. Paul cried out and cussed up a storm. Cheezie roared.

WE WENT INSIDE THE HOUSE AND TO THE KITCHEN. CHEEZIE pushed his walker to the stove and started cooking: fresh tomatoes and garlic and handfuls of basil from that garden of his. A pot of salted water began to boil. I said I'd already had lunch, to which Cheezie responded I was nothing more than skin and bones, and I could either eat or be force-fed. I said in that case I'd eat. Cheezie remarked on the good sense that ran in my family. This was the way of the old Italians, as it had been my mother's way. There wasn't any point in arguing about it. Paul went to the bathroom to worry over his butt. Cheezie watched him go with sad eyes.

"I warned him about that stupid can," he said. "Warned him it'd come to evil, he tried it with the wrong hombre. He got caught cheating at warshers last year, too. Company picnic. Got beat up pretty good over it."

"How in the hell do you cheat at washers?"

Cheezie shrugged. "A guy's willing to work hard enough, he can cheat at anything."

"Why does he do it?"

"I don't know. I guess because he's unhappy."

I said, "Cheezie, I'm involved in something—something bad. With the White Dragons. I need help."

Cheezie didn't say anything for a while. His wooden spoon made stirring sounds in the sauté pan.

"Last time you needed help, people died," he said. "A woman and a man. Probably some others."

"They took my daughter, Cheezie. They took Anci. I could, I'd dig them up and kill them all over. But this isn't about doing any murders. I just need to talk to someone."

"Been a long time," he said, "since I knew any of those idiots. And that's not even to mention their feelings about us Italians."

"I understand," I said. "I also know you and my dad knew some of these guys back in your union days."

"Back then, you had to get along with a little bit of everybody. Even redneck racist yahoos. But Slim, I ain't in the union no more."

"Once in, always in, Cheezie," I said. "You taught me that." I took out my little notebook and opened it and sat there with a pencil in my hand looking at him. He sighed.

"There was a man in Bonnie name of Cecil Pines."

"Pines?"

"But I think he's dead now."

"Dang."

"No, it's better this way. He was a bad man. Let's see. Years ago, I read something about a ladies' auxiliary starting up outside Elco, but I don't know what ever came of it."

"Hard to believe," I said. "You ever hear of a fat little fucker named Dennis Reach?"

"Reach?" He pursed his lips and searched his memory, finally shaking his pom of white hair. "It don't ring any bells, no." He turned and looked at his boy, who'd slipped quietly back into the room. "You?"

"Nope. No bells," Paul said, but his cheeks had turned the color of overripe plums.

"I knew a Reardon once, though," Cheezie said. "When they killed him for trying to turn in his white sheet, the cops tried to write his death off as a bear attack."

"Tried to?"

"Bears typically don't use hammers."

"Ah."

"There were one or two others," he said. "Most of the ones I knew well are dead, though, a long time. I could do some looking around, if you wanted."

"I don't want that," I said. "But if you think of anyone else, I'd appreciate it if you'd give me a ring."

"I promise," he said. He lifted the pan off the stovetop. "Now, no more talk about that scum. Not in my kitchen. It's time to eat."

We ate. Well, I ate as much as I could, until I felt like a full tick, ready to pop. We chatted some more about this and that, the Miners baseball team over there in Marion, the new Ford line, the sorry state of hunting that year. Afterward, I told them good-bye and rose to go. I apologized to Paul for my goof with the pellet gun. I said I hoped his butt healed up quick, but he only frowned at me and grunted.

I left the house. I knew he'd follow me, and he did. I was walking to the Triumph when Paul came out and walked quickly over to me.

"You're just lucky the old man is here with us, Slim,"

he said. "Otherwise, you and I would be dancin' right now. And not fun dancin', neither."

"I know."

"Fightin' dancin', is what I mean."

"I know," I said again. "I get it."

"I don't hold with folks showing me up in my own house."

"Last I knew, this was your dad's house, Paul."

"Be mine one day," he said. "Might as well be mine now. Mine in all but law."

"Maybe you can get some of your White Dragon acquaintances to come teach me my manners."

"What?"

"Reach," I said. "Dennis Reach. You recognized his name. I can't help wondering why that is."

Paul swallowed. He tried to laugh a little but failed. He scratched his butt and winced.

"He's that club owner, ain't he?" he said.

"Was. Don't own nothing now but some dirt and an oblong box."

"I don't know him."

"You just said you did, dummy. Now tell me how and why or you'll get that dance you were just talking about. And not fun dancing, either. Fighting dancing, is what I mean."

He didn't like that, but he didn't have any choice but to take it. He talked big, but he wasn't big, either physically or in what you'd call spirit. A dishrag has more backbone.

Finally, he said, "If it'll get you out of here, I got to run into the house real quick, though."

He went inside. After a while, he jogged back out with something in his hands, an article from a newspaper. He gave it to me. It was about the most recent sheriff's race in Jackson County. Accompanying it was a photograph of a tall man in oil-spattered blue jeans and a ball cap standing in front of a hand-painted sign that read *Bet on Black*.

He said, "Dad saves them. Newspapers. I don't know why. Your dad ever save anything?"

"No."

"The man in the picture is J.T. Black. Used to be a deputy over there in Jackson County. Made a run for the big chair couple years back, but lost to that colored sheriff."

"Lindley."

"That's him," Paul said. "Anyway, this here is Black and his campaign slogan."

"Bet on Black?"

"Clever, right?"

"No, it's not clever. Man's running against a black candidate and puts up a sign says *Bet on Black*? It's confusing as hell."

"I thought it was good."

"That's because you're a peckerwood idiot."

"Well, he got beat."

"And no wonder."

Paul sighed.

"Anyway, Black was a brother."

"White Dragon?"

"Yeah, and a friend of Dennis Reach's. They used to

run a little meth together out of Frankfurt. Ran the meth
gangs, I mean."

"While he was a deputy? Or after?"

"Both. Rumor was, that's why he left the job. Sheriff at
the time wanted to drop him for it, but couldn't get neither
him nor Reach. Those two liked to keep their hands clean.
Let everybody else get bloody. Anyway, I thought he might
be a place for you to start."

"I'm keeping this article," I said. "Sorry again about
your butt."

He sighed and shook his head, but then he laughed
about it some.

"Stay out of trouble, Slim, okay? You may not know
it, but the old man loves you like a son." His thin-lipped
mouth made a sad shape. There are sons and there are sons.
He turned and went back up the steps and into the house
and closed the door. Family.

Speaking of which:

"So you learned the story of some haters, got a possible
lead," Anci said. "Good crime solving right there. Gold star."

"Thanks."

"Not that it matters any," she said. "We already know
who done it."

"You think you know. I don't know anything yet."

"That's because you aren't reading all this Holmes.
Read enough Holmes, you'd know it for sure," she said. She
paused to give me a quizzical look. "Why are you sitting
that way?"

"What way?"

"Holding your belly like you swallowed a football."

"I've had two and a half lunches today," I said. "A football would be a relief."

"Detective work is dangerous, and you're so brave to do it," she said. But she didn't mean it, I could tell.

After a while, I took my aching belly into the office at the back of the house and opened the safe to look at the Cleaveses' overstuffed envelope. I reflected a moment on all the nice things I might do with it. Fixing the A/C, one. That was first on the list. A new motorcycle maybe, or maybe even a vacation to some faraway land where they had foreign murders and the femme fatales double-crossed you in an exotic language that sounded like a song. After a while, though, I decided I didn't want a vacation or a new bike. I wanted Peggy to come home, and I wanted to not be chasing White Dragons for a living. I wanted a cup of coffee.

I closed the safe on the money and my vacation wishes. I went into the kitchen and found Anci reading at the table, plugging away on yet another Holmes. *The Valley of Fear*, I think. Another good one. The article with the photo of J.T. Black was where I'd dropped it on the counter, and it was only when I looked at it again that I recognized him. Maybe it was the light. Or the fact that he'd changed his facial hair. Whatever, all I know is that for some reason it had taken me nearly an hour to recognize him as the guy with the giant mustache I'd seen that morning at Shotgun & Shakes, the one who'd awkwardly smooched Carol Ray Reach on her perfect cheek.

Anci noticed me standing there, staring. She said, "Still feeling puny?"

I said, "More and more all the time."

6.

So J.T. Black knew Dennis Reach, and they both knew Carol Ray to some greater or lesser degree of intimacy. Now Reach was dead and Black was sniffing around his ex-wife. I wasn't sure yet what it all meant or what the living members of the triangle were up to, but I was willing to bet my retirement it wasn't anything you'd embroider on a throw pillow.

Sheriff Wince wasn't available. I tried his mobile and his office but he didn't answer, and the deputy I spoke to instead said he'd been threatened with terrible things if he forwarded my call.

I said, "Mine specifically or just anyone?"

"You specifically."

"That's not very flattering."

"We're cops," the boy said, "not flatter-bugs."

Lindley was in at the Jackson County sheriff's station.

He said, "Please tell me you want to confess."

"Why? Would that make you happy?"

"Let me put it this way: I've got kids. *Six* kids. That's a lot these days. Hell, it was a lot back when I was young.

And, what's more, they're boys. It's like living with a herd of
wild beasts. You want so much as a morsel of food for yourself, you got to fight for it. You want to watch a program
on the TV, it's like going to war. The last twenty some-odd
years, I can't even fuck my wife without assurance of an
audience and some kind of snide remark in the morning."

"Must be quite a show."

"Don't make me come over there now."

"Sorry."

"And finally, *finally*, after a lifetime of this business, I'm
about to pack the last of those little bastards off to college.
Another month, I'll be able to watch whatever the hell I
want on the idiot box whenever I want, everything in that
refrigerator will be mine, and I'll be able to screw my wife
in the middle of the living room floor and twice on Friday
night, and there won't be a word said about it except, 'My
God, R.L., you're the greatest.' I'll be like a goddamn king."

"Yeah?"

"And busting you would still make me happier."

"Dang."

"Just telling the truth. What's on your mind? Assuming
I give a damn."

I said, "I'm interested in what you can tell me about J.T.
Black."

"And why, pray, should I tell you anything about him?
You're my prime suspect, after all."

"Humor me, would you? Maybe pretend I'm writing a
story about it."

"Okay, write this in your story: J.T. Black is a big, mean,

racist, shit-for-brains motherfucker. And that's *on* the record, man. His daddy is a coal operator, has his own little string out this way, and the way I hear things he about owned this entire county, one time or another. J.T. was a deputy for a number of years before I busted his ass in the last election. Not bragging about it, just stating fact. End of story."

"He's a White Dragon, isn't he?"

"He is," R.L. said after a moment. "Leastways, he was. Way I understand things, Black and the Dragons had a bit of falling out."

"Any idea over what?"

"Nope. You understand, we were never what you'd call close."

"He's not on your Twitter feed?"

"What?"

"Nothing. I don't even know."

"Man starts talking nonsense like that—Twitter and whatnot—needs to get his head screwed on right. What's all this about, anyway? Why you suddenly interested in a gang of crazies like the Dragons?"

"Have you got anything new in the Reach case?"

"My momma told me never to answer a question with a question," he said. "You think Black is tangled up in all that?"

I said, "Don't know. But Reach was a White Dragon and so was Black, and I just ran into J.T. the other day hanging around one of Reach's ex-wives."

Lindley chuckled. "So you met Carol Ray, did you?"

"Briefly but beautifully."

"She's trouble, that one. And deeper into her former husband's doings than she likes to let on. Cop in me thinks I should warn you about that. Other hand, she gets done with you, you're like to be out of my hair for good and always. I'm thinking I'll go with that idea. The second one. See where it leads."

"I'll be careful."

"I don't care."

I ignored him. I said, "She seemed to think Dennis might have been done in by his bad-ass buds."

"That'd be mighty convenient for you, wouldn't it? Slim, I've worked more than my fair share of homicides. One thing they all had in common, the biggest asshole in closest proximity was almost always guilty. Guess who that is."

"I have a picture of it in my mind."

"Good. And one more thing before I bring this pleasant chat to a close: I catch you nosing around this business in my county, trying to fuck up my investigation, I will have your ass back in a cell so fast it'll give you jet lag. You'll be looking at obstruction of justice and accessory to murder. And that's just the appetizer."

"What if I make you a personal promise to behave?"

I won't even share what Lindley said to that.

It took me another couple hours to track down Reach's other exes. One was a nurse's aid at a cancer center in Ohio, the other ran a pricey yoga camp in Hohenwald, Tennessee. Neither of them was hiding out. Getting anything out of them, though, was a story unto itself. The nurse's aid didn't want to talk about it, said she was glad the motherfucker was dead—in so many words—and invited me to the Forest City for the party. At least the yoga instructor put on mournful airs.

"It's hard," she said, her accent thick and slow, "terribly hard to feel sad and happy all at the same time. Conflicted. Do you understand what I mean?"

"I guess I do."

"Of course, I didn't want Dennis to suffer. Did he suffer?"

"I don't know," I said. "Maybe a little."

"Sad."

"Uh-huh."

"And you say he suffered?"

And on like that for longer than comfort allowed.

Jessie, the son Carol Ray had mentioned, belonged to the yoga instructor, but he was stationed in Germany and wouldn't rotate home for another year and a half. Another dead end.

By the time I was finished for the night, Anci had been asleep for hours and the house was that nighttime quiet when you can hear the clocks ticking. I finished the book I was reading—one of Anci's mystery stories—and took out my phone and dialed Peggy.

"Well, listen to what the cat dragged in."

"Is that me? Am I the thing the cat dragged in?"

"That's you, baby."

"Just as long as I know where things stand. How's your sister?"

Peggy said, "Let me put it this way, she's single-handedly

keeping the box wine industry in this country afloat. But we're beginning to work a few things out. How's everything back home?"

I took a deep breath and gave her a quick rundown of everything that had happened.

She said, "You're kidding? A missing dog case turned into murder? I've only been gone three days."

"I know."

"I tell you, this is just like that damn thing with the chickens last year."

"Not exactly. I didn't end up in the slammer over that one."

"No. Just the emergency room," she said. "And you're on the hook for it, too, this Reach business. What do you think it's all about?"

"Not sure yet, but I think it's possible our man Reach was trying to skip a few rungs on his way up the White Dragon ladder and somebody took umbrage."

"Sounds like a working theory, anyway," she said, "but are you sure these are the kind of people you want to get tangled up with?"

"Assuredly not," I said. "But I think I've got a lead or two around the periphery. Little luck, I can ask a couple of questions and settle the whole mess in another day or so. Far as I can tell, the worst of it's already over."

"Here's hoping."

I did hope it, too. Hoped it all profound. But it wasn't to be, because that's when I sniffed out the first trace of wood smoke on the air, a sharp tang that stung the eyes and tickled the nostrils. My mind instantly told me "wood-stove," but nobody with any sense would be burning a woodstove in that weather, not unless they were trying to see visions or sweat out demons. A campfire, then, may-be. But from where? The closest camping was nowhere. The scent grew stronger and kept growing until it stung my eyes and throat. I got up and walked off the porch to follow the smoke around back of the house, and then I saw and smelled it for what it really was: burning cedar.

I said into the phone, "Hey, babe, let me call you back, okay? Someone's set my house on fire."

7.

SURE ENOUGH, THE HOUSE WAS ON FIRE. THE HOUSE MY FA-
ther had built. The house at Indian Vale. My house. More
precisely, it had been *set* on fire. A man in a dark hood-
ed jacket was scampering away through the overgrowth of
musclewood and frost grape in the back property. I called
after him, called him and his mama terrible names, but he
neither slowed nor stopped. A metal can slipped from his
hand and hit the ground and rolled onto its side, pump-
ing out the last of its contents. Gasoline. I stopped thinking about the man. I scrambled back around the house and
through the door and up the stairs into Anci's room. A light
sleeper, she woke in a bolt.

"What's is it? What's wrong?"

"Nothing." I remembered her trauma of a year earlier.
I calmed my voice and said, "Okay, it ain't exactly *nothing*."

"What, dammit?"

"Well . . . the house is on fire."

"You're right." She threw back the sheets and leapt out
of bed. "That's not nothing."

"Get outside. Now."

She looked at me sharply.

"The cats!" And she was gone down the stairs.

Damnation. I chased Anci. Anci chased our house cats, Morris and Anthony. I tripped and fell down the stairs. The house filled with smoke like it was a race. I remembered the phone in my back pocket and called in the emergency, then raced off again to join Anci on the cat hunt. When we finally found the critters, they were huddled together in my office, mad as hell and ready to fight. And fight they did, like little tigers, but a half dozen deep scratches later, I'd shut the cats into the cab of my truck and my family was outside and reasonably safe.

Anci said, "What can I do?"

I coughed out a lungful. Black smoke. The house was on fire for real now. A knife of flame sliced through the east-facing gable, and a section of copper flashing bucked its nails and curled quickly into a ball, as though to protect itself. A window exploded. The cedar shingles had nearly caught, I realized, and once that happened it would be all she wrote.

"There's a big bundle of hoses in the shed," I said to Anci. "Garden hoses."

"I know it."

"Go get them."

She tore off. I sucked a deep breath and plunged back into the house. I fumbled through the hallway and into the living room and finally the kitchen, where I found the fuse box and switched off the main circuit. I circled around again and through the back door and outside, where after a few desperate gulps of air I found Anci screwing hoses together. She was crying a little.

"Goddamn it," she said.

"It'll be okay."

"The couplings don't all match."

"It'll be okay," I said again. I knelt in the grass to help her. "The trucks will be here any moment."

She nodded and wiped her eyes with the back of her hand. "Top of that, I had five bucks in there."

"What?"

"You heard me. A fiver. On the bed table. I ran off without grabbing it."

"Don't matter," I said. "We got each other."

"Minus five bucks."

We finished attaching all the hoses that were attachable. I dragged them around the house while Anci screwed the other end to the spigot, but I knew it was too late and it was. The fire had climbed too high for the water stream. For a moment, I had a panic-induced vision. Or hallucination. The flames weren't flames at all but orange orangutans, and these orangutans had climbed onto my roof to dance their tribal dance of war and devastation. I hated them and wanted to spray them with water, but my hose wouldn't reach. A nightmare.

A roar snapped me out of it. Not an animal roar. An architectural roar. A large section of soffit at the back of the house collapsed, sending a shower of sparks skyward. Anci yelped and grabbed my arm. I was fixing to head back inside on a final, desperate salvage mission, when at last the fire trucks appeared at the end of Shake-a-Rag, globes blazing, horns wailing their sad song of panic and loss against the country night. Anci and I high-fived. Then we hugged each other and cried.

A HALF HOUR OF HARD WATER STREAMS AND MUSHROOM clouds later, they'd managed to save the old place. "Save it" is maybe overstating things. The fire had taken most of the rear kitchen wall and the metal pipes were exposed and jutting out at all kinds of crazy angles like a dug-up animal skeleton. The windows in the kitchen were gone, too, and the aluminum porch door had warped and exploded from the heat. The floors squished and buckled menacingly beneath our feet. I called Peggy to tell her what had happened, and she cried a little, too, said she loved us and that she was coming home in the morning.

"Your sister needs you," I said. "You should see to that business, then come home."

"I'll wrap up my business here," she said after a long moment's hesitation. "Quickly as I can. Then I'm coming your way like a rocket. And save a little for me, darling, because I am going to put a bullet in someone's ass."

"I love you."

"I love you, too."

Pretty soon, the fire chief came tromping in to make his report. He was a stub of a guy with arrow-shaped white mustaches and the stiff bearing of a retired soldier. Some of his men called him Major.

"It's still in one piece, anyway," he said, shaking my hand. "Sorry about the mud pit in your yard. Fire engines and pressurized water got a way of making a mess."

"It's nothing."

He nodded and said, "For sure it's the least of your worries. You say you witnessed someone starting this? Some fiend?"

"I did. His fuel can's still around back. He dropped it when he ran away."

"We found it. A gasoline accelerant, most like. Homemade napalm, even. Looks like it started in the woodpile around back. Those cedar shingles?"

"Cedar shake, yeah," I said. "We redid the roof last year."

"How's your insurance?"

"Cheap," I said. "But at least we don't have to worry about the air conditioner for a while."

"Son?"

"Nothing," I said. I felt like I was coming apart at the seams.

After a while, Wince and a few of his deputies put in an appearance. Indian Vale isn't technically inside any town limits, so any policing we might require is handled by the sheriffs. Honestly, I was happy to see him. He spoke with the Major and took down some notes. He ordered the deputies to collect the arsonist's gas can and search the surrounding area for footprints or clothing fibers or other such clues. Then he followed me outside and around the house.

"Bad," he said. "Real bad, but I reckon it could have

been a lot worse. I don't suppose you've got an explanation for any of this."

"This time, honestly, no."

"Anyone make a threat at you lately?"

"No one not wearing a badge."

"Lindley's tough, I grant you, but this don't seem like his style."

"Agreed."

"What about this business you're tied up in now? The Reach murder. Any sense that this might be connected?"

"It's most likely," I said. "If only by proximity. But damned if I can see how."

"Me, neither. Not yet, anyway. So what are you going to do?" he asked. "Bug out or stay?"

"Stay. Try to, anyway."

"Probably not smart."

"Probably not, but where would we go? You know as well I do that it's damn near impossible to disappear around here, unless you're willing to go completely native. Besides, going someplace else is only like to put others in danger, too, and I don't think I want to live with that."

"That really it?"

"Mostly," I said. "Or maybe I just hate the idea of being run off my own place again."

Anci wasn't crazy about it, either. After Wince had collected the evidence and gone, we went back inside to see what there was to see. Anci went to check her bedroom, me to my office.

"We can relax," she said, coming downstairs again. "I found that five dollars."

"Oh, good. I was worried something awful about it."

"And you can just forget your plan to pack me off with Jeep or Opal Mabry or the mailman or whoever you've got in mind."

"Oh, do I have a plan?"

"You do. You know, I know it," she said. "So just forget it. You try to make me go, I'll throw a shit fit makes Lindsay Lohan look like Little Miss Sunshine."

"Okay," I said, slightly terrified.

"I'm serious now."

"I can see that."

"No tricks."

"No tricks," I said.

She wasn't satisfied until I gave her pinkie-swears, though. This settled, we walked through the house to see what we could see.

She said, "What a mess. And what's that smell?"

"Smoke, mostly," I said. "But some of the wiring burned, too, and that makes it worse."

"It smells like someone tried to barbecue a mummy."

"We'll have it cleaned, and then it won't anymore," I said.

"Or a dead horse."

"Or . . ."

"Or what?"

"Nothing," I said. "Never mind.

I was going to say it smelled like A. Evan Cleaves, but the words caught in my throat like a brick of charred cedar.

We cleaned up what we could and spent a few hours doing it, too, but in the end it didn't amount to much of anything. The living room was a sodden mess, so we put down towels and heavy blankets to soak up what water we could. Anci swept ash out of the kitchen and tried to put back the furniture and the pictures that the hoses and fire-fighters had knocked around. Blessedly, most of the damage was confined to one area of the house. The bedrooms were more-or-less intact, as was the living area. We'd be eating takeout pizza and burgers for the next six months, but the old place was safe to live in. Structurally, anyway.

Midnight came and went. Anci camped out on the living room sofa. She texted her school friends to let them know what had happened, and even though she was still afraid I could tell that she was enjoying their sympathy. After a while, she tucked into another of her books—*The Woman in White*—and the next thing I knew she had fallen asleep. I waited until she was snoring and then got off the couch and went outside to walk the perimeter of the house. Nothing but country sounds and a hot dark sky like the inside of a soup pot set to boil. Back inside, I found Anci's sodden copy of *The Hound of the Baskervilles*, turned to page one, and made myself comfortable at the foot of the sofa.

THE NEXT MORNING, I RAN INTO TOWN FOR BREAKFAST: PAN-cakes and scrambled eggs in Styrofoam clamshells, coffee for me, coffee and orange juice for Anci. Anci ate on the porch, where the stink wasn't so bad. I tried to eat but ended up just having the coffee. When Anci was done, we cleaned up our mess and went into the house. I showered and washed my hair. I was still wet and wrapped in a towel when the phone buzzed, a blocked number. I'd been waiting for something like this—knowing it would happen sooner rather than later—and so I took a deep breath or two before answering.

"We clear on a thing or two now, ball-sucker?" The voice wasn't quite a hiss, but it was low and rough and unnatural. If it was a person, it would have had on a hat and fake mustache to disguise itself.

"Wait, wait, wait. Ball-whatter?"

"You heard me," he said, but then he acted like I hadn't. "I said I guess we're clear now. Ball-sucker."

"Rude."

"I reckon you're lucky the whole place didn't go up, and you with it, too. You ever seen a human body burn? It takes a while. Takes a while for it to die all the way. The brain. Like I said, you are one lucky sonofabitch."

"Well, I guess it depends on what you call luck," I said. "Me, I wouldn't say that. Perhaps you could come over, and you and I could debate on it. I'll supply the Cokes and the foot to shove up your ass."

"Your good luck just ran out, Dad," he said. "Your little girl's, too."

"That's mean."

"We're mean people. Dangerous, too," he said. "Later."

"Hey," I said before he could disconnect.

"Hey, what?"

"A. Evan, I'm going to kill you for this. Twice."

But the voice just laughed.

I was so mad, I didn't need to finish toweling. The shower water just sorta steamed away. Somehow I dressed myself in matching clothes, managed not to put my underdrawers on my head. Then I put in a call to my old mining buddy and the reigning Most Dangerous Man in Little Egypt, Jeep Mabry.

"What shift you on, brother?" I asked when he picked up after about twenty rings.

He muttered something about a monthlong four-to-twelve rotation, and oh the agony, and what business did I have waking a workingman from the dead? And on and on until I gave him the score and he snapped awake and got pissed at the same time.

"And you think it was this Cleaves asshole?"

"What it looks like. Sounds like, I mean. Some guys shouldn't try to do fake voices. On a good day, A. Evan sounds like someone sat on a rattlesnake, and that's mildly hard to disguise."

"Well, let's go fetch him and introduce him to justice."

"Good idea," I said. "First, though, I ask you a favor?"

"Anything."

"Keep an eye on Anci for me."

"You got it," he said. "You want to drop her off?"

That took some clarifying. I explained my promise to Anci, about not forcing her to leave Indian Vale. Jeep was amused.

"You're kidding? Listen to you. Getting bossed around by a thirteen-year-old that way."

"A thirteen-year-old *daughter*," I said. "It's one of their magical powers."

"I'll keep it in mind," he said. "When?"

"Right now is best."

He showed up twenty minutes later, which means he flew. He was so big he filled the doorway, and his face was puffy and red with sleep. He was still in his PJs, too, gray sweats and a yellow T-shirt. He looked ridiculous and terrifying at the same time.

"Holy shit," he said. "They burned your roof. You just did that roof."

"Kitchen, too," I said, pleased that he seemed so honestly outraged about it. "I bought those new countertops last spring. Well, they're toast, and the wiring is shot, and I think the coffeemaker melted. Anci had one of those Hello Kitty clock radios from way back. You ought to see it now. The kitty looks like a gargoyle."

"Poor kid."

At which point she appeared. I grinned at her like a dope. She looked at Jeep and then me, from one of us to the other and back, and her face got as red as a devil's behind, and holy shit, did she raise a squall. It took ten minutes to calm her down enough to cuss.

"You tricked me, goddamn it," she said.

"I didn't," I said. "I said you could stay. I never said you could stay alone. Besides, it's just for a few hours."

"That's what you always say. And then you'll go off and

get in a scrape and be gone three days. What am I supposed to do in the meantime?"

Jeep said, "We could do a puzzle."

Anci glared at him.

"I don't have any puzzles. Did you bring a puzzle?"

"Maybe we could break something and put it back together."

"I got something in mind," she said.

"Be cool," Jeep said.

"Shove it."

She kept it up until it was time to go. Jeep followed me out. He made it look like he needed to talk to me alone, but I think he was really just trying to get away from the hurricane inside.

"Kid's a tiger."

"She's a tiger in a Sherman tank," I said. "I can't decide whether having you here is protecting her from anyone who might come out here for trouble, or protecting them from her."

"That last thing."

"No contest."

"Nope."

He said, "So this thing with Reach and the Cleaveses and the White Dragons. What do you think it's all about?"

And I told him what I thought.

IT'S TRUE THAT PRIVATE DETECTING EXPOSES YOU TO WHAT you might call the contradictory nature of human behavior. Fine. But a hundred-thousand-dollar payoff followed quickly by an attempted murder by arson was a new one on me. Assuming A. Evan really was behind the fire, as I suspected him to be. I can't tell you how pleased I was that the hundred thousand dollars in question had been locked away in a fireproof safe.

My plan was to cruise by the Cleaveses' Union City farm, see what there was to see. What wasn't my plan was to get tangled up with them before I had a better idea what the hell was going on, Jeep's suggestion aside. I guess I could have called Ben Wince with my suspicion, but his office was already on the case, and anyway, it's not as though I had anything like proof. Plus, if possible, I wanted a crack at them first.

I drove out to Union City in the heat. The heat was real but the city wasn't much. There's not even really much town. A couple of locals gave me a lazy summer version of the small-town stink-eye, and a lonely mutt lifted his leg in salute as I dove by, but that's about all I got out of it. I knew the Cleaveses' address, but this was pretty open country and it took me another half hour or so to find their homestead a mile or three east of the limits.

Houses either look lived in or they don't, and this one was as still as a petrified log. Even pulling a drive-by I could tell they'd cleared out. I swung around and came back and parked on the road. I put my gun in my pants and went up to the house and inside.

I wasn't expecting anything fancy, of course. But this was a bad place, a nightmare place, though why I imagined it so was more a matter of feeling than something concrete. The inside was empty except for a foul odor and a damp that sat on the skin like a corpse's tongue. Every time I turned a corner, I expected to meet something unspeakable coming the other way, a haint with A. Evan's face maybe. There wasn't any furniture, no marks in the light dust that had blown in from the nearby fields, no scuffmarks on the wood floors. There weren't any personal photographs on the walls, no evidence of family history and no nail holes to indicate there had ever been any. There wasn't a TV or a radio. A computer was out of the question. The only thing to look at were some dirty playing cards, pinned to the plasterboard, probably by Sheldon, judging by the age of the cards. A whole wall of them. The women were done up in corny Wild West apparel—frilly bodices and hoop dresses and a flat mile of gingham, and derringers or six-shooters in their gloved hands—but with their business hanging out. There was a single mattress on the floor in one of the back rooms, now nearly black with age and contamination.

I went out of the house and around back. There was a double cellar door with a stick through the loop handles. There was a rusty padlock on a chain, but the shank was loose. I pulled out the stick and went down the stairs into the dark. The odor I'd detected in the house above now hit me full on, and I nearly retreated. Pushing forward, I stumbled around on the soft earthen floor until I found a pull-string and light. It was a small space and very warm. Someone had dug up most of the floor and pushed the dirt toward the edges of the cellar, so that the middle of the floor was a shallow pit. There weren't any bodies, but the dirt was full of dried blood and crunched under my feet. Here and there were square postholes, but whatever rig had been there was gone now. I was down in the kill pit maybe four minutes. The smell got to me. It was the smell of death and fear and despair. I found a corner to throw up in. Then I went back up into the light and used my cell to call Jeep.

"What you thought?" he asked as soon as he picked up.

"Dogfighting," I said by way of confirmation. "The Cleaveses are dogfighters."

PART TWO
THE SHOW

8.

I HAD SOME DARK MOMENTS TO MYSELF—ANIMAL CRUELTY
will do that to a person, or at least most people—then made
my way back into Union City. I needed more information,
so I spent an hour or so asking around, hitting up the locals,
but no one wanted to say anything. Couple guys even acted
like they didn't know who the Cleaveses were, but they
weren't going to win any gold statues anytime soon. Another guy looked into the sky like he'd spotted a UFO and
suddenly couldn't be bothered with any old business here on
earth. Finally, I found someone—a gray-headed man who
ran the town's only little grocery market—willing to chat.

"I can't get anyone else around here to talk to me," I
said. "It's like they're all taking amnesia lessons."

"Oh, they just don't want to go picking on the Cleaveses," he said, "get on their bad side. Sheldon's crazy enough
to make a statue of a blind man twitch. A. Evan's another
story entirely. That boy's so mean, the devil don't want him.
He dies, they're going to have to find some whole other
place to put his soul."

"You don't seem so afraid of him."

"I'm not. Let me tell you something. Couple of years back, this place here wasn't doing so good. You may find that hard to believe, with that the new Walmart up the road a piece, but it's the truth. Well, about that time, I started having trouble with my wife. More than trouble, maybe. She run off. So there's that. But the trouble with the store and the trouble with my wife got me in trouble with my house mortgage, too. Ain't never had no trouble like that before, but all of a sudden I couldn't keep up."

"Lot of that going around these days."

"What I found out. So I talked to these people on the phone. My bank. I want to keep my house. I like it and it's mine and I want to keep it. They think they can help me. They put me into some kind of remodification program. I told them I ain't ever been modified before, so I'm not sure why I need *re*modified, but they say that's the way to do it, and that's what we do. So we start this process, and let me tell you, son, if there's a paperwork hell, I was in it. I ain't ever seen anything like it. They got teams of accountants and adjusters to climb in your asshole and hunt around until they find your teeth, and you got to fill out paperwork about the whole deal. Mountains of it. Making matters worse, they were the ones suggested I go through this business in the first place, and then when I agreed to go through it they treated me like a crook, like I was trying to pull some kind of swindle. But went through it I did, two years of pure misery and sleepless nights and paper cuts, and now nothing don't scare me anymore, not even them Cleaveses. Or maybe I'm just stupid."

"I doubt it," I said. "But whatever happened to the house?"

"Lost it. By the time I figured out they were just stringing me along, trying to squeeze a few more payments out of me, it was too late. I lost everything and live with my brother now a few miles up the road. It ain't the best situation, you might imagine, and I think his wife would just as soon shoot me as look at my smiling face in the morning, but neither of them is that goddamn bank, so I don't mind it none."

"Looks like the Cleaves have lit out of their house, too."

"Oh, they do that sometimes. Probably they've gone on a visit up to the Harvels'," he said.

"The where now?"

"Not the where. The who. Bundy and Arlis Harvel. They're Sheldon's cousins. They go there sometimes to visit, sometimes stay a few weeks."

"Any sense of where these Harvels call home?"

"Not specifically, no," he said. "Though I think they have a patch west of here, somewhere near Mockingbird Hills."

In other words, somewhere thataway. You could search for them for three days and come up without anything more than an expanded sense of how big and empty a country this can be.

The old man cleared his throat then and said, "Listen, you mind taking a word of advice?"

"I'll take it. Long as it doesn't have anything to do with not chasing down these Cleaveses. I don't care that they're dangerous or crazy or what. I already know that. Should have known it the first time I saw them. I don't care that they live in a haunted house with nothing in it besides dirty playing cards on the walls or that they seem to sleep in the same bed. I guess I don't want to think too much about that last business. Makes me feel a bit like a failure, too, like I've spent all these years studying human nature but still don't really know anything about it. And I don't mind about these Harvels, either, though I assume they're as crazy as the Cleaves, they've got the same blood in them. But, dammit, these folks tried to burn down the house my daddy built, and I need to find them."

The dude smiled a little sheepishly. "Well, actually, my advice was, hot day like this, you might want to grab you something frozen out of the box back there."

"Something frozen?"

"Got some of them Otter Pops in. Orange and purple and blue. Blue one's got a Frenchie otter on it in a beret. It's adorable."

"Well, I'm a little embarrassed now."

"I would be, too. It was a pretty good speech, though."

"Thanks. The Otter Pop sounds okay. Think I might take you up." I went and got some out of the box and brought them back to the counter. He rang me up and I gave him some money.

"They really burned your house down?" he asked.

"Tried to," I said, tearing open the blue Frenchie one with my teeth.

"Might want to rethink going after them, then," he said. "Those people are crazy."

★ ★ ★

I FOLLOWED THE OLD GUY'S LEAD AND RODE AROUND MOCK-ingbird Hills for a while, but it didn't come to much. I didn't have an address, and I didn't know what the Harvels' house looked like, or the Harvels themselves, or whether they drove cars or rode bicycles or Shetland ponies. I stopped at a couple of places along the way, but either no one had heard of them or they wanted me to think they hadn't. After a while, I gave it up. There was another avenue to follow.

I hated to feel like I was picking on him, but I dropped in at the Twin Pines Sawmill in Frankfurt and looked around until I found Paul Bruzetti on the floor working the jig. I smiled and waved to put him at his ease, but I don't guess I was all that convincing. He looked like he'd just shit a brick, and when he turned to face me his right thumb went quickly to his mouth.

"Damn near cut it off," he said.

"That's be pretty amazing."

"Amazing? For me to cut off my thumb?" he said. "First my ass, now my thumb. That's sadistic. You're a sadistic person."

"Not amazing for you," I said. "Amazing for me. But it'd take too long to explain why."

"Or it could just be that you're a sadist. I'll be honest, either way I'm starting to regret that you ever decided to come around again."

"Me, too, kinda. But look, I've had a difficult couple of days. First, I nearly get shot by a racist dognapper, then I get arrested for his murder. And a few days later, someone tries to burn my house down with my kid inside."

"Someone tried to burn down your house? Your place over there to Indian Vale?"

"That's right. My place over there to Indian Vale. What that means is, for the next many months, I'm going to be fighting with insurance adjusters and looking at wallpaper samples, and the whole thing makes me mad as hell. So call me sadistic or frazzled or at the end of my rope or just plain ole-ass mean. I don't care. I think you know these people. I think you know them and like them enough that you've chosen your racist redneck pals over your own father. I also think you have information I need, so you're either going to give it to me or I'm going to feed you through that plane until you come out looking like a bleached carrot stick."

He about turned the color of a carrot, too. Even a chump and a coward can only be pushed so far. He blew out a spitty breath and shot his chest out like he meant to throw it across the floor and staggered toward me until he we were nearly sharing the same pants.

"That's a threat. Another threat," he said. "You keep threatening me, and goddamn it, I'm tired of it. Tired of it up to here. I think I'm going to make you do something about it this time, you redneck Hungarian sonofabitch."

He tried to make me. He raised up a soft fist and took a swing. I did something about it. I punched him in the forehead. It wasn't much. It would have torn through a grocery bag, probably, but not a doubled-up grocery bag. But it was enough. Paul's bulbs went dim and his mouth slack, and he dropped over backward like a wooden box of shovels. A couple of the other workers looked up from their machines at us, and one ran his sleeve across his nose in a curious way, but no one made a move to interfere. I guess Paul wasn't too popular at work, either.

"You hit me," he said after a while. He touched his head.

"You kinda asked for it."

"I guess I kinda did. What did you say you wanted? I'd really like to get you the hell out of here."

"Black's name is no good to me yet," I said, not bothering to mention that Jackson County, which Black called home, was off-limits to me for now. "And him just being a former Dragon don't get me much of anywhere. I need something more and something more direct."

"I don't guess I have to tell you the trouble I could get into over this? That stuff my dad talked about the other day? All true. Every word of it. These people are animals."

"Your pals."

". . . Guy's name is Tibbs."

"He have a first name?"

"There is no first name. There's not even really a last name. Just an alias and a phone number." He took out his phone and scrolled to a name on his contacts list and showed me the number. "He won't answer. Just leave a message telling him what you want and wait."

"He'll call back?"

"I don't know. I don't know what he'll do. He does, though, you might wish he hadn't."

"Well, we'll see.

He said, "Slim, this is it. This is all I'll do. You can come back in here, tie me to the table saw, but I'm done because what they'd do to me would be worse."

"That depends."

"You won't mention my name." Not a question.

"I'll try not to let it slip."

He started to pitch another of his little fits, but I'd had enough. I'd had enough of him and his foolishness. I turned and walked out of the mill, and for all I know he never dragged himself out of the sawdust.

I went back to the bike to make my call. The recorded message was just long enough for a voice to come on and announce its name. Sure enough: Mr. Tibbs. So far, so good. I waited for the electronic beep and said, "Dennis Reach." I recited a number into the handset and broke the connection, and as I did a shiver ran down my back like someone was doing the dance macabre on my grave.

9.

I DECIDED FINALLY TO FOLLOW SHERIFF WINCE'S ADVICE. I picked up pizzas on the way home to try to make it up to Anci. She wasn't speaking to me, unless grunting is speaking. Jeep was snoozing on the sofa. I thanked him and he hurried off to his four-to-twelve. I put the food out and we ate a quiet meal. When we were done, I set about looking for the Harvels. Turns out, they were easier to find than I'd expected. They weren't listed in the white pages, and I don't think I'd have been able to bring them up on Anci's computer except that Arlis had been popped a few years back for exposing himself outside an elementary school and got himself on the state's sex offender registry, complete with address. I was celebrating with a slice of the leftover pizza when the phone rang.

"You goddamn shithead."

"Speaking."

It was Susan. She said, "Slim, do you know how old I am?"

"How old?" I asked. "I don't know. Ain't that a question a gentleman isn't supposed to wonder about?"

"Just answer, will you? It's not a trap."

"Okay. Uh, fifty-two?"

A long pause happened on the other end.

Then finally: "Forty-four, Slim. I'm forty-four."

"That's what I said. Forty-four. Might have said forty, even. This connection is terrible."

She said, "Slim, shut up."

"Yes, ma'am."

She sighed and pressed on. "Point is, I'd like to make it to fifty-two. I'd like to make it to a lot more than that. Way things are going with this job, I'm not so sure I will."

"They called already."

"They called. Someone name of Tibbs. He wants to meet you."

"These folks don't waste time. When and where?"

The address was someplace in Marion near the industrial park. The time was seven in the morning. The haters were early risers.

"He said to remind you to come unarmed," she said. "Oh, and one more thing, I'm burning this phone. I'll let you know when I get a new one."

"That good, huh?"

"Let's just say I'm sleeping with the lights on tonight. Maybe several nights." Then she paused for maybe ten seconds and finally said, "Jesus, Slim, don't get yourself killed."

I started to say I wouldn't, but she'd already ended the call. I dialed Jeep Mabry's number to leave a message.

★ ★ ★

Anci was still in bed the next morning when I made ready to leave, but I'd promised not to sneak off without telling her where I was going. Jeep's wife was downstairs cooking breakfast.

"Your aunt Opal is here for a visit with you," I said. "Might want to talk over some of those detective stories even. So try not to sleep the morning away."

She was groggy-headed, but the change in babysitting personnel to Jeep's wife got her attention.

"Not Jeep again?"

"He's tied up for a while."

"Oh, tears. Now we'll never finish our puzzle. Where are you off to, anyway?"

"Bran-Wichelle Industrial. A tool and die."

"Living the high life as always."

"It's for a meeting," I said, "with a notorious character."

It hurt my feelings a little that she didn't seem to mind about the notorious character. Instead, she looked thoughtful for a moment, brow furrowed.

She said, "Bran-Wichelle. Why's that familiar?"

"Well, it's that big factory over there on 13. We ride past it, time to time."

"That's maybe it," she said, but she didn't sound so sure.

Bran-Wichelle Industrial was a gray and white aluminum box covering roughly fifteen acres of land outside the town of Marion. There was a guard box outside the twelve-foot-high electric Bran-Wichelle branded fence, but the man in the box waved me through without hesitation or identification. Clearly, my arrival had been foretold. I drove up to the main yard and stopped. I waited in my idling truck until a fat guy with greasy hair and even greasier clothes moseyed over to the driver's-side window.

"Get out," he said.

I got out. He and another guy gave me about as thorough a frisk as you can get with your clothes on, separated me from my keys, and drove me up to the main building past a line of morning-shift stragglers dragging their hangovers onto the floor, where the machines were roaring away as though they never slept.

I hoped they wouldn't want to do the meet inside and risk opening themselves up to me that much. And they didn't. I was led across the work floor and out the other side to a small, open-air patio between buildings where fat boy and I stood until another door opened and a young man came out.

"That's far enough," he said, though I hadn't moved. He was dressed in a light blue suit with patent leather shoes and sunglasses so big they covered half his face. His hair was chestnut, combed neatly to one side; combined with the glasses and the duds, it made him look a bit like a Jim Jones impersonator. He had one of those Bluetooth things in his right ear and just one hand, his left. The other was a prosthetic, plastic and smooth and white as an apple half. The one-handed man Carol Ray had mentioned, the one whose coke deal she'd blundered into at Classic Country all those years ago. He nodded, and the man at his right disappeared into the building.

I said, "Don't want the hired help listening in?"

"Not exactly. There are limits to our trust. There's a man on the roof, though. Of course, we search everyone who comes here, but sometimes weapons are cleverly hidden, and the best weapons can't be taken away at all. Do you understand?" His accent wasn't Little Egypt, but it took me a moment to realize that it wasn't anything: a voice freed of accent, smoothed out, and made expressionless and robotic.

"Sure, Mr. Tibbs," I said, and shrugged. I tried not to think of the man on the roof, tried not to imagine the bead being drawn on me, but I couldn't help it. What would it be, head shot, one to the heart? Dealer's choice? A trickle of sweat made its way down my throat, and as I glanced down as though to follow its course I spied the tiny red dot of a laser scope resting at the top of my chest.

Throat shot. Arty.

Tibbs said, "I apologize for that. A bit of theatrical flair of which I personally disapprove. But I trust the point has been made."

"Whatever."

"My name is not Tibbs."

"It's Tibbstein?"

He ignored me.

"Tibbs is merely a figment, if you will. A code. When someone needs to speak to us on a sub-official basis, they ask for Tibbs."

"And you represent the sub-official basis?"

"I do," he said. "You must understand that large segments of our population have accepted the Jewish liberal media image of us as a terrorist organization. To them, everything we do is a crime. I'm afraid that it has become necessary to police ourselves."

He noticed my expression.

"It's funny to you?" But he wasn't trying to pick a fight. Just asking a question.

"Nothing you guys do is ever funny."

He didn't care about that one way or another either. He lit a cigarette. I said a silent prayer to cancer.

"I must also ask you to understand that if Dennis Reach had been a member in good standing of this organization at the time of his death, we would not be having this meeting. Do you understand that?"

"Yeah."

"Do you believe it, though?"

"I don't know," I said. "Does it matter?"

"Not really," he said. "The White Dragons protect what belongs to them. It is their nature. It is *our* nature. Many times, we will even protect what we once possessed. Do you see?"

"I see."

He nodded. He was awfully serious now. Grave even. Henrik Ibsen would have told him to lighten up.

"But you're not going to protect Reach?" I asked, catching on at last.

"It goes without saying that the issue of protection is relative by its very nature. A surgeon would gladly cut away a finger to save the entire hand."

"And Reach was the finger?"

"Take five steps forward," he said, his voice gentle. When I hesitated, he said, "Five steps. Please. Nothing will happen to you. It's all arranged."

If they'd wanted me dead, I'd be dead. I took five steps. I looked down. I was standing on a large manila envelope, nearly invisible against the dust-covered concrete pad. I picked it up and opened it. Inside was a picture of Dennis Reach in a tuxedo, smiling as he plunged through a thick cloud of rice or confetti. Hard to tell which. His pleased expression made him look like a different man, or at least a younger, less careworn version of the train wreck he'd become. On his arm was his bride, a young woman with dark curly hair and coffee-colored skin.

My, my.

"As you might expect, our organization has rather strict rules regarding miscegenation and interracial relationships."

"Rather?"

He shrugged.

"There are exceptions, of course, to every rule. Negresses possess certain . . . qualities. I would say *attractive qualities*, but I would only mean it in the strictest and most literal sense, and no doubt you would intentionally misunderstand me."

"No doubt."

"To the untrained mind," he went on, like I hadn't said anything, "they can pose quite a danger."

"Plus, if you started booting out every good old boy who had a black lady in his past . . ."

"Precisely." A small grin appeared on his face, but it only made him seem greasier. "Officially, we are intolerant of the practice. Unofficially . . ." He let it hang there, unfinished.

"So marrying this woman wasn't the only reason Reach was expelled."

"No."

"Why then?"

"First," he said, "we want to know why you care."

"Let's just say that I like to see things through."

"Even at the risk of your own life?"

"Even that," I said. "Although I can't say I've seen anything too dangerous yet."

"You're forgetting the man on the roof."

"That so?"

I waved a hand over my head.

Tibbs looked up. The red dot left the top of my chest, drifted downward, crossed the concrete between us, and came to rest in the middle of his crotch. We both looked toward the roof, but only I was smiling. A man was still there, and a rifle barrel, the same rifle, except now the man was Jeep Mabry.

No one likes to be caught with his pecker in his hand, especially when he's gone through a lot of effort not to, but I have to admit Tibbs took it pretty well.

"I see," he said. He cleared his throat a little. "Very good. Can I ask a question?"

"All's fair in love and gunfights."

"Thank you. Is my man up there dead?"

"No. I had to hazard a guess, I'd say he's probably going to have to step up to the next size hood for a few weeks, but he's alive."

"I see," he said again. "You realize that this changes nothing about our agreement."

"Sure, but you have to admit it does make things a hell of a lot more interesting."

"I suppose it does. Would it make you angry if I said that should anything happen to me, even with your friend up there, your chances of getting out of here alive aren't terribly promising?"

"Would it make you angry if I said that if the shooting starts, you die first?"

"I'd expect nothing else." He was a tough guy, all right, but no one was that tough. Even with those big shades sitting on his face, I could tell the idea of dying first wasn't going to remind him of any funny songs.

"Good."

"I'm going to say some words to you now," he said. He reached into the pocket of his jacket and took out a slip of paper. "They are just words, you understand, random sounds without meaning." He was talking like that in case there was a directional mike pointed at him, in addition to a rifle barrel. "You cannot write them down, and I won't repeat them. After this, we're through. Am I making myself plain?"

"As a pressed white sheet."

He frowned at that and shook his head. Another disappointment to the race.

"Black," he said, enunciating his words clearly. "Number five. Third. B. Two days. You'll need this."

He halted my advance with a raised hand and placed the slip of paper he was holding on the ground at his feet.

"When I'm gone," he said.

"One more thing."

"I told you . . ."

"Why are you helping me?"

"Our own reasons."

"Fair enough."

"Suffice it to say," he said, mildly annoyed by the interruption, "that in many parts of this country, our organization has become an enclave of criminal activity. We consider this an unacceptable condition."

"Postpones the revolution?" I asked.

"Something like that. Just look around you. Look at what's happened, what's happening, to our world. How violent do you think our major cities were fifty years ago? How dangerous were our schools? How many of our children were in danger of being shot on the streets or in their classrooms? People like you know what's true, but you also listen to the liberal Jewish media machine, and that, my friend, is a monster that speaks nothing but lies."

"If you knew what your anger was doing to you," I said, "you would shun it like the worst of poisons."

He cocked his head, interested.

"Who said that?"

"Someone you wouldn't cross the street to piss on."

He looked at me a long time, half-turned to go, then paused and spoke softly.

"If you do in any way go back and cleave unto the remnants of these nations, even these that remain among you, and shall make marriages with them, and go in unto them and they unto you, know for a certainty that there shall be snares and traps unto you, and scourges in your side, and thorns in your eyes. Until ye perish off from this good land which the Lord your God has given you. Joshua, chapter twenty-three, verses twelve and thirteen. We all have words at our disposal. Pray you don't run into us again, Slim."

He tipped his hand to Mabry on the roof, and disappeared inside the building.

I picked up the slip of yellow paper and scooted out of there as fast as I could go.

10.

FUNNY THE THINGS THAT WILL MAKE YOU WANT TO EAT. Since the fire, I hadn't been able to keep down much more than a morsel, but after my meeting with the White Dragons I felt like I could eat a horse, the rider, and the saddle. Jeep was hungry, too, but if Jeep ever got carried away by a tornado he'd find a way to eat a four-course meal before he hit the ground. We drove northwest into Herrin and parked it at Hungry's, a greasy spoon on South Park where the townies still gathered to shake out the latest gossip to see what would fly. Our waitress was an old woman with thick purple eyeliner and a large gold cross pinned to her frilly blouse, but when she arrived at our table with plates of perfectly fried hash browns and biscuits covered in milk gravy, we forgave her many sins and sang songs to her loveliness.

"Mine eye hath played the painter and hath steeled thy beauty's form in table of my heart," Jeep said, taking the plates from her hands.

"Drink to me only with thine eyes, and I will pledge with mine," I said.

"You fancy shitbirds want anything else?" she said.

"A cholesterol workup," Jeep said.

"And a life flight out of here, should it become necessary," I said.

"Boys, Jesus hates an asshole." She dropped our ticket and slipped off to see to the rest of her section.

"Better sip our coffee slowly," Jeep said. "This is likely our last refill."

But it wasn't caffeine making my hands shake. I shoveled down some food and reached into my pocket for the paper Tibbs had given me, a long yellow slip stamped with a chain of numbers.

"Any idea what it means?" Jeep asked as he nibbled a sausage patty off the tines of his fork.

"Not sure, precisely," I said. "Except that it looks like a ticket to something during the third shift at the Black #5 coal mine, B shaft."

"In two days."

"That's what the man said, if indirectly."

"I guess we know what it is, don't we?"

"I guess we do," I said, suddenly losing my appetite. The dog, the doggers, the coal mine. Goddamn, what a world.

"Want some company?"

I nodded. "Couldn't hurt. Meantime, we're going to go our separate ways, for a few hours, anyway. Think you and Opal can watch Anci for the rest of the day?"

He wanted to come with, but I finally talked him out of it and we parted company. Jeep headed toward Indian Vale, and I turned the Triumph toward Mockingbird Hills and the Harvel residence. My plan was to surveil and surmise. But all I really did was screw up.

Boy, did I screw up.

I espied the beat-up blue Honda Civic just outside of town, but when I swung into a Huck's to refill my tank, the little car puttered in beside me, and a middle-aged guy with a friendly face and a silver-white beard stepped out. He even smiled at me and said hey when I held open the door for him, and I let down my guard entirely. When I turned back onto Highway 51, the blue car sped off in the opposite direction and I forgot about him altogether.

That was my first mistake. My second was not giving anyone a clearer idea where I was going, but since I didn't figure to do much more than watch I didn't give it a first thought, much less a second.

The Harvel spread was a huge cut of land and a tiny farmhouse five miles east of Union City. South was the puddle of Pleasant Valley Lake and a pretty good patch of woodland: high stands of oak and elm shot through with red mulberries and eastern white pines. But this was open land, gently rolling with moraines deposited sometime during the last ice age. No country for old men, and no place for sneaking.

No need for sneaking, either. The flatbed with the crazy yurt wasn't anywhere in sight, nor was any other sign of the Cleaveses. Maybe they'd come and gone. Maybe they'd never really existed in the first place. If not for Lew Mandamus's assurances, I really might have believed I'd imagined them all along. A man was raking grass clippings in the front yard. He seemed angry, the way he attacked those clippings, the strokes of his metal rake hard and fast. He was a little squirt, short but thick in the shoulders, and his mustache was like a daub of mustard beneath his fat nostrils. I wondered if he was a hireling or a Harvel, and I aimed to find out. I pulled up, side of the road, and stuck my head out the window.

"You a Harvel?" I asked.

"Don't want none."

"Ain't selling none. Are you Arlis or Bundy?"

"Yup."

"Well, which is it?"

He shrugged, and I gave it up.

"Sheldon or A. Evan around?" I asked.

"They don't live here."

"I know, but I heard they might be on a visit."

"They come to visit time to time," he said.

"This one of those times?"

"Maybe," he said. "Might be on an errand, though."

"Could I leave them a message?"

"What message?"

"Could I write a message down and leave it inside?" I asked.

Something moved around inside his mouth and cheek, a plug of tobacco or a tongue as thick as a wrist. The rake spun between his blocky hands.

"Guess so," he said at last. "You said you ain't selling nothing, right?"

"Just salvation, my son."

"Don't think anyone here's in that market." He waved a hand over his head as he turned toward the house. "Come on up anyway."

I came on up anyway. The house wasn't as awful as the Cleaveses', but if the Cleaveses really were staying with their cousins, they were doing it end-to-end. There were some beds and a couch and a television set I expected to see Eisenhower giving a speech on. But that was about it. The whole thing was as spacious as an ice-cube tray. There wasn't any evidence to suggest that a female presence had ever inhabited it, something I might have asked about had I been in the mood for tragedy. There wasn't a vase full of pretty flowers, or curtains in the windows, and the only book I saw was a ratty copy of *Bloody Williamson*. The little guy with the yellow mustache parked it in front of the TV while I checked the house, the backyard, and the barn.

"They're not here," I said when I got back.

"Told you."

"Well, you didn't exactly."

"Back to that again?"

"Mind if I go ahead and leave that message?"

"Said I didn't."

I scratched down my number on a dry-erase board stuck to the refrigerator.

"Tell Sheldon the hired help came by," I said. "And tell A. Evan I can't wait to see him."

"He'll know what that means?"

"I hope he does."

"Okay." He shrugged and switched channels on the TV to show me how much he cared what I hoped.

I was a few miles down the road when I realized I hadn't seen Shelby Ann around the Harvels' house, or even anything that would suggest she'd ever been there in the first place. I thought about turning around and bugging the dude with the yellow mustache again, but then I figured he'd had enough hassles for one day, so instead I pulled off at a Shell station to take a leak. Too much morning coffee.

When I finished, I stepped back into the parking lot and spied the baby blue Civic, but it was already too late. The face with the white beard flashed into view as I felt an explosion at the back of my head and dropped onto the hard gravel chuck on both knees. The world went kaleidoscopic.

"Shee-it," said a voice from somewhere far above.

"What's the matter?" said another, this one to my right.

"Fucker's got a head like a goddamn air conditioner."

And like an air conditioner, I tried to stay cool, but just then something hit me again, harder this time, and I felt the fight ooze out of my arms and legs as the neurons stopped firing and my brain went slack. The twin gas pumps blurred and disappeared from sight as the world yawned blackness.

But even the void couldn't keep me from recognizing A. Evan's voice.

I DON'T KNOW HOW LONG I WAS OUT, BUT WHEN I WOKE UP from nightmares, my neck was so sore I yelped when I turned my head. White Beard and Blond Mustache were sitting nearby, idly flipping through issues of *Guns & Ammo* and *American Bow Hunter*. Arlis and Bundy, together at last, though I still had no idea which was which.

It took me three tries at sitting up to realize I was tied, spread-eagle, to a narrow metal table, kind of like you'd find in an ME's lab. A nice touch, I thought, truly terrifying, though the effort felt like overkill, wasted effort on the part of the bad guys. Wasted rope, too. I couldn't have stood up to save my life.

Speaking of which . . .

"He's awake," White Beard said.

"Hey, dumbshit," Yellow Mustache said. Meaning me, I guess. I was the dumbshit. "You reckon you've got a concussion?"

I didn't answer, but they weren't expecting me to. They liked the idea of my concussion just fine. They were bad men, and to a bad man nothing brought more pleasure than the idea of other people's suffering. They stood and stretched and chuckled a little to each other and went out of the room. I took the moment to try and figure out where I was.

The lights hanging overhead were as big as punch bowls, the air smelled strongly of manure, and even with my limited range of vision I could make out a disc harrow lurking in a corner. There was a breast plough and some daisy rakes and a two-pronged hayfork and other such instruments of a similarly sinister appearance. You could have led tourists from certain parts of country through it all and convinced them it was a torture chamber. I wasn't any too happy about any of it myself. It wasn't the barn on the Harvels' property. I'd caught a pretty good glimpse of that one a few hours earlier, and this wasn't it. So I was on some other property in southern Illinois or northern Kentucky, in some other barn. Course, that only narrowed the possibilities to a few thousand. I was still doing the math when White Beard reappeared.

"You're Slim," he said. His face wasn't pleasant now. This was his true face. He was as ugly as a monkey's ass and he had sour breath and a brain gone badly psychotic. Somewhere, a mother was filled with pride.

"Not sure," I said. "I might be Slim. I might be Martin Van Buren. You want people to remember their names, you probably shouldn't give them amnesia."

"Naw, you're no Martin Van Whatthefuck. You're Slim. I heard of you, know 'bout your shenanigans. You may not realize it, but you've got some renown on you."

"I give it back."

"Bet you would, too," he said. "Listen, though, you talked to a guy today in Marion."

"Couple of 'em, in fact."

"Maybe, but you know the one I mean. The one you talked to. What'd he say?"

"Don't remember," I said. "He wouldn't let me write anything down."

He shook his head. There was regret in his face, but it was false regret.

"That kind of talk ain't going to get you nowhere," he said. He held something in his hand just outside my range of vision. "You know what this is?"

"Flower bouquet and an apology pie?"

He grinned. His teeth had slash marks across them like they'd been cut with a knife. He raised whatever it was for me to see. I think he knew I couldn't see it the first time. He was having a game at my expense. It was a pistol-shaped thing with a trigger and a curved metal loop extending from the base and handle. The end of the loop was hot and bright.

"Not a pie," he said. "Not any kind of apology. Try again."

"Ray gun?"

"*Soldering* gun."

"I was only kidding about the ray gun. You like science-fiction stories?"

"Brother, you're in one."

"You fixing to do some metal work?"

He shook his head.

"What I'm fixing to do is ask a question. For the second time. I don't like to repeat myself, neither, so I'm unhappy already."

"Times a-wasting. Fields full of sheep to fuck, I guess."

"You're a tough guy, all right. They said you were tough."

"I'm not tough," I said. That was truthful. I didn't feel tough. Toughness was something in my rearview mirror, and I was riding a rocket ship away from it. "Ask me your question."

"First, I want to tell you what happens if you don't answer."

"Look, I really don't need to hear it. I only got into this

mess in the first place because I like dogs. I don't care about Dennis Reach, not really, and I don't care about you or the Cleaveses or the White Dragons. You want to run around like crazy people doing what it is you're doing, why, that's fine with me, too. What say you cut me loose and we just call it even?"

"Sorry, but it's too late for that," he said. I didn't think he was sorry, though. Not really. "The boy in Marion, the one you spoke to today, what did he tell you?"

"He said he didn't care Dennis Reach was dead. He quoted the Bible some. That's pretty much it."

"That's it?" he said.

"That's the gist of it, yeah."

He shook his head.

"Don't believe you," he said. "And even if I did, we got to do this the right way."

"You got a funny reckoning of right, you know that?"

"Maybe, but I got to be sure. I got to be so sure I can take what you've told me to my people and have them believe me beyond a shadow. Because if they don't, and I tell them different, it comes back on me . . ." He leaned in a little closer. Our noses were nearly touching. "You understand?"

"Look . . ."

"What we're going to do is this. Arlis is going to come back in here . . ."

"Aha!"

"What?"

"I didn't know which of you was which. Now I know. You're Bundy."

He ignored this and said, "Arlis is going to come in here. He's going to grease you up some. Not *on* you, you understand. He's going to grease *in* you. Grease your nether. Then we insert the solder. Right down your mine shaft. The tip heats up, sizzles the oil, cooks you from the inside."

"Seems like you might skip the oiling-up step. Feels like overkill to me." Truth was, I could barely speak. My mouth had gone dry as powdered bone.

Bundy shrugged.

"To me, too. But Arlis likes it, and he has so little to make him happy."

"He was my brother, I'd find that worrisome."

"I'll be honest, I do, sometimes. But you do what you do for family. So oil you up he will, and fry you shall."

"Nothing to be done about it?"

"Lessin you can convince me you're telling the truth. And you can't do that lessin we use the solder."

"Vicious circle."

"It ain't going to be your fondest memory, I'll say that," he said. "Look, Slim, time to get real. You ain't walking out of here. Talk to us, don't talk to us. It doesn't make much difference, far as you're concerned. You're a dead man. See, you don't mean anything to us, me or my people. You got into this thing kinda on a whim, and some things have gotten tangled since then."

"You can say that again."

He turned his head and hocked a loogie into the dust.

"But that boy in Marion, he's something else. That one-handed motherfucker. Tibbs. He's not something you can just push into a corner and forget about. He's the real deal. Bottom line is, I got to know what he told you, and I got to be sure about it, and that's all there is."

"Look . . ." I said again, but it wasn't any good.

Arlis came in, like he'd been waiting nearby the whole time, the little shit. He held a glass jug of oil in his arms, cradling it like an infant. The glass was frosted with age, and the oil was grimy and there were dead flies bobbing around in it. Arils set the jug on the table, and he and Bundy used carpet knives to cut me out of my clothes. They took turns working me over as they did. I struggled against the beating and the ropes—bungee cords, I guess they were—and one of them popped loose. I shrugged halfway off the table and hit Arlis so hard in the face he fell over and jarred the table and knocked off the jug. The glass broke, and the oil splashed all over the floor. Bundy hit me from behind and I lay down again.

"He spilled the oil," Arlis said. I couldn't see him, only hear him.

"I saw."

"He broke my jug, too."

"We'll get you a new jug."

"Not like that one. That was my good jug."

"We'll get you another good jug. Maybe even a better one. I know a place. Meantime, get some of that oil off the floor."

Arlis got some oil off the floor. The next couple moments were unpleasant ones. Even more unpleasant, I mean. Arlis did his business. The greasing business. It was like an eel was sliding inside of me. I gritted my teeth. Then Bundy reappeared, hovering over the table.

"Last chance," he said.

"Won't matter what I say, will it?"

"Nope."

"Let's get it over with then."

I think I said that last part. I'm not sure. There was a flash, and a scream like a herd of wild animals was crying out all at once because a redneck psychopath had stuck a hot soldering gun up their ass. The metal table jumped up and hit me in the back of the head and there was a sound like a hundred metal drums banging out some fearful cacophony. The room went away and came back and went away again in a flurry like the flurry of the wings of a green bottle fly. The last time it came back, Bundy was there again, smiling at me with his knife-slashed teeth.

"Give me your thoughts."

I opened my mouth to speak but the only thing that came out was a gasp. Bundy thought it hilarious. Finally, I said, "It ain't nothing I'm eager to do again."

"I bet. But here's the thing. That wasn't even the full deal. Arlis likes to start off slow. That was just the edge of your bunghole. Not even really through the window. Think how bad it'll hurt when he goes all in."

"Why don't you show me first?"

"The guy in Marion. The one-handed man."

"I've never even been to Marion. Is that a town or a lady?"

He looked at me a moment.

"Have it your way. Arlis?"

I couldn't see him, but I could feel him drawing nearer between my legs. I was about to die and I knew it. Die or go insane and then die. I said some prayers. I said some words to Anci and Peggy. I had some words with my dad. Not all of them kind, but words. I wished things had turned out different. I wished I'd taken that job filling potholes for the county. I wished Peggy and I had gotten married, had time to do that. Make our family together. But mostly I wished I'd never met Sheldon and A. Evan Cleaves. I lifted my head off the table. Best to see it coming, I thought. Look it in the eye. And that's when I saw Jeep Mabry watching us through the window.

"Boys," I said, "how's your life insurance?"

The door slammed open so hard it came off its top hinge. Jeep came in like a devil harvesting sinners. There was an ax by the door and he grabbed it and swung hard as Bundy turned and rose from his place near the table with a cry of alarm. He was fast, but Jeep was faster. Twice as fast. The ax hit Bundy in the neck near the top of his right shoulder and damn near severed his head. Arlis screamed. He lunged at Jeep with the soldering gun, but he slipped a little in the puddle of spilled oil and lost his footing. Jeep kicked Bundy loose from the ax's beard with a sickening crack and stepped forward smartly, almost casually. He might have been going for the last gallon of milk in the dairy aisle. Arlis tried to get up, but he was too slow. With a hard downward stroke,

Jeep buried the ax in his brain. The boy spat some words you couldn't quite make out and then died right there in his own mess of oil and dirt and dead flies.

Then Jeep was at my side, untying me.

"Hope you didn't need one of them alive for anything," he said.

"Now that you mention it," I said, but truth was I wanted those monsters dead, too, so I didn't pursue it further, or regret the leads we'd certainly just lost. "How the hell did you find me? Even I don't know where I am."

"I didn't," he said. "Anci did."

I sat up. It was agony. Breathing was, too. I didn't dare try to turn my head. The ribs on my left side were broken, and everything below my waist was on fire.

"Anci?"

"She put an app on your phone that lets her track you. Parents use them these days to keep tabs on their kids. Guess who's the kid in this situation."

"I'm getting a sense of it."

"She's scared you'll be mad at her," he said.

"Mad at her? I'm going to raise her allowance. By to-morrow morning, she'll be bathing in orange soda."

"You're a good papa."

"I know."

He helped me off the table, slowly. There were some coveralls hanging from a nail near an empty horse stall, and he fetched them for me and helped me get dressed. They were absurdly big on me, and they smelled like shit, but they hid my shame good enough. I looked at the Harvels on the floor. They weren't getting up anytime soon.

I felt Jeep leading me away from the sight.

"Doctor?" he said.

I nodded.

"Doctor."

11.

"THIS IS MY FAULT," ANCI SAID.

We'd retreated to Lew and Eun Hee Mandamus's place near Tolu. A regulation hospital would have raised too many questions and made too many witnesses. We didn't want either. Thanks to some medic training during his days in service, Lew had me stitched up good, treated my other wounds. Eun Hee administered some homeopathic stuff she said might help. I took it all and was grateful. I was grateful not to be dying, hog-tied naked to a metal table at the mercy of the nightmare Harvels.

I said, "It is not your fault. Stop saying that."

"It is. It was my idea, and it's my fault."

"Nope. Listen, squirt, only bad actors are responsible for their bad actions. No one else."

"You're sure?"

"Completely and entirely."

"I'm going to give you a hug now," she said.

"Okay, but go easy. I'm fragile."

"I promise. On three?"

"On three."

She didn't wait for one. The hug hurt like hell but felt like heaven.

The remainder of my convalescence, I was surrounded like a city under siege. Jeep was there and Anci, of course, and Jeep's wife, Opal. Jeep snuck off not long after dropping me off to dispose of the Harvels' bodies. I didn't ask what he did with them, but if Jeep didn't want bodies found, they never would be.

Periodically, Lew appeared with pain meds and other medicines. He seemed worried especially about infection. No telling what was growing in that barn, or on the Harvels.

"You looking thoughtful, Slim," he said, changing the bandages on my ribs. "What's on your mind?"

"Lew, what kind of a thing might a dog have sewn up inside her?"

"Come again?"

"The dog. The Cleaveses' dog. Shelby Ann. She had an incision under her collar, like someone sewed something up inside her nape. I didn't think much on it at the time. Now I'm thinking on it."

"Could have been a tracking chip. Those are pretty standard these days. Help you to locate a missing pet. A runaway."

"Not the Cleaveses' style," I said. "Besides, if she had a tracking chip, they wouldn't have needed me to look for her in the first place."

"I guess not," he said. "Well, when you find her, we can find out together."

"First I have to find her."

★ ★ ★

A LITTLE WHILE LATER, PEGGY FINALLY SHOWED UP, MADDER than I'd ever seen her. Her Charger roared up to the gates of Shinshi in a bellering sandstorm of shredded road gravel and river loam. Then the real storm arrived.

"Those goddamn pieces of pig shit ought to be glad they're safely dead," she said.

"Believe me, they're dead. They're deader than Trotsky."

"That's not dead enough."

"Deader than Trotsky's pet turtle, then."

"That's closer," she said, and calmed herself down some. "I'm just satisfied they didn't do serious damage to your rear end."

"I am, too."

"It's such a cute rear end."

"Thank you," I said. "Pretty fond of it my own self."

She smiled and leaned over and kissed my hot forehead. She said, "You're going to hunt these men now, aren't you?"

"Yes, I am."

"Don't suppose you'll let me talk you out of it?"

"A few days ago, you might have," I said. "But now I don't think I've got a choice. Not if I want to live any kind of life worth living. Besides, Dennis Reach might not have been worth much, but he didn't deserve to die like that, and not because of me."

"You're a good man."

"I don't feel like one."

"That's how good men always feel," she said. "Take Jeep with you at least?"

"If he'll go."

"He'll go. You'd have to tie a safe to him and throw him in a lake to keep him from going. And even then he'd still go."

"Course then he'd be wet. And still tied to a safe. And madder than hell about it."

"Situation like this, these kind of people, a little hell is called for," Peggy said, "you want to know my opinion about it."

THE FOLLOWING MORNING, I THANKED LEW FOR ALL HE'D done. I hugged Eun Hee and accepted her care package of homeopathic pills, potions, and unguents. Then I drove over to Shotgun & Shakes, where Carol Ray was back in her office, sipping coffee and being adorable.

"No offense," she said, "but you look kinda beat up."

"I feel kinda beat up. It's a set."

"You want some coffee?"

"I wouldn't say no."

She got me some coffee, then leaned against the front of her desk, crossing her long bare legs at the ankle. If I'd had a pen, I'd have written a poem about it.

She said, "Let me ask you a question, Slim."

"Shoot."

"What makes a man go into your line of work? Private-eye work, I mean."

"Dunno. All kinds of things. Boredom. A yen for trou-blemaking. Professional misfortune, maybe. I used to be a coal miner."

"Pull the other one." She blew on curls of steam rising from her mug.

"I did."

"Shaft, low, or slope?"

"I'll be damned. One of the cognoscenti."

We toasted our shared misfortune.

"A gal doesn't marry three times in southern Illinois without a coal miner being in the mix somewhere."

"Maybe I know him."

"Don't all you guys?"

"It's a curse."

"What is? Having friends?"

"Depends on the friends," I said. "Let's take this J.T. Black, for example. Now, way I hear it, he's got a pretty rough history."

She nodded.

"J.T.'s been into a little bit of everything. I agree, some of it was on the rough side."

"I hear tell he ran a little meth with Dennis Reach, one time or another. Back during their days with the White Dragons."

"I don't know anything about that," she said, but I could tell that she did.

"I suppose it's stupid to ask whether J.T. was one of your three husbands."

"Pretty stupid," she said, and smiled and blushed some. "Another of my youthful mistakes."

"I'm not here to judge you."

"Thank you."

"Well, maybe a little."

"We're in a fight now."

"R.L. Lindley told me that Black had fallen out with the Dragons. Any idea what happened between them?"

"Not specifically, no. Except someone high up in the organization was trying to horn in on one of their rackets a little more than comfort allowed. Dennis never wanted to rock the boat, but J.T. pitched a fit and brought down hell-fire and damnation on himself. It got pretty ugly for a while there, too, I can tell you."

"Wasn't anything to do with their dogging, was it?"

She actually looked ashamed.

"Know about that, do you?"

"I'm figuring a thing or two out. Kinda unusual, ain't it? You being married to Reach and Black both? Guy might get the idea you were the brains of the operation."

"If I was the brains, I wouldn't have been married to Dumb and Dumber. But I can see how a body might be led in that direction, yes."

"What'd J.T. do before deciding to take a stab at law enforcement?"

"He worked in one of his daddy's tool-and-die outfits. Ran a punch press, as I recall. I think that's how he lost part of his right pinkie finger."

"Lost his concentration?"

"Lost his ass," she said. "Funny thing is, the old man has a missing finger, too. Left ring, I think."

"He run the press, too?" I asked.

Carol Ray shook her head. "Dog bit it off. And swallowed. If memory serves, it was a full-grown bitch Rott-weiler. Name of Truman."

"Truman?"

"No one ever accused Leonard Black of being too snuggly with his feminine side." She chuckled, but the sound was full of rue. I don't guess a gal gets married three times in southern Illinois without letting all kinds of things into her life, some of them a lot more lowdown than a bunch of scruffy in-by dudes, roof bolters, and fire bosses.

"Think you can get me an audience?"

"With J.T.? I don't . . ."

"With his daddy. Leonard."

"You're sure that's something you want to do?"

"No," I said. "But it might be useful. Besides, I've al-ways wanted to get a look at him up close."

"Well, hell, I can try. Honestly, though, I don't know if I have that kind of pull anymore," she said. "Once upon a time, the old goat liked to watch me dance at the barbecues he'd throw at his place out in Cape Girardeau. Juice New-ton records and cheap semiautomatic pistols ruled the day, if you can believe it. Anyway, the dancing about drove J.T. fucking nuts, but it kept me in smokes, and at least he never tried to touch me."

"I don't suppose anyone named Cleaves was ever at one of those shindigs."

"Who?"

"Just somebody I'd like to run into again one day."

"Another someone from the mines?" she said.

"I guess you could say that," I said. "Though maybe not the way you're thinking."

I SPENT THE REST OF THE DAY HUNTING SHELDON AND A. Evan Cleaves: Bridgetown, Elizabeth, Colton, New Delta, Madrid. I talked to anyone I thought might know something about the connection between them and J.T. Black. In the afternoon, I rushed home to relieve Peggy from watching Anci and to let in the contractors. I'd already got them going on the cleanup. When they were done, we'd see about the roof, the kitchen, whatever else. The insurance would ultimately pay, but in the meantime it was going to amount to real dollars.

"And you'll have to pay for most of it out of pocket, too," said my agent. "Hope the homeowner's policy eventually covers everything."

"Well, that's a kick in the privates."

"I knew it wouldn't make you happy, Slim, but you've got yourself a documented arson here. The insurance company won't pay out until the investigation comes back with a determination that you didn't set it yourself."

"Me? But I'm not even a suspect. Not in the arson, anyway."

"You and I know that. The company knows it, too. It just don't care. You'll have to wait until the police make a final determination."

"What if they never do?"

"Well . . ."

LATER, I TALKED TO ANCI AND PEGGY ABOUT IT ALL.

"I don't know how we're going to do it," Anci said. "Right now, we can barely afford the stuffing in our pillows."

"I can help some," said Peggy. "Not as much as I'd like. I got to help my sister move, and my savings account is already thin as a promise."

"You should keep your savings," I said. "But thank you."

"Then how?" Anci said.

"I think I know."

I PAID THE ROOFERS AND CLEANERS IN CASH. A. EVAN'S CASH. The roofers came in and strung together some giant blue tarps and were ready to tear out the burned sections and install the new rafters and braces. But first the cleaning people arrived to fight the smoke monster.

"You'll want to be out of the house," an old woman in a white lab coat explained. You always know you're about to be taken for a ride when they're wearing that white lab coat. Her boys weren't wearing coats, at least, but probably only because they couldn't find any to fit. These were some big boys. Basically bank vaults with legs. When they lugged in a metal contraption just slightly smaller than a VW Bus, it looked like a jewelry box between them. "It's an ionizer.

It'll take away the smoke smell, but it'll give you one hell of a headache."

"How long?"

"Twelve hours is best." Her head tilted back so her nose could sample the air. "Maybe longer. Every job is different. I ain't saying you have to go. You could stay. You'll just have the headache of your life is all."

I said, "I've been running around like the proverbial one-legged man lately anyway. Another few hours on the road don't seem like too much to ask."

"Hectic life."

"Can be."

"Listen," she said. "Smoke odor can hide just about anywhere in a house. Especially an old place like yours. Cracks in the wall, the insulation. Hell, even under the switch plates. You got pets?"

"I've got pets."

"I've known pets to hold onto smoke for longer than you'd think. Dogs, especially. You got dogs?"

"Cats."

She wrinkled her nose.

"I never could figure them out. They're like a four-legged puzzle. They don't like you and they let you know it, too, so that reduces my willingness to scoop their shit."

"That's not my favorite part, either."

"I knew a guy once had ducks. Pets, too, not farm-type ducks. Smoke hid in their feathers."

"What'd he do?"

"Butchered them. He loved those ducks, but that smell

will turn you into a killer. You need to, you give us a call. We'll come out and run that machine again."

"Sure those boys of yours won't eat me for dinner for squawking?"

"Freddy and Teddy?" she asked. "Hell, those two only look like trouble. You should have seen their daddy."

"He must have been something."

"He was," she said. "Something and then some. Fought brain cancer for almost a year before it took him down. Doctor said he shouldn't have lasted three weeks. Freddy and Teddy barely made it through the funeral."

"I'm sorry."

"Hell, don't be."

But I could tell she didn't mean it. You drilled down to it, loss was one of the few things we could ever really share with one another.

MEANTIME, THE ROOFERS GOT TO WORK.

"I can't sleep with that racket going on day and night," Anci said the next morning over breakfast. "They started in at five this morning, and it's like the hammers were inside my head."

"Well, it's only a couple of weeks, and then it'll be gone."

"And then we'll have a new roof to burn."

"Not this time," I said. "Night of the fire, I had a vision, and the vision gave me an idea. How would you feel about us hiring a protector monkey to watch over the new roof?"

"A protector monkey?"

"Like an orangutan."

"Okay, one, that's not a monkey. That's an ape. Two, give me your phone."

"Why?"

"I'm going to call your doctor, see about having you committed."

"Uh-huh. Couple weeks under the watchful eye of our new protector monkey, you'll secretly be wishing you'd jumped on board in the first place." I showed her a catalog. "I like these kitchen countertops. What do you think?"

"Bamboo?"

"It's renewable."

"Renewable's good," she said. "I like it fine, but it's A. Evan's money. Maybe we should get something in honor of him."

"Dirty concrete?" I asked.

She spooned cereal into her mouth.

"Or petrified cow shit. With a sluice grate for the floor. Damn it all."

"What?"

"Bran-Wichelle. It keeps jumping into my head—ever since you mentioned it—but for the life of me I can't remember why."

"Well, keep pondering. It might be a clue."

"Wouldn't that be something?"

I WAS CLEANING UP THE BREAKFAST DISHES WHEN BEN WINCE called. That's something you love to see on your cell phone caller ID: RANDOLPH COUNTY SHERIFFS.

"I think we've got a problem here, son," he said.

"You, too? Maybe I should start a 1–900 line, take credit card numbers."

"I'll be frank. I don't recommend that. You typically have enough misfortune of your own without getting tangled up with everyone else's. Listen, I'm sheriff of a county known for its high murder rate and general lawlessness, and even I ain't never seen anyone up to so much troublemaking."

"I'm a lovable rascal," I said. "But at least I mean well."

"I guess intentions matter some. During sentencing, at least."

"I've heard tell. So what's the problem?"

"Rather show you in person," he said. "You think you can make it down here?"

"Sounds urgent."

"Well, it is. Maybe more than. And speaking of urgent . . ."

"Or more than."

"Or that. You don't happen to know an old cat named Soapy Howard?"

"Soapy? I don't think so."

"He runs the package liquor up around Bald Knob."

The image of a hillside hole-in-the-wall flickered to mind. I'd been there the day before, looking for snacks and information.

"I might have seen him."

"Might have," Wince said. "You don't know him, but he knows you, Slim. You and his brother used to work together at a Sommes shaft mine in Kentucky."

"So?"

"So he says you dropped in on him last week, asked a lot of questions about someone named Cleaves. Said you looked pretty rough, too," he said. "You scared hell out of the kid he's got working the counter for him. He said you looked like you'd been beat up pretty good. Your face."

"I cut myself shaving."

"You ought to get yourself some electric clippers, then."

"Maybe I will."

"Damn it, I'd hoped Soapy was wrong. Now I really need you to come in, and the sooner the quicker, too."

"Double urgent?"

"Don't make me come get you, boy. If I come get you, or send someone to, we'll have to put you in cuffs. I'd rather Anci not have to see that."

"You've given me rope before."

"Maybe. But this is different."

"Do tell."

"Okay, here it is. I think you got sprung a while back from Jackson County and had your knickers in a twist about being locked up on the Reach murder. I think you're a rabble-rouser who doesn't like to get the runaround for something you didn't do. Plus, you were on the hook for it. Reach's murder. Maybe you even had good intentions. Just between you, me, and the riot guns, I think you mean well, usually, even if you do go about your business like a Ward Nine New Year's Eve party. I think you went looking for the Cleaveses and couldn't find them, but you kept looking until you somehow ran afoul of bad men and got yourself worked over but good. How's that?"

"That's a lot of telling."

"It is," Wince said. "There's also the little matter of J.T. Black going missing."

"What was that now?"

"You heard me. Don't pretend you didn't hear me. After your phone chat the other day, Sheriff Lindley went looking for him. Wanted to ask him a question or two, but his house is cleared out. Truck's gone, too, and his still is broken down."

"Where's he gone?"

"If we knew that," Wince said, "he wouldn't be missing."

"Okay, I'll come in. When?"

"I'm thinking right now."

"Give me a day," I said.

"A day? Why not a year? A guy like you can do more damage in a day than most folks do in three lifetimes, one of them as a reincarnated Genghis Khan."

"Genghis Khan?"

Wince shrugged with his voice.

"On my mind probably account of a documentary I watched the other night. History channel. Interesting fella, if you ignore the mass murder."

"What if I promise not to cause trouble?"

"That's like a dog promising not to drag his nuts on the carpet. Make you a deal, you got till five o'clock."

"Thank you."

"At 5:01, I come looking."

I said thanks again, but he'd already broken the line. I found Anci in the kitchen.

"Saddle up," I said.

"For real?"

"You heard me. Let's do it."

It took her a moment to believe she wasn't being conned, but the prospect of troublemaking lit up her face.

"I get to come with?"

"Peggy and Opal are working. I've got to meet Jeep, but he's out on business of his own and can't make it over here."

"Hot damn."

And off she went to put on her motorcycle gear and scrounge up her private detective kit: notebook, pen, flashlight. I did the same, except I put on more than leather gloves and boots. I strapped a 9000S under my jacket and an S&W 442 to my ankle. I also put my knife on my belt and a mean look on my face. Had time, I would have gotten a scary tattoo, too. As it was, I felt like a walking arsenal, the flawless expression of American manhood.

While I waited for Anci, I fretted some more about the night to come and what it was certain to bring. The evil of it, and the cruelty. Man's inhumanity to . . . well, everything, all of it. My mother had raised me to believe that a person was only as strong as his willingness to be merciful to the weak, but as far as I could tell this was a view not widely held, and there were times I wondered whether even she believed it, given who she'd married and raised a family with. Maybe none of us really believed it. I don't know. When it comes to philosophizing, a newborn kitten understands things better than I do.

I was still pondering it all when Anci came down again

and took one look at me and said, "You're worried about something."

"Oh, I am, am I?"

"Don't lie. And don't play dumb, neither. I know you better than anyone, and I know that look. You're chewing on something, and I want to know what it is."

"And here I thought I was supposed to be the grownup in this relationship."

For once, she didn't have a smart remark. In fact, she didn't say anything at all. She just sat down beside me and put her hand on top of my hand.

"Sometimes the world is a pretty rough place," I said, and I wanted to say more but nothing else would come out.

Anci waited a moment and then nodded and said, "It really is. Sometimes, anyway. Maybe even most of the time. But that's where we come in. To put things right."

I looked at her and she looked back up at me. She smiled. I leaned down and kissed the crown of her head.

"I'm damn proud of you, kid."

"Hell, I know it."

12.

"YOU TWO COME IN. I'LL SCARE UP A SNACK."

We came in. Carol Ray Reach's house. She and Anci shook hands. I got a quick peck on the cheek and Anci's raised eyebrows. We went into the kitchen and the aforementioned snack was scared up: coffee for me and Carol Ray, milk and cookies for Anci. I thought she'd protest this treatment—she would've at home—but instead she tucked in gratefully. We'd managed to skip lunch somehow, and the cookies were her favorite, oatmeal raisin.

"I never saw you as the milk-and-cookies type," I said to Carol Ray.

"You've had me all wrong then, Slim. Sweet innocent old me with my pantry full of oatmeal treats."

"There's a rather large gun in the pantry," I said. "I couldn't help noticing."

She nodded.

"That's my Ruger Redhawk double-action, sugar. And rather large is right. You could use it to turn an Egyptian pyramid back into sand. I might be sweet and innocent, but

I'm nobody's baby. Truth is, I've got them stashed through-out the house, case of a rainy day."

"I bet I can guess why, too," I said.

"I bet you can." She glanced quickly at Anci, then back at me. "You don't mind if she listens in on this nasty business?"

"He doesn't mind," Anci said. "Fact of the matter is, I'm kinda the brains of the outfit."

"Well, now, I can see that."

"Don't take much imagination, does it, way he carries on?"

"Not really, no."

"I'm literally standing right here," I said.

Carol Ray turned her attention back to me.

"I talked to old man Black like you asked," she said. "He's heard of you, sugar. And let me tell you, your name did not exactly make him gladsome. Says you were tangled up with Roy Galligan a couple of years back."

"Uh-oh."

"Uh-oh's right. He wants to meet you. Says he wants to meet the person who brought down Matt Luster."

"That's not what happened," I pointed out. "It's not even the same time zone as what happened."

"Maybe you can tell him that, you meet him this afternoon. Four o'clock. Whatever you do, don't bring a gun, and for God's sake, Slim, don't wear a wire. You're not planning on wearing a wire, are you?"

"I don't think so."

She nodded, said, "Good. That is good. The on-site security is . . . meaty."

"Meaty?"

"Imagine a fleet of bulldozers in leather ties."

"I'll wear a hardhat," I said. "One more thing. Any chance you've seen J.T. around?"

"J.T.? Nope. Why?"

"No reason," I said. "Except the local law told me he's missing."

"Missing?" she asked. "This something I need to worry about?"

"I honestly don't know," I said. "Maybe keep the Redhawk handy."

"Believe me, I will."

I tapped Black's address into my phone. Anci did the same. Then I told Anci it was time to hit the highway. She stuffed the rest of the cookie in her mouth and chugged her milk.

"Stay out of trouble, Slim," said Carol Ray.

"Too late," Anci and I said at the same time.

Anci looked up at me.

"Jinx. You owe me a Coke."

ANCI DRANK HER JINX COKE—CHOCOLATE COKE, TO BE exact—and ate some French fries. They were the good kind, crinkle-cut and fried in grease that'd had time to mellow in the trap. Probably since the states were arguing about nullification. Jeep had come out to meet us. He ordered a barbecue and some coleslaw. I was too anxious to eat anything much, except I stole some of Anci's fries, so my lunch was fries and the stink eye.

"Four o'clock at Leonard Black's and an hour later at the sheriff's?" Jeep said. "You'll never make it."

"I have to," I said. "My squirrel's in a bag as it is. I can't stand another bust. Besides, I have to be on the outside come tonight."

Jeep pondered this for a moment this and then said, "Maybe I should give him a call."

"Who?"

"Wince."

Anci snorted. I snorted. I threw up my hands.

"Oh, merciful hell," I said. "Please don't. You're not exactly his favorite person, you know? He's still not convinced you didn't disappear that meth dealer last year."

Jeep growled, "Fine. I'd recommend you call your lawyer, but that'd probably just make things worse. Wish I knew what it was all about, though."

"We'll find out at five o'clock."

"Righteous."

I looked at Anci.

"This is the part where you're supposed to pester me about coming along. Then I tell you no, it's too dangerous, and you make a wisecrack and say a dirty word like a kid on TV."

"Kids on TV don't get to say dirty words, stupid. You go on along to whatever caper it is you've set up," she said. "I'm on to something and I mean to follow it through."

"Oh, yeah?"

"Yeah."

Jeep smiled at me and shook his head—*kids*—but Anci

was serious. She munched her fries and stared bullets through the big plate window and out into the world of mystery.

ONE MORE TIME, WE PARTED COMPANY. JEEP AND ANCI struck out on some mission or other. Anci wouldn't say what, except to promise it wouldn't be dangerous. I figured whatever it was, if Jeep was with her, she'd be safe enough. Hell, she'd be safe if there were Nazi werewolf bikers involved. Jeep tried to argue that he was too busy to play chauffeur, but in the end she corralled him into it, and off they went. It wasn't ever very hard to talk Jeep into troublemaking.

Meantime, I headed for Leonard Black.

All my years underground, I'd stayed clear of Black coal mines and their sorrowful repute. Underground work is dangerous by nature, but some of these local strings were less like jobs than advanced forms of suicide. That's how I thought of the Black mines. Things just seemed to go wrong inside of them—too many injuries, too much misadventure—like they were broken or sick. One miner I knew up in Colton, Billy Goat McElroy, thought they were haunted. He got to worrying about it so much he hatched a scheme to bring his pastor down for some kind of Church of Christ sortilege, but the bosses caught wind of it first and got him fired. Not much later, Billy Goat died under what you'd call less-than-ideal circumstances, hanged from the bottom of a back-road bridge, and the locals whispered that the ghosts had got him after all. I always thought he was just depressed about his lung and heart problems, but folks tend to prefer their superstitions.

Haunted or not, these days there wasn't much of it left, the Black strand. The old-style gopher holes had long bled out their seams, and the bigger drops had mostly been bought up. Black remained a name in the downstate, though. He was a character. The story went that he'd won the land lease to his first coal mine by shooting the balls of the former owner's prize bull with an Eagle Arms Company Front Loader, but I suspect that was just the hoax-craft of local legend. Still, Black had a local reputation as a recluse and a bit of a nut: at nearly eighty, he affected both an enthusiasm for vintage motorcycles and a version of the paranoid-style of American politics that made even the local militia head cases keep their distance. That is, the stories swirling around him tended to be whoppers, but they also tended to ring true.

His spread was west, near Cape Girardeau between Commerce and Thebes, and *boy*, was this a dreary slice. You think you know ugly land, I'll show you ugly land. It was like the Lord had paused in the work of His creation to take a shit, and He took it right on Cape Girardeau. The rock-spotted hillsides were clotted with gray mud and touched with scrub and saw grass. The Ohio was pretty, I guess, but Leonard's view of it was spoiled by smoke stacks, power stations, and the slow drifting hulks of coal barges. Even the old farmhouse had sucked in enough smoke and fumes that the shingles had turned black. It sat there on its plot like a funeral cake.

Black looked funereal, too, though more like the guest of honor than just a guest. He met me at the door in an open robe like a coal-mine Hefner and grinning a skeletal grin. His skin was pink as faded rose petals, and the eyes behind his misaligned antique spectacles were gray and lifeless. J.T. was a pretty big guy, but Leonard surprised me with his smallness. If I'd wanted to, I could have put him in my pocket and run away.

The two boys he kept as hired help weren't pocket-sized, though, and if there was anything especially floral about them I couldn't make it out. Maybe their matching purple and gold sweats. I was ushered into a living room as big as a hunting lodge and garnished with all manner of murdered animal parts. I admit, I've never understood it. I'm not a vegetarian, and I wear leather boots and such, but killing an animal just to hang its face over your fire pit seems more an act of meanness than decorative ingenuity. For an instant, I pondered what Eun Hee Mandamus would have made of it, but the violence of the resulting thoughts made me put my pondering away.

"Is that a bat?" I asked, pointing to a place just below the I beam.

Leonard grinned.

"Ozark big-ear. You have any sense of what it takes to hit one of those little fuckers on the wing and leave enough to put on a plaque?"

"Fancy killing."

Leonard did not grin.

"You disapprove?"

"Well, bats are pretty. Also useful. For example, they eat bugs."

"That one don't."

The muscle had left us for a moment, but now they came back. They were so big they made the room hotter. One of them stuffed a cold drink I didn't want into my hand. The other one slipped a cigar I wanted even less between my fingers. Both of them shoved me into a chair. The chair was okay, I guess. Leonard sat opposite.

"We don't stand much on ceremony around here," he explained. "You are lucky they didn't sit you in your drink and set your thumb on fire. Or make you smoke your chair and stick that Habano up your ass." One of the tanks filled Leonard's highball with something as green as a newborn cicada. He sipped it and frowned. He looked at me and frowned some more. He was good at frowns. Almost as good as Paul Bruzetti. A master. "You're here about my boy."

"You get right to business."

"I prefer to keep my business dealings straightforward and to the point."

"And this is business?"

"My boy is. His future is," Black said. "So yes."

"It's about your boy," I said. "I think Carol Ray mentioned it maybe."

"She did. You mixed up with her?"

"Mixed up?"

"Intimately?"

"No, sir. I've got a woman. A good woman. And by the way, I'm not sure any of this is your business."

"And I'm not sure I like you deciding what's my business. Everyone in my line knows you, Slim. Everyone knows what you did to Roy Galligan."

He rose suddenly. He set his drink down and crossed to an ornately carved cabinet at the back of the room. He opened the cabinet and drew out a rifle, a Parker & Snow musket, I think. Maybe 1861. He came back across the room and pointed it at me. I almost felt honored.

"Tell me," he said, "I was to shoot you now, Slim, would it save my boy some trouble?"

"Maybe."

"You don't mind having a gun pointed at you?"

"I mind it plenty," I said. "But it keeps happening to me, and maybe I'm starting to get used to it. I don't like it, though."

"I wanted, I could put a ball in your brain—and with my eyes shut, too—then we'd cut you open, fill you full of hand weights, and sink your carcass in the Ohio."

"Hand weights?"

"They work better than rocks, and the boys here have a few to spare." He shrugged. "It's convenient."

"And what should murder be if not convenient."

I thought he might go ahead and do it, shoot me with the Parker & Snow, but just then one of the tanks approached. He used his hand to lower the barrel of the Parker & Snow and whispered something in the old man's ear. Then he walked away again. Leonard looked at me. He rested the gun against the arm of his chair and sat.

"I've elected not to shoot you."

"I'd hoped you might."

"For now, anyway."

"Fair enough."

He sipped some more of his drink. His hands shook around the glass.

"So this is about J.T.?"

"It's really about Sheldon and A. Evan Cleaves."

"The Cleaveses? Shit."

"I've had that same reaction."

"I don't doubt," he said. "They have that kind of reputation. Like wildfire. People have made the mistake before of bringing them in on something. Work-type things. Wet work. They're impressive. They're frightening to those who can be frightened, and they talk a good game without saying much. I don't know that makes much sense."

"I follow it, though," I said.

Leonard nodded his appreciation at my following it and said, "My opinion is that A. Evan might actually be crazy. Sheldon acts crazy, but he's more an old fox than a loon." Here he paused to take another sip of his drink. "Usually, though, it don't work out. Or it gets out of hand. Wildfire can't be controlled, nor crazy. Folks usually end up regretting ever hearing their names."

"I know I do."

"And you think my J.T. is tangled up with them somehow?"

"I don't know," I said. "My guess is, the lot of them are tangled up in something. I don't know whether J.T. brought them in or whether they all got brought in on it together by someone else. I'm sure as hell confused why they dragged me into it. It's not like there weren't enough men with guns lying around. But they did drag me into it, and now the only way for me to get out of it is to talk to the right people and convince them to leave me alone."

"And you've decided that person is my boy?"

"Well, he did run away for a reason."

"J.T. didn't run away," Leonard said. "A Black don't do that. He's just being strategic."

"Any idea where this strategery is taking place?"

He thought about it. Thought for five full minutes. I reckoned he'd eventually have to answer, but he didn't. He just sat there like lichen on a gravestone. I didn't know what to think. It was like he just went away. At last, I got alarmed and started to rise, but one of the tanks came over and put me back in my seat. He shook Black by the shoulder—gently at first but then more roughly—until the old man popped to life again like an out-of-tune television.

"I need to talk to him first, deliver your message," he said, like nothing had happened.

"Okay."

"Then I'll reach out to you."

"Through Carol Ray?"

"Through her." He paused thoughtfully. "Probably I should have shot you."

"Oh, probably."

That got him in a huff, some reason. Likely he'd had his fill of my flip attitude. He reached back from his sliding position for the rifle. I'd had enough rifles pointed at me for a day. I stood quickly and took it from him, snatching it from his hand. I stepped past his chair and gently hit him with the butt of the rifle in the back of his head. He dropped forward into his own lap. After a moment, I could hear him snoring loudly. The lumps of steroid muscle just stood there, watching. I showed them the gun, and they raised their hands.

"No need for fireworks, Dad," the one with the big forehead said. "He gets like that. You didn't hurt him. You avoided getting shot. It's win-win."

I agreed that is was. Forehead showed me out. I held onto the musket on the way out, though. Mama didn't raise no dummies.

"You know, he'll probably forget you were ever here," he said before I was able to escape. He tapped his forehead with two thick fingers. "Memory goes in and out."

His forehead wasn't the only thing being tapped, but I know when I've been out-maneuvered so I handed over my last ten bucks without too many hard feelings.

"Remind him, would you?"

"Maybe," forehead said, "but a sawbuck hasn't bought much around here for a long time."

"It's all I've got," I said. "It's gas money. I'll probably have to walk back part of the way."

"Cry me a river."

"What's your name, boy?"

"Ron Spike. And I ain't your boy."

"Have it your way. Can I ask you something?"

"Sure, big spender. Ask away."

"Does the old man ever forget J.T.'s visits?"

"Every now and again," he said. "Not often. Tell you the truth, the kid and him don't exactly see eye to eye on much these days. You ever meet J.T.?"

"Ran into him once. That's about it."

"Once is usually enough."

"Okay. Thanks. Don't forget to have him call me, will you?"

"Sure. What the hell? I feel generous today." He pocketed the ten. "You really a private eye, hayseed?"

"Sometimes." I took his outstretched hand. It was like grabbing a ring of drop-forged iron. "Sometimes I'm just a guy who runs around visiting sick old men. What ails him, anyway?"

"Oh, he's a sweet old guy. Fucking Santa Claus with a dime bag in both pockets and a sweet spot for bitches young enough to be his granddaughters. Except the syph is eating his brain. Few more years, we may have to lock him away."

No skin off his balls one way or another. He'd probably end up with the house and the land, and maybe one or two of Leonard's antique cycles, but saying so was just asking for a fight, and much as I might have enjoyed testing my manly skills against a walking laboratory, I had other appointments to keep.

Sheriff Wince was waiting. And maybe a holding cell.

13.

As these things usually go, I busted my ass to get to the Randolph Country sheriff's station, barely made it in under the wire, and then sat there for an hour reading a copy of *Modern Maturity* I found outside Wince's office. I'd just flipped to an article about your sex drive after sixty when the door opened and the sheriff appeared.

"'Bout time."

"Complications have arisen," he said, then paused. "What in the hell are you reading?"

"AARP magazine. Somebody must have left it."

"One of our master criminals, probably. Learning anything?"

"Yeah. I haven't saved enough to retire, but if I start now I might be able to quit when . . ." I paused to do the math. "Never mind. It's too depressing."

"That's not the half of it. You know those jokes you like to tell?"

"I do. For example . . ."

"That is, if you can call them jokes."

"That hurts. I lie away nights working on this stuff, you know."

"You ever think of quitting this business, giving clown college a try?"

"Lots of effort, little difference."

"Final question: are those orange sodas?"

I nodded.

"I stopped and got Anci some sodas. Didn't want to leave them outside in the heat."

Wince licked his lips.

"I have one of those?"

"You still on your diet?"

"Supposedly."

"Then no."

"Fair enough. As I was saying, you might want to keep a lid on it in there," he said. "Consider yourself warned."

I stood up and we went in. Wince's office was occupied. Too occupied. Lindley was there, and another guy, a bony thing with a face like a death mask. The serious character who'd made such an impression on Carol Ray. Ammons at last. Lindley was sitting. Ammons was pacing. When Wince led me in Ammons trained a pair of eyes on me might have been pulled from a taxidermied beast, cold, hard, and lifeless. Also, faintly yellow. I liked him immediately and wanted to make friends.

"Slim, you remember Sheriff Lindley?" Wince said.

"You're kidding, right?"

"And this is Senior Agent Ammons of the Illinois State Police MCU.

"Movimento dei Comunisti Unitari?"

Ammons looked confused.

"I beg your pardon?"

Wince put his head in his palm.

He said, "Oh, holy Jesus."

It was going to be a long meeting.

IT WAS, TOO. LONG AND BAD.

"You're pulling it." Me.

"I wish I were." Wince.

"The goddamn FBI?" Me again. "Here in SOIL?"

"Yes." Ammons. "The FBI."

"No. I'm sorry," I said. "In this case, it's got to be the *goddamn* FBI."

"Slim . . ." Wince. Of course.

I ignored him.

"Why?"

"Interstate violation of some kind," Ammons said. "But they're keeping mum about the specifics. Usually, they at least tell us what it's all about, but this time they're keeping it to themselves, which means it's big. Maybe nightly news big. Meanwhile, they're working on scotching our case against the Cleaveses and Harvels."

"Uh-huh," I said. I rose to go. "Well, I wish all y'all the best of luck with that. I really do."

"Slim . . ." Wince again.

Ammons pressed on. "We believe that the Cleaveses are up to their red necks in a criminal conspiracy involving the

White Dragons, weapons, drugs, you name it. And we're close. We're very close to bringing them in. We even think we have a shot at bringing them in before the Feds do."

"But if it's their investigation . . ."

"We can't really know it's their investigation unless they *tell* us it's their investigation."

"And since they won't talk to y'all . . ."

Ammons tried not to smile, but he didn't get very far with the project.

"That's it."

"So basically this is all about spite."

Ammons's smile went away fast.

"Call it what you want."

"Cool. How about spite?"

Lindley jumped in before Ammons could eat his own face. "There's just one leak in the dike."

"Not much suspense here."

Ammons had calmed down enough to make his neck work. "If the Feds get to you—and trust me, they're going to get to you—they'll argue that you've tainted our entire operation." He paused a moment to glare at Wince. "And they wouldn't be too far off, either."

I said, "I'm not sure this is my problem."

"It is if we make it your problem."

"Fair enough," I said. "So what's the plan?"

Wince cleared his throat.

"Well, we were kinda . . . uh . . . we were kinda think-ing about locking you up for a while."

I took the phone out of my pocket.

"I'm calling my lawyer," I said.

Ammons looked at Wince. Wince shook his head back at Ammons.

"Fine," I said. "Wince, I'm calling your lawyer. What's your lawyer's name?"

"Slim . . ."

I put the phone away.

"This is some bullshit now."

Ammons shrugged.

"It's suboptimal, yes. But there are a lot of butts on the line over this one."

"A lot of butts, Slim." Wince.

I said to Ammons, "Your butt included, I guess."

"*Especially* my butt."

Lindley said, "Maybe we could stop talking about our butts and start working on how to put Slim here into jail."

"That's not very nice," I said.

"Well, I don't like you."

I looked at Ammons.

"If those are my choices, I choose the butts."

"I'm willing to entertain counteroffers," he said.

I thought about it. They pretended to think about it, too. Oh, they did a powerful job at pretending to think. Wince traced the wood grain in his desk, and Ammons stared off into space like he was working on a mathematical formula for the secret of the human project. But I think it was mostly just politeness. What they were really thinking about was putting me in a hole.

Finally, I said, "I have a counteroffer."

They looked at me, ready to listen. Or to pretend to.

"It's a shit-a-brick kinda deal, but at least it's something."

IT WAS A SHIT-A-BRICK KINDA DEAL, ALL RIGHT. A HOSPITAL'S worth. Or a jailhouse's. At first they thought I was nuts, but somehow I talked them into it. Actually, Ammons did. Maybe he thought it would put a bug up the FBI's ass. I'm not really sure. Ammons did the deed and stalked out. Lindley laughed and shook his head and rumbled away like a storm cloud. What a crazy place the world was. When they were gone, Wince and I found ourselves alone. We blew out hard breaths and sank into our chairs. Wince got up and went to a cabinet and opened it.

"Well, I'll be . . ."

Inside was a small stack of cookies.

Wince stared at them as though he might cry.

"Secret admirer?" I asked.

"None of your goddamn business," he said, but he was too happy to be genuinely cross.

"Five cookies?"

"Six."

"Might have left you the whole box."

"Why are you trying to prick my condom, boy?"

"I guess you don't want to hear a warning about high blood pressure, then, do you?"

"That in your old-people magazine, too?"

"Matter of fact."

I opened an orange soda and took a sip. Wince looked hungrily at that, too.

"Well, I ain't got time for high blood pressure, boy. You, neither. You better get out of here before Ammons comes to his senses, comes back to relieve you of that badge."

I took it out of my pocket and held its weight in my hand. They'd wanted to put me in an orange jumpsuit, but in the end I'd talked them into deputizing me. It made a kind of sense, anyway. At least in the mixed-up world of law enforcement politics. This way, anything I knew, anything I learned, anything I *had* learned, would be the property of the Illinois State Police, with all the protections that came along with that.

"You as a lawman," Wince marveled. "The world's turned itself over, belly up, and peed on the sky."

"Grab an umbrella."

"You realize the powers and authorities that come along with that, at least in your case, are less than those wielded by a school librarian?"

I pointedly ignored this.

"I got to get home," I said. "Get myself a ten-gallon hat. Maybe some spurs."

"You ought to go home and hide until all this is over."

"I'll hide under the hat probably."

"That's not a bad idea," he said. "You also understand that badge puts Ammons's career in your hands? You fuck up his case, he'll go from cop to killer before I can do anything to stop him."

"I promise to be a good boy."

"There we are with that again," he said. "Listen, Slim, I want you to stay out of trouble. You've done me a good turn or two in the past, and maybe I owe you one." He shrugged. "Maybe that's something you don't want to talk about."

"No, we can talk about it."

He pretended not to hear that. He was having fun with his piety and didn't want to let it go.

"But this thing, it's bigger than I think you realize. These men aren't going to write you a ticket and smack your fanny, you get in their way. This is one of those things where the distinction between the cops and crooks won't be all that obvious."

"It was obvious before?"

"Those jokes are going to be the end of all of us," he said. "I don't suppose you know what any of this is really about, do you?"

"When I find out, I'll tell you," I said, but the truth was I knew. Knew it all for a certainty. Shelby Ann. The kill pit beneath the Cleaveses' house. The Black coal mine. Tibbs's magic ticket. Even a dummy can only be led around by the nose for so long. Or by the leash.

"I'll hold my breath," said Wince.

"Good idea. Make the bad men go away."

"Hey."

"Hey, what?"

"Before you go . . ."

"Yeah!"

"Give me one of them sodas."

"Give me one of them cookies."

We stared hard at each other for a long moment, but in the end an exchange was made.

"YOU WITH A BADGE? WONDERS NEVER CEASE." IT WAS ANCI. We were on our cells, so I couldn't see her face. But her voice sounded almost proud.

"You wanna know what I think? I think you want to give me the dozens but you're too impressed with your old man's new offices and powers. How'd it go with Jeep?"

Her voice dropped to a hush. "About him."

"About Jeep?"

"You know he likes to sing when he drives?"

I was quiet a moment, but she had me. I had to tell the awful truth.

"I know," I said.

"Show tunes?"

"I know."

She laughed, but still quietly. Jeep must have been near-by.

"Why didn't you warn me?"

"I wanted to," I said. "Really, I did. But it's not the kind of thing people talk about."

"He's actually got a pretty good voice, for a guy with a head like a cement block."

"Listen, don't mention it to anyone else, okay? It's the man's secret shame. I was kinda hoping he'd remember not to do it in front of you."

"Well, I'd have hoped that, too, I'd have known. Truth is, I think he forgot himself and started singing out of habit."

"Probably you were making him nervous, you and your secret mission," I said. "Speaking of which, how'd it turn out?"

Her voice was grumpy about it.

"Disappointment. I thought maybe I'd found a real lead, but I came up craps."

"Better luck next time," I said.

"We'll see," she said. "Where are you off to now?"

"Loves Corner."

I WATCHED FOR LONGER THAN I THOUGHT I WOULD. I PARKED on a grassy shoulder down the road and sat there sipping Anci's orange sodas and waiting. I didn't see Wesley or his car or any of his pot plants. Likely the boy was at work. I hoped the plants had been burned and buried somewhere far away. Seven o'clock rolled around. Then eight and nine. Maybe he was having trouble getting out of the house. Maybe he had kids and they wanted to hear *Hop on Pop* one more time. Everybody's got a story. Even the bad guys. Or the good guys. Or whichever it was. But night came on at last, and so did the silver pickup. The one Wesley had mentioned to me that day. The one I thought he'd made up in his paranoia. Silver truck was laying it on thick: Stars and Bars decals, a gun rack, bumper sticker reading ASS, GRASS, OR CASH. The works. He parked twenty yards or so up the street, doused his headlights, and sat there. I jumped down from the Dodge and walked over, keeping low. I had my gun out, but I figured I wasn't going to need it. Still, always better to be prepared.

One thing, when you're staking out, you might want to keep the doors locked. Cuts down on nasty surprises. You'd think they'd teach that at the academy, but budget cuts have to happen somewhere, I guess. The passenger door was unlatched, so I opened it and swung on up and closed the door behind me. The man behind the wheel looked at sharply me and my gun. He smiled and raised his hands, but I could tell he recognized me and that he wasn't afraid. He was wearing a dark suit and a red baseball cap.

"Agent?" I said.

He smiled at me.

"*Special* Agent. Carney."

"Special Agent Carney, you and I need to have a little chat."

14.

CARNEY DIDN'T WANT THE LOCAL SQUIRRELS TITTERING over their nuts about the mysterious goings-on at Loves Corner, I guess. Or more likely he was worried Tremble would come home from his shift, interrupt our parley. He insisted we drive north a ways and meet at Evergreen Park, on lonely County Road 16 near the Carbondale city reservoir. I told him he was crazy and laughed at his paranoia, which got our relationship off to a great start, as you might imagine. He was still huffing about it a half hour later when we parked our trucks nose to nose on a flat stretch of nowhere and approached each other like we meant to pull pistols and shoot one another for honor or money.

Carney was around thirty, with a bland face and a short, stocky frame that made his suit seem two sizes too big for him. He was sweating like an Alabama minister in August, but at least he'd ditched the ball hat. We got close to each other, and he showed me his badge: Robert L. Carney.

F.B Fucking I.

"Just so there's no mistake," he said.

He'd showed me his, so I showed him mine.

"Just so there's no mistake," I said.

"You're shitting me. They gave you a star?"

"You should have seen them, too. I tried to refuse, but they persisted begging and crying until I took them up. Something about the future of law enforcement being in jeopardy if I didn't go along."

"Christ, they told me you could talk a blue streak."

"Those files are awfully complete."

"You have no idea."

"Now you're just trying to rattle me."

Carney laughed and shook his head.

"Somehow, I think you're hard to rattle. This was that little shit Ammons's doing, I take it?"

"I honestly don't recall. The glow of my pride has blocked out the details. Memory serves, though, someone was upset you won't play nice with the other children."

"Fucking Ammons. Look, company policy is to cooperate with local assets when cooperating with local assets makes sense and won't compromise our case."

I nodded slowly and sucked my teeth some, doing my best dimwitted country boy act. I even scraped my foot a little on the gravel road. I'd have brayed at the moon and done a little jig, I thought it'd get me what I wanted.

"And you're not sure whether . . ."

I paused as though to fret it out. Carney smiled, but it was a certain kind of smile. It was a getting-over smile. I'd got him and got him good. Nothing lures 'em in like the ol' Simple Son of the Country. Some reason, it just makes folks want to talk, preach, explain, whatever.

"We're not sure the local assets aren't up to their necks in it."

I guess I couldn't hide my surprise.

"Lindley?"

"Or Wince. Or one of a half dozen others."

"Or me."

Carney nodded.

"Or you. Someone paid for that roof."

"So what do you want?" I asked. These bastards could have my life, but they couldn't have that new roof. "I figure you weren't waiting outside Tremble's place just to scout the local pot trade."

"I'll be honest. It wasn't until recently that we figured out the connection. We were interested in a phone call he received a few weeks ago from a certain local character. Someone you met the other day in Marion, as it happens."

"Tibbs?"

"What he calls himself. Tibbs is the Illinois White Dragon's chief fund-raiser. Mr. Tremble is a drug dealer with a criminal connection to his former boss."

"I'll be damned," I said. "And what about me?"

Carney shrugged.

"Just back off. Rather, understand that you're backing off, even if your brain doesn't know it yet."

"Is this the part where you describe the box I'll be put in if I fuck with you?"

He grinned, and in the shadows cast by my headlights, he looked as much like the devil as A. Evan had on my front porch a few days earlier.

"I don't have to, and that's assuming there even is a box. When this thing starts to go, it's going to come down like an avalanche. Everyone's going for the ride."

I looked at the ground again and scratched my head.

"You're mixing your metaphors like Momma's shut-up-and-eat-it leftovers," I said. "I can't keep up."

"And you can drop the dumb hillbilly act. It's not even summer stock caliber."

I raised my hands.

"I'll back off."

"And be ready for a call from Carter."

"Jimmy?"

"My boss. He's going to want to talk to you. You won't like what he has to say. He likes people peeing in his sandbox even less than I do."

"Well, now I have something to look forward to."

Carney sniffed. He climbed back in his truck and turned over the engine. I walked over to the driver's side door and he rolled down his window.

"That's it?" I said.

"For now that's it. I wouldn't get too comfortable. And you better have paid your taxes on that hundred grand."

"No worries," I said, and winked. "I'm laundering the money through a number of fake charities for wayward federal agents."

"Jesus . . ."

"Is my bagman."

"See you around, Slim."

"Hey, one last thing?"

"What now?"

"Dennis Reach," I said. "You haven't asked me about him. I assume that means you know who popped him."

Carney sniffed and shook his head and looked at the windshield like he meant to drive away. Then he turned again to me and said, "You heard of Helen Dees?"

"Nope."

"She's the woman who reported the AR-15 stolen."

"The one used to kill Reach? I was told it wasn't stolen."

"You were told wrong," he said. "Helen Dees is the mother of Amanda Dees. Amanda Dees used to be married to a guy called Jacob Terrence."

It took me a moment.

"J.T.?"

"Yup. Amanda got the gun in a very nasty divorce. She didn't want the piece, so she gave it to her mother. Mother doesn't really want it, either, but she hates Black and she'll do a headstand in cow shit to let him know it. Your pal Black shows up one day in a huff and collects it. Helen Dees reports said crime to the Jackson County sheriffs . . ."

"Who refuse to do anything about a theft involving one of their own."

"You really are sharp, hayseed."

"If I were really sharp, would I have stepped into this nest of vipers?"

"That hurts."

"It was supposed to."

"Whatever. Warning delivered. Now go somewhere else and stay out of our way," he said. "Stay out of jail."

He rolled up his window and drove away. I stood there thunderstruck.

By the time I headed home from my meeting with the mean FBI man, I was plumb tuckered. Seriously, you could have put me to bed for a year and when I woke up I'd have hit snooze. Anyway, despite my weariness in both mind and spirit, I stopped by the Huck's for some replacement sodas and ice cream, hoping to make it up to Anci. She likes that fancy Ben and Jerry's, and I do too—I'm American enough that I like it when even my ice cream is attached to some cause like saving the rainforests or fighting various kinds of cancer. Makes me feel better about my waistline. The problem with the Huck's was, they only carried those lowbrow ice creams, big boxes or those plastic gallon drums, from creameries that didn't seem to care about anything but profit. I thought about driving to one of the big stores, but that was a half hour in any direction, so I finally settled for some chocolate for me and some strawberry for Anci. As the clerk was ringing up my stomachache, my phone rang.

"Yo?"

"You *hit* Leonard Black?"

"I said yo. You're supposed to say yo back."

"Stuff your *yo*s," said Carol Ray. "You did, didn't you? You sonofabitch. Hit him, and with his own rifle, no less."

"Technically, I think it was a musket. I had this funny urge about keeping him from shooting me with it. How'd you find out, anyway?"

"Spike called me with the after-action report."

"So his name really is Spike? I'll be damned."

"Of course his name's really Spike. Why? Is it important?"

"I don't think so," I said. "It's just a neat name is all."

"Oh, Slim . . ."

"Bad?"

"Well, I don't really know yet. I haven't spoken to Leonard, just Spike. Leonard's still snoring and farting."

"Okay."

"But yeah, it's shitstorm bad."

"Maybe I can find a way to make it up."

Carol Ray snorted.

"With what? Flowers?"

"I don't think Leonard's much of a say-it-with-flowers kinda guy."

"I meant for me, stupid."

"Ah."

"Let me work on it from my end," she said. "I'll let you know. Until then, stay tight."

"Speaking of your end."

"Not tonight, darling. I've got a headache."

"That's not exactly what I meant. You don't know Amanda Dees, do you?"

"Nope."

Click.

I DROVE HOME. I FELT WORN OUT. DEPRESSED EVEN. IF I'D had a spoon, I'd have opened the ice cream, eaten some along the way. The ice cream boxes were sweating through the plastic bag, so I rolled up the windows and turned on the truck's AC, but it was still so hot outside that the windows fogged over, so I turned it off and gave up. We'd just have to settle for melty ice cream. I was pretty close to Shake-a-Rag when my phone rang again.

"What's the scoop?" Anci.

"Funny you should mention. I'm on my way home with ice cream."

"Strawberry?"

"What else?"

"It's a start," she said. "By the by, there's someone waiting for you in the driveway."

My throat seized up a little. Anci wasn't alone, but the idea of someone hanging outside the house wasn't something I was too thrilled about.

"Who is it?"

"Dunno. Opal talked to her, wouldn't let her in the house."

"I'll be there in five."

I made it in three. There was a woman standing in my driveway beside a Dodge Rambler so big it looked like two cars masquerading as one for Halloween. She was wearing jean shorts, a cutoff T-shirt, and a sneer.

"Where the Sam Hill have you been?" she asked before I could step down from my wheels. She snapped some chewing gum at me. "I been standing here a fucking hour already."

"I'm . . . sorry?"

"You don't look it."

"Likely that's because I don't feel it," I said. I looked at her more closely, hoping for a twinge of recognition. Nothing. It wasn't the sort of face you easily forgot, either, lean and as long as a Wagnerian opera. She wasn't pretty, but she was trying hard to be. Her hair was the antigravity marvel favored by southern Illinois cheerleaders, but even that and her high-school-senior fashion sense couldn't quite disguise the fact that she'd long since crossed the thirty-year mark. "I don't believe we've been introduced."

"Mandy. *Duh.*"

"Okay."

"You're Slim," she told me. "Who's the redhead in the house?"

Her gum went *snap snap*.

"She's a friend."

"Yeah, well, she wouldn't let me in. Kinda rude about it, too. Tell your friend her day's gonna come."

"I wouldn't bother with it, Mandy."

"I ain't afraid of her," she said. "I ain't afraid of nothing."

I thumbed back toward the house.

"She's Jeep Mabry's wife."

"Don't tell her I said nothing, okay?"

"Okay."

"I was only kidding."

"Your comic stylings are a mystery to me," I said. "What do you want?"

"I don't want nothing," she said. "J.T. wants to see you. He's been wanting to see you for a couple of days now. You really ought to come home more often."

"In many ways, I'm a troubled person," I replied. "But I want to see J.T. Just say where and when."

"He's been hiding out at the Elks in Z.R. for about three days. He's there now."

"Hiding in plain sight, eh?"

"What?"

"Nothing," I said. I kissed her hand, and she blushed.

"He said he'd wait until I called," she stammered.

"Okay, go ahead and call. I'll head right out."

"I will," she said. She took out her phone and then looked up at me, as nervous as a June bug in a room full of ducks. "That really Jeep's wife?"

"Yeah. You ever met him?"

"No, but I've heard tell. I'd like to see it for myself one day. See him in action, I mean. But it's like deciding where you'd like to watch a fertilizer plant explosion from."

"It is that."

I thanked her and walked up to the house with the ice cream. Opal and Anci were reading in the kitchen. Nice as pie.

"Purple eyeliner still out there?" Opal said.

"I talked to her, but she's gone now."

"That the aforementioned ice cream?" Anci asked.

"Strawberry and chocolate, as promised."

She collected the boxes and put them in the freezer. When she came back, she kissed me on the cheek.

"What's that for?" I asked, mildly shocked.

"For not being a total dummy."

"Well, thank you. It's the ice cream, isn't it?"

"It's not the ice cream. Well, not just. Don't let it go to your head."

"I won't."

"It's not like you brought Ben and Jerry's, after all."

"I'll do better next time." I said to Opal, "All quiet here?"

"Yes," she said. "We've got our books and DVDs and a lot of music I've never heard of."

Anci rolled her eyes, but truth was, she was thrilled about Opal's visit. In a while Peggy would join the two of them for a sleepover. Jeep and I had business that night.

"I'll be back," I said.

Anci kissed me on the cheek again. Opal did, too.

"That's two kisses for you," said Anci.

"Three, counting the first one."

I went out. Mandy was still in the driveway.

"Why the hell are you still here?" I asked.

She stared up at me from under sparkly purple eyelids, her gum snapping noisily between her lips.

"Why am I still here? Aren't you going to say you're sorry?"

I blinked at her once or twice.

"Sorry? What for?"

"For making me wait." She blew a pink bubble. "I had things to do, too, you know?"

"Just call J.T. and tell him I'm on the way, okay?"

"I already did that," she said, and rolled her eyes at the world's injustice. "Mr. Insensitive."

★ ★ ★

ZEIGLER-ROYALTON WAS A FORTY-FIVE MINUTE DRIVE, AND for all I knew J.T. Black would have packed up and split by the time I arrived. If I was right, he had as busy a night ahead of him as I did, but I didn't figure I could pass up a chance for a sit-down heart-to-heart. Besides, he'd been thoughtful enough to send a personalized invitation. I cranked up the radio and hauled ass toward Z.R.

The Elks in town wasn't run by the men's club anymore, hadn't been for ten years or so, but the name and the stuffed buck still occupied the space above its doorway, most likely because everyone was too lazy or too drunk to take them down. Black was inside, hunched over the bar next to a guy with no arms, but otherwise the place was nearly empty. I drew up a stool and sat between them.

"Slim."

"J.T."

Black said, "Slim, this is Sticky," and nodded at his drinking buddy.

J.T. and I shook hands. Sticky shook hands with his eyes.

"You just about missed your chance with me, hayseed," J.T. said.

"Can you blame me?" I raised my finger for a beer. The bartender got J.T.'s approval before he'd serve me. "Look at the kinds of places you want to take me."

"You don't like it, man," the bartender growled, "you can just pack up your shit and take it on down the road."

The guy without arms thought it was hilarious.

"Hey, no offense," I offered, and I even showed him my open hands, but I don't think he believed me. In places like

that, offense wasn't taken; it came free with every drink. I
said to J.T., "I've been looking all over for you, man."

"I know you have," J.T. said. "That's what I wanted to
tell you. You can call off the fucking search, man, 'cause I
am getting my ass out of this dump."

I nodded like I knew what he was talking about, but all
he did was give me the twice-over with unsympathetic eyes
and stroke the beer foam off his mustache. Hard to tell in
the gloomy light of the Elks, but I got the distinct feeling
that J.T. Black hadn't been getting his eight solid hours a
night.

"Might not be the best idea, son," I told him. "You
know, lots of folks are looking for you pretty hard."

J.T. shook his head sadly.

"Yeah, I've heard tell. Wince. Lindley. The goddamn
FBI . . ."

"That's what I've been calling them."

"You ever hear of a guy named Carter?"

"Just recently, in fact."

"Yeah, well, do yourself a favor and stay clear of him.
He's a tornado with a badge."

"How about a guy named Tibbs?"

"Him, too." He looked at me. "Without the shield,
though. You know, it's the goddamnedest thing, man.
You've been running your ass off looking for Sheldon and
A. Evan for, what, a week now?"

"Longer."

"Yeah, well, I'd be willing to bet my last five bucks you
don't even know why."

"Dennis Reach is why."

The bartender brought our things, a couple of drafts with foamy heads, an ashtray as clean as they came, and two fingers of something brown in a shot glass for the former Jackson County deputy.

"Denny Reach was a cocksucker," J.T. said. "Not even worth pissing on, so give that shit a rest, will you?"

"Fair enough," I said. "That why you killed him?"

He looked at me a long time.

"You're just lucky I didn't kill him, motherfucker," he said at last. He showed me a mouthful of teeth. "If I did, you wouldn't be walking out of here."

I opened my mouth to make a crack about his friend being unarmed, but just then the bartender, who didn't like me anyway, slung an evil-looking sawed-off from under the bar and tucked it neatly beneath my chin. If he'd pulled the trigger, what was left of me would have flown backward off the barstool, across the room, and out the door onto the lonely Z.R. streets.

"Put that thing away, Fish," J.T. said softly, looking over his shoulder. It'd be inaccurate to say that the place froze—it wasn't exactly moving in the first place—but its alcoholic old muscles tightened somewhat, and one or two of the sprightlier drunks cleared their throats and gazed longingly at the spaces beneath their tables. "Fish is from East St. Louis," J.T. explained when Fish had put it away.

"Ever been to the top of the Arch?" I asked, and for an instant I thought the shotgun would reappear, but J.T. sur-

prised us all by braying like a jackass, rearing back to slap
his knee, and, in the process, nearly falling off his stool and
onto the floor.

"Goddamn, boy, you are a piece of work," he said. "Hey,
Fish, did you hear that shit? You've got a fucking scattergun
under the guy's throat, and he wants to know if you've ever
been up in the Arch." He shook his head. "Man, that is rich.
That is some rich shit."

Fish still didn't see the humor in it all. His right eye
flickered in little spasms, and the ropy veins in his forehead
knotted like they might burst.

"Hey, it's great laughing with you all," I said, "but I
get the feeling you didn't call me out here just to tell me to
fuck off. Especially since you were pretty much doing that
anyway."

"You're right, man," he admitted, awfully cheerful for
one of the condemned. "You ever hear of a motherfucker
named Norris?"

"Morris? Like the cat?"

"No, man, Norris. With an N. He owns a gun shop in
Carbondale, right there across from the mall."

"So what?"

"So, I sold the gun to him."

"The AR-15?"

"Long time ago, man," J.T. said. "I haven't seen that
fucking thing in, like, three years, Slim. Honest."

"Why'd you steal it in the first place?"

The kid shook his head

"Steal? Hell, man, I didn't steal shit. The gun was mine. I picked it out. I bought it. I'm the only one who ever discharged it. And when the time came to give it up during the divorce, all of a sudden, it was a fucking gift. Shit, I don't have to tell you how messy divorce is, man."

"I read a book about it once."

He slid a piece of paper between us. It was stamped with the name of the pawnshop and a date three years ago.

"That doesn't really prove anything," I said. "You could have retrieved the gun and kept the ticket, or had someone else buy it for you and kept the ticket as an alibi."

"Three years ago? That's seems a little complicated."

"It kinda does, yeah."

"I didn't do it, man."

"You know what?" I said. "I think I actually believe you."

He surprised me by saying, "Thanks."

"Tell me about Sheldon and A. Evan Cleaves," I said. "Or the Harvels."

He shrugged, but I could tell he didn't like hearing their names. He made a face like he meant to spit.

"What's to tell? Sheldon used to be a fire boss at one of my old man's mines. The Harvels are nuts. A. Evan's crazier than all of them stacked end to end. This one time when we were kids, he made us play circus. I know it sounds weird, but he was obsessed with circuses. We never wanted to play with him, my brothers and me, but one day he hung some sheets in an old carport at an empty house down the way and put out some chairs and drew some rings on the floor with chalk, and we came to the circus. He even had tickets. Except when we get there, it's a geek show. You know what that is?"

"I've heard, yeah."

"Yeah, well, I was seven at the time. Maybe eight. I didn't know. A. Evan had pinched some chickens from one of the neighbors, live chickens, and we sat there watching while he bit off their heads and spat blood and chicken brains all over the walls and all over us. Eventually, he threw up, but I think he threw up from laughing so hard at the looks on our faces."

"He was seven at the time, too?"

"No. He's younger. He was five or six."

"Jesus."

"Jesus never heard of A. Evan Cleaves, Slim," he said. "Or if he has, he's staying away."

"So what's their connection to Reach, and why did Reach steal their dog?"

"I honestly don't know, man. I really don't. Dennis and I had a falling out before he brought them on. All I know is that everyone thinks that I know, so it's time to boogie."

"Just a victim of circumstance, huh?"

"Exactly."

"Catch you later, then."

He looked up at me with eyes that were almost sad.

"That's it?"

"That's it," I said. "I just wanted to hear you say it."

"You know, man, I don't really blame you for all this. I blame Reach and the rest of the rats. And Tibbs. And A. Evan Cleaves. But my life in this part of the world is pretty much over, man, and it'd be nice if you'd at least act a little sympathetic."

I dropped some money on the bar.

"Catch you later," I said again, and walked out.

NINE O'CLOCK OR SO, WE HEARD A FEW DROPS, THE FIRST time in a while; it was a drizzle with all of the promise of rain, but none of the follow-through, and it didn't do much to break the heat or soften the baked earth. Some of it came through the tarp on the roof, and Anci and I put out pots and pans to collect the drips. Peggy was there, and Jeep and Opal arrived shortly after. It was time for business. I kissed Peggy and kissed Anci on the head, and then Jeep and I started off without speaking. I guess we both had a pretty good idea what we were about to see, and neither of us was the least bit happy about it.

Two hours later, a last set of taillights bumbled their way down the shadowed lane, glimmered briefly in the wet-kissed air, and disappeared around a stand of redbud trees. The gravel parking lot of Black #5 was nearly half full, and even with the security lamps turned out and the distant moon dim against the rim of some faraway hill, Jeep and I were able to make out shapes in the gloom: groups of men and dogs trotting toward the coal mine, eager to go below.

Jeep swept a dripping bush from his eyes and, scowling, handed me the binoculars.

"What you thought, slick?" he asked.

I nodded.

"Goddamn dogfight," I growled through grinding teeth. "Goddamn underground fucking dogfight."

PART THREE
DEAD GAME

15.

WE WENT DOWN THE HILL IN THE DARK AND TO THE GATE OF the mine, where we were met by some men with guns. I showed them my ticket—that slip of paper Tibbs had given me—and they led us into the yard. They didn't talk to us. They didn't talk to one another. Nobody told a joke or sung a song. We were down to business. Moonlight pooled on the barrels of their weapons. We followed them to the mine elevator, where a group of our fellow ticketholders was waiting, as well as some men holding dogs on thick leather leashes.

Finally, the elevator came up, and a redneck holding a TEC-9 stepped forward and said, "Boys, we gonna get on this thing now and go down into the mine. Here's how this works: I tell you to do something, you do it. You don't do it, you might get peppered with this here TEC. 'My clear?"

He must have been clear because nobody said anything. He nodded some and said, "Okay, we want spectators grouped in the middle of the cage, doggers at the edges facing outward."

That didn't make the boys happy. They didn't want to

stand ass-to-elbows with a bunch of strangers as scummy as they were, I guess. Firearm threats notwithstanding, some of them got vocal about it. Some redneck George Washington decided to lead a mini-revolt for the freedom of the elevator platform and got a rifle stock in the nuts for his trouble. He dropped to his knees with a grunt and was dragged away to his fate.

Everybody else hurried to the middle of the cage. No one wanted a rifle stock in his nuts. Next the doggers were led on and instructed again to stand facing outward, with their backs to one another. Well, none of them wanted to do that, either, and there was another little fuss over it. In the end, though, everybody agreed to obey the guns aimed at their faces. The walking boss's TEC-9 and one or two Cobray M11s. And with the fancy suppressors, too. You've never seen so much agreeing. We were like conservative ministers deciding we hated sin, Satan, and folks on food stamps. When we were finally in position, a beer gut in a quilted Day-Glo vest snapped shut the lanyard. The cage lurched, and we were on our way.

More ways than one, down we went into the dark. The first thing that strikes you about the inside of a coal mine is the cool. Rock and earth are good insulators, and as we sank into the shaft the cold air rose up to meet us like a corpse's breath. Everyone started shrugging into their coats and hats. Jeep put on a ball cap that barely contained his head. I was already wearing my cap, and I hadn't brought extra clothes, so I just jammed my hands in my pockets, which was just as well since I couldn't stop them shaking. A thousand feet or so later, we rattled to a standstill. "Rattled" is maybe understating it. We hit down with a bang that sent our skeletons into our hats. The cave cold came howling at us like Baskerville's hound.

"This way, gentlemen."

The gate opened, and the gentlemen disembarked. One of them hocked a serious loogie into the dark. Someone else farted. Just like Camelot. Another armed group led us off the platform and into the work area. It was a different group. They looked the same, but they were missing different teeth. It was a subtle difference, but if you looked closely you could detect it. They waved their guns at us, and we followed them into the main run and five or six hundred yards deeper into what was once a pretty good size room-and-pillar mine. Or still was, maybe. This wasn't an old mine. It was a relatively new outfit—last twenty years or so—and the cuts were clean and the works new. The lighting systems were functional and you could feel the steady breath of the ventilation system as the air coursed through the veins cut in the rock. So maybe we were just in a closed section. You couldn't ask anyone. Asking would get you stitches. Or worse.

Our group was full of stitches and worse. The doggers, especially. No one was pretty, but every one of those doggers was a Frankenstein of wounded parts: scars, cuts, abrasions, missing fingers and flesh. It was like the world had taken a bite out of them. If they'd started comparing scars, they'd have stayed down there until the coal turned back into plant and animal life. Their personal style didn't do much to smooth out the rough edges. You could have filled twenty barrels with their tattoo ink, and the hairstyles they favored ran the spectrum from twenty-to-life to life-without-parole. Their dogs seemed to be in better shape, but I didn't guess that was going to last much longer.

We finally made it to the room. It was a big one, fifty yards by fifty yards, maybe. The ceiling was low and gave the whole thing a claustrophobic feel. There were lights bolted to the ribs and a fight ring in the center. An ugly woman in a one-piece bathing suit ordered us into a circle at the edges of the room. One of the doggers thought he'd make a romantic pass at her, but she wasn't in the mood for love. She tucked an automatic into his crotch and invited him to take his place. He took his place. He looked vaguely shocked that his manly wiles hadn't panned out. Then Ugly Woman joined another woman, even uglier but younger, and together they started dancing and grinding to some kind of dance music that was bass and nothing else.

"We're in hell," I said to Jeep.

"Not yet."

More men came in, and the edges of the room began to swell. The onlookers stood arm's length apart, careful distances. They stacked their firearms and cash at their feet.

"Case the place gets raided," Jeep explained. "You just walk away. You still get busted, but there's no clear weapons charge."

"Walk away? You can't just walk away. You're in a coal mine."

"Principle's sound, though."

"And I guess no one can prove you were gambling on the fight."

"Less a sure thing, anyway. Complicates the legal process. Makes deals more likely."

The MC stepped into the chamber and brushed past us. You could tell he was the MC on account of his clothes: a cream-colored cowboy suit and one of those bolo ties with a scorpion trapped in a chunk of amber. He was wearing a pistol in a patent leather holster. A big .45. He was as short and round as a highway barrel—the MC, not the gun—and his face made me want to give up on humanity once and for all. He had a slung jaw and tiny black eyes and eyebrows that seemed to carpet his entire forehead. Flannery O'Connor would have considered him implausibly grotesque. He pushed through the crowd and into the ring, then squatted down and rubbed his hands through the piles of straw on the floor. He was awfully attentive about that straw. Then he stepped across the pieces of plywood that formed the walls of the ring and raised his hands. There was a roar from the onlookers. It was on, I guess. I felt my stomach drop.

Jeep pushed earplugs into his head. "You sure you got the stomach for this, slick?" he asked, and when I looked a question at him he grumbled, "Once. Down in goddamn Broward County, Florida. I was drunk off my ass; the place was full of asshole Marines. Only reason I left without killing anyone is I got hit from behind with a fucking parking meter."

"Parking meter?"

"Yup."

"An actual parking meter?"

"Full of coins, too. Must have been a busy street, wherever it was. I chewed a bottle of aspirin every day for a month, washed it down with a fifth of Cabin Still, and the headache's still never quite gone away. But at least I stopped seeing double."

"And now you get to see this."

Highway Barrel barged into our conversation.

"Tickets, boys."

I handed over the slip of paper Tibbs had given me. Highway Barrel held it in his palm like a dog turd.

"This ain't quite the right one," he said. "This was the one from a while ago. You should have the new one."

For an instant, I nearly panicked. Then I got myself together and said, "Leonard said it would be all right."

"Leonard?"

"Black."

He looked shocked by that.

"I . . . might need to call for confirmation," he said.

"Go ahead," I said. "Call him from the mine tonight. Call his home. Leave a record for the cops."

"That's not what I meant," he stammered.

"What *did* you mean?" Jeep said, catching on.

"I don't know."

"Well, maybe now you do know," I said.

He stared at us a moment more, but then he took the ticket and went away. The next guy handed over his ticket without hesitation. Highway Barrel still found a reason to read him the riot act up one side and down the other.

Jeep whispered, "Think that was smart, slick? Bringing Black into it? Now the little guy almost has to call."

"Yeah, but he won't call tonight, I'm guessing. And even if he did, it's hard to imagine they'd care too much. This is bullshit, man. The Cleaveses might be psychopaths, but even they aren't stupid enough to kill somebody over a game this small."

Jeep inclined his head toward the ribs of the mine tunnel, first one way, then the other.

"Check it out, slick," he said.

I couldn't make out what he was talking about at first. But then my eyes adjusted to the shadows, and sure enough, there they were: webcams, digital cameras built to transmit live images directly to the Internet.

"You're kidding? We're on the YouTube?"

"Not that. But we're definitely online somewhere. Could be a hidden link," Jeep said. "Part of an at least halfway legit streaming service. Subscribers only."

"Wouldn't the cops be able to find something like that?"

"Most cops couldn't find their own butts with a road map and an extra hand," he said. "But, yeah, maybe. That is, if they were looking, which they probably aren't. Their best shot would be if some animal cruelty outfit were monitoring the web for shit like this. But then again, you can bet your ass that site isn't advertising itself."

"So what—it might be part of some otherwise-legit gambling thingy?"

Jeep grinned. "Site?"

"Yeah. Site."

"Yeah, it could be part of something semi-legit," said Jeep. "But it probably isn't. I had to bet, I'd say it's probably hiding behind something pretty run-of-the-mill. Something you'd never suspect. And the link to the real shit could be invisible."

I was about to ask him to explain all that when another cage-load of men and dogs arrived. Suddenly the room was too full. Everyone lost their breathing room and stood scowl to scowl. One guy's tattoo took up on the next guy, and so on, forming a giant, horrible tapestry. Something like that could never last. This wasn't a meeting of the Southern Baptist Convention—it wasn't that mean—but it was close. Someone would say something or smell something, there'd be a wink or a laugh or a nothing, and hell would break lose. The room was itching for reasons to murder. Highway Barrel must have known it, too, because just then the lights flickered, the sad dancing girls started jumping and waving their arms, and the show was under way.

"Hold your breath, bro," Jeep said.

Now the man in charge took the center ring, grinning like a moray eel, his double chins spreading across the bottom of his face.

"Pure." He smacked the word between his swollen lips. His face beamed in maniacal glee. I wanted to hit him and never stop. "In a world of bullshit, liberal media lies, homo propaganda, and PC revisionism, what we have is pure. Muscle, bone, teeth, fur, and blood."

The crowd loved it. They wouldn't have known a liberal revisionist from a chicken in a dress, but they loved it. His speech had the word "liberal" in it, and they'd been trained to hate that word and all it stood for. These were poor guys, most of them. You could tell by their clothes, their hairstyles, and their choice of pastime. A lot of them were on public health. One older guy in a corner was rocking a brace he probably got from the state. But somehow none of that counted as the dole. The dole was what *everyone else* was on, and they hated them for it.

"And by moving underground, into the secret places of the world, we'll show them that pure things survive and thrive, even in shadows. We . . ."

Someone switched on the boom box, interrupting him. Thank the gods. The girls reappeared, dancing and fondling each other in a display of sad eroticism while Highway Barrel grumped his way out of the ring and the first dogs grumped in, led by boys no older than fifteen or sixteen. Tomorrow's sociopaths, today. The dogs were underweight pits, bony things with sharp ribs and knobby knees. The muzzles came off, and they flung themselves together with the nauseating sound of crunching cartilage and flattening muscle. The men around us rushed the edges of the ring in a sudden stampede. If Jeep hadn't been there, I'd have been trampled.

And after what happened next, I sort of wish I had been. The dogs locked jaws and snarled. There was a spray of blood. And that was about it. Almost as fast as it started, the bout ended. One of them lost part of an ear, and the other was bloody around the eyes, but when the men in the hunting vests separated them using long metal rods, the animals trotted back to their disappointed masters as though nothing much had happened.

"Rookies," a kid with pimples said to me. Maybe he'd pegged me as the new guy and wanted to be buds. "That bigger dog's got some promise. Not much, but some. The little guy's going to get himself killed, though."

"Yeah?"

"Hells, yeah," he said. "He's twenty pounds underweight if he's an ounce. He'll get in a serious fight one day and . . . poof. Doggie all gone, man."

I didn't want to be buds back. I wanted to start a chain reaction that, in the fullness of time, would lead to the boy shitting his own teeth. But just then the next contenders emerged. These were bigger things. Scarier things. Pimples went nuts with applause, along with the rest of the room.

"Playtime is over, man," he said over the noise.

The dogs were called King's X and Ripper, and they were old pros. Their owners were muscleman types with loads of oozy tats on their arms and shoulder blades. When they looked at their animals, it was with the frozen appraisal of a pair of robot killers. I felt Jeep buzzing beside me. He wanted to kill them, too.

This fight was longer and bloodier. King's X was a brown and white pit with a head like a cement block. This was a big animal. I've seen smaller cars. Ripper was darker and even bigger. I suspected he was a weightlifter in a dog suit. When he collided with King's X at full speed, both dogs crashed to the straw mat in a bundle of exploding muscle. Ropes of foam splashed across the ring to dowse the psychopaths who'd moved in too close. The dogs smashed against the plywood barrier with a sound like raw steak hitting concrete, separated, and went after one another again, harder this time, teeth flashing.

"How long will it go?" I whispered up at Jeep.

"Dogs like these," he said, "it's what they call a dead game. They'll fight till one of them is a corpse."

He was right. After a few moments, it was clear King's X had had enough. He turned and spun. He snapped at Ripper, but it was weak. He ran, trying desperately to get away.

"Uh-oh." Pimples. "Game over."

Ripper was on him, jaws clamping around the other dog's left hind leg and tearing until the limb held on only by a few bloody ligaments. Ripper took his throat between his jaws, and shook. And it was over. King's X sighed. His eyes rolled back in his head as blood pumped out his gasping mouth, and when he shit himself before he died, the men around us laughed their asses off.

"What do you think, man?" Pimples asked.

I showed him what I thought. I turned and threw up all over him.

THIS WAS A NIGHTMARE NIGHT, AN ENDLESS NIGHT, THE KIND that would hunt you through the rest of life and come to stand at your deathbed with black eyes. There were five more fights. Three more dogs died. A fourth lost most of his jaw. He'd probably end up in a garbage heap somewhere.

The straw in the ring went black with the blood. By the time we headed back to the surface and into the hot air of early morning, I was shaking so bad I thought the rattle of the lift would vibrate something inside me loose that couldn't be fixed. Jeep put his arm on my shoulder.

"Easy, brother."

It was still dark and the light rain had pressed east, leaving behind a humid stew. When we arrived at the surface, it jumped on us and stuck there. The men with guns were nowhere in sight. A few of the doggers and spectators hung around to chat or smoke before saddling up and heading off into the night to God only knows what. Families, probably, a few of them. Little kids. I stopped thinking about it. The nightmares would come soon enough anyway. Pimples shot me an unhappy look before climbing into a bright yellow Ford pickup and roaring away in a cloud of dust. He didn't like being puked on, I guess. I was busy repeating his plate number under my breath when I realized that Jeep wasn't beside me anymore. He'd vanished.

Well, hell, he'd been on the elevator with me, so he couldn't have gone far. I waited five minutes. Then ten. At fifteen he finally came jogging up, shush-finger to his lips.

"This way, slick."

I started to ask a question, but he was already gone, jogging off again. I gave chase. That was easier said than done. Black #5 was a two-shaft outfit with a surface area about the size of ten football fields laid end to end. By the time I finally hobbled up to Jeep waiting behind a Quonset hut, my still-recovering legs were screaming just a little less urgently than my lungs.

"Hey, slow down, asshole," I said, although the big man had already stopped moving. "What's the rush?"

Jeep aimed a finger, and I saw. Highway Barrel and one of the muscle dudes. Ripper's owner, I realized. Someone had moved several giant rubbish containers near one of the shafts, probably to hold used-up or trashed equipment brought up from the bottom. Highway Barrel was busy filling it with the bodies of dead dogs. Muscle Dude was sitting on one of the containers, smoking a hogleg joint. He didn't want to help. Highway Barrel was huffing and gasping, and his sweat made him look like he'd been dipped in cooking oil, but Muscle Dude didn't care. He was indifferent to suffering, human and inhuman both.

Jeep said, "Time to gather a little information. Maybe bust some heads."

"I'm for that. The head-busting thing, especially. Who gets to be the bad cop?"

Jeep thought about it.

"How about no good cop, bad cop? How about just two crazy redneck motherfuckers?"

"Sounds like a scheme."

Highway Barrel wasn't happy to see two strangers approach, but at least he didn't open fire. That was something. Muscle Dude puffed away on his hogleg. That was something, too. I admit, the guy worried me a little. He was too calm, one. Two, he was as big as a bank vault. I'll fight just about anything human, but Muscle Dude looked like he'd just rolled off the assembly line at the Mack factory.

"What's up, amigos?" he said. "Come to help bury the collateral damage?"

Highway Barrel glared at him. The boy didn't notice glares. Highway Barrel didn't want it to go to waste. It was a dandy of a glare. He turned it toward us.

"What do you want, men? Fight's over. Show's done. Time to vanish into the night."

"We know." I showed him my hands. He didn't relax. He didn't add my name to his Christmas card list or ask to be Facebook friends. I turned to Muscle Dude. "Hey, sorry about your dog."

He shook his head. "Don't be. Fucking thing was a loser from day one."

"What do you want?" Highway Barrel.

"What's your name?"

"Fuck you. That's my name."

"I'm Slim," I said, ignoring him. "This is Jeep."

Muscle Dude laughed. The veins on his neck crawled around.

"Oh, how I love this part of the world, man."

"What do you want?" Highway Barrel again. His hands twitched. I wondered when he'd remember he was armed. "You're cops, aren't you? Oh, Lord have mercy, Jesus Christ."

Muscle Dude stiffened. He didn't like that we might have been cops. I don't know how he felt about Jesus. Probably it was a troubled relationship. He hopped down from the container.

"We're not the police," I said. "But we are looking for someone."

"And you're gonna help us," Jeep added.

Highway Barrel sucked his lower lip. His upper was covered with tiny beads of sweat.

"Who?"

"A. Evan Cleaves," I said. "And his gang."

The little guy took a step back like I'd take a swing at him. He wasn't wrong. I was about to.

"No. Uh-uh. No fucking way."

"Just tell us, and we'll be on our way."

"I can't."

Jeep said to me, "I knew he wouldn't tell us."

"Hey, you were right. I was wrong. What can I say?"

"You want me to take care of these two, Carlos?" Muscle Dude finished his joint. He pitched away the roach and flexed his muscles. Jeep laughed at him.

"Pretty," he said. "There's almost nothing you can't inject these days."

"Shut up," Highway Barrel hissed.

Jeep ignored him.

"About that dog of yours, son," he said.

"Shut up," Highway Barrel hissed. "Please."

"It's like I said, man," said Muscle Dude, "fucking garbage."

The boy sprang like a jolt of lightning. He was so fast he knocked over his bud. Highway Barrel went down on the gravel pad with a shriek. I caught a hard knife-hand strike to the shoulder and dropped to one knee. But the boy didn't want me. He wanted Jeep. Jeep wanted him. It was a match made in heaven. The two men collided like dogs in the ring, both growling. I looked up. Highway Barrel was fumbling with the big .45. He'd finally remembered it.

I hit him hard enough to make him forget it again. I hit him with a snapper of a right, then spun and side-kicked him into the garbage cans. As he flailed over backward, I ended up with the .45 in my hand.

"Stay down, you idiot," I said.

He didn't want to stay down. They never want to stay down. He might have been a little guy, but he was strong as a brown bear. And none too bright. I waved his own gun under his nose, but he kept coming. He kicked my right leg with the silver cap toe of his Western boot. But that was pretty much his only move. I backed out, stepped quickly under his slow right hook, and came up again with a right hook to his balls. I followed this with a jump kick to his chest—a little like targeting the broad side of a billboard—and an elbow to the face that dropped him in a pile. He looked up at me and held out a hand.

"I don't like fighting," he said, spitting blood.

"You're shitting me."

"What?"

"You don't like *fighting*? You're the MC of a goddamn dogfighting ring."

"I mean *human* fighting."

I reached down to pull him upright. My plan was to beat him to death, administer CPR, then beat him to death again, but just then I got hit hard from behind and lost my feet.

Not on purpose, either. Jeep and Muscle Dude were engaged in some serious hand-to-hand combat, and they'd run right into us. For a moment I worried that Jeep was getting the worst of it. Muscle Dude's bulges weren't merely ornamental after all. And he'd been trained to fight. Two quick roundhouse kicks upside Jeep's head sent the big man staggering before a beauty of a spinning stiff-leg to the midsection that would have split open a football took him off his feet altogether. But they don't make them much tougher than Jeep Mabry, and flash and high kicks aren't any match for plain old country-boy meanness. When the big man found his footing again and raised up into the light, he was actually grinning. Lashing out, he caught Muscle Dude by his short curly hair and drove the boy's face down into his knee. Then he unleashed a spinning kick of his own, a whirling arc that met the side of Muscle Dude's head and sounded roughly like a sledgehammer smashing an overripe melon. The kid should have done the smart thing and taken a nap. But when he came up again, this time with a boot knife in his hand, and lunged forward, he ran full-force into Jeep's jump front kick, a shot that sent the boy end over end one too many times. He skidded on the rain-slicked lip of the shaft head and plunged, headfirst, into the hole. He didn't even scream.

Carlos did, though. He screamed bloody murder. And he screamed even louder when Jeep hauled him from the ground and dragged his terrified ass to the hole.

"Last chance," he said.

"A. Evan," I said to Highway Barrel. I touched Jeep on

the forearm, trying to hold him together. I might as well have been touching a lead statue.

"Woodrat Road," Carlos whimpered. "They've got a hideout place in Woodrat Road. Near Pyramid and the park."

"You know it?" Jeep asked, still looking at the little man, digging holes with his eyes.

"Yeah," I replied, because the question was for me. "I know it."

Jeep tossed the little man aside like a used hanky. He lay on his face near the garbage bag of dead pit bulls, whimpering softly. At least he had sympathy for something.

16.

WE DROVE THROUGH THE NIGHT. WEST AND SOUTH, INTO the hills. The dark world blurred. This was rough country. Trail of Tears State Forest jumped up and swallowed the land. No one wanted to live out there. There wasn't any moon, and the roads all ran headlong into black holes. Finally, I broke out of my thoughts and broke the silence.

"Here's the part I don't get."

"Tell me."

"If the Cleaveses are up to their necks in the dogging business, and it looks like they are, why hire me in the first place? Why not just kill Reach themselves, snatch Shelby Ann, and go on about their miserable lives? For that matter, why bother with the dog in the first place?"

"Doggers are like breeders everywhere," Jeep said. "Always looking for a prize line. But yeah, I saw her picture. In terms of dogging, she wasn't anything too special."

I nodded, hating it, hating the bloodless math of it.

"So why her, then?"

"Maybe there's something else special about her?" Jeep said. "Or maybe it was just to fuck with your buddy Reach?"

"All right. So maybe it's a simple matter of clipping the competition. We're right back to the first question. Why hire me?"

"Don't know," said Jeep. We thought about it a bit more. Probably neither of us was going to give Sherlock Holmes a run for his money. Finally, Jeep said, "Convenience, maybe. Or maybe they just like other people to do their dirty work for them."

"Hundred thousand bucks could pay for a lot of dirty work. Especially when you've already got a pair of psychos like Bundy and Arlis Harvel at your disposal."

"True."

"I can't figure it out," I said. "In fact, it only makes sense if . . ."

Jeep nodded.

"The Cleaveses didn't kill Dennis Reach," he finished for me.

"Sonofabitch," I said. It's amazing how dumb a grown man can be. "They think I did it."

"Which only leaves one question."

"Who did kill Reach?"

"Yep."

There wasn't much mystery to it. The Colt rifle, Reach's words to me the night he was shot, J.T. hiding out and hauling ass. It all added up to one name, and I'd like to say I was more than just a little surprised. But I sure as hell was embarrassed.

Carol Ray.

Jeep must have been reading my mind.

"Better see if we can find her, slick," he said. "It might go a long way toward getting you out of your hole with Lindley."

"The hole's pretty deep at this point," I said. "And like to get deeper. Frankly, though, I'm more worried about the FBI."

"Fuck it," Jeep said. "If we're going to get our assholes in a knot, let's at least have something to show for it."

"And what might that be?"

"A. Evan Cleaves's nut sack, stapled to my living room wall."

"A. Evan still attached?"

"Briefly."

And on we drove into the night.

WOODRAT ROAD RAN RIGHT UP TO THE DOORSTEP OF PYRA- mid State Park. Way back, the area was all strip land, and even to this day the overgrown tailings left behind by the Pyramid Coal Company form a kind of gently rolling grass- land. Denmark was just west, Galum Creek a little to the north. The Cleaveses' hideout was in between, inside a dark, wet hollow surrounded by chinkapin and hackberry trees and a humid gloom. The moon finally appeared, low on the horizon, and the silver light on the rim of the hills was kind of pretty. Then A. Evan's hideout jumped out of the landscape and punched pretty in the nose. Here the country dove toward lowland and wet muck. The insects attacked us like a little air force, and the hot kiss of the summer damp

laughed in our faces. But the trailer was worse. It was a geri-
atric fiberglass doublewide whose only saving grace seemed
to be that it had a roof and four walls. Maybe not even that.
Any port in a storm, I guess, but a newspaper story about
a tornado would have torn A. Evan's trailer to confetti and
thrown the confetti into the next county.

"Why not just live in a cave?" Jeep said.

"At least there's not a dog in the yard."

"Yeah. Ain't that a kick in the ass?"

"Speaking of ass-kicks, how you want to handle this?"

"With our usual charm."

Our usual charm involved broken doors and red-hot
gun barrels. Or at the very least kicking anyone's ass who
looked at us crooked. I thought about it.

"How about we try the bedroom window first?" I said.

"Your caper, slick."

The backyard was a mud hole. There was a pile of abandoned pickup trucks in various stages of advanced oxida-
tion. It was like a museum. There were kennels—shit- but
not dog-filled—and a device, wild with copper tubes, that
could only have been A. Evan's attempt at a still. Like he
didn't have enough vices.

I half-expected someone to come out of the dark at us,
chainsaw in hand, babbling some sort of wild-ass, backwoods glossolalia, but maybe I've just seen too many Hollywood horror movies. The back door was missing. It was just
a rectangular hole in the fiberglass. As a security measure,
someone had leaned an old fishing boat against the hole.

I said, "Now that is something you don't see every day."

Moving the boat seemed like a bad idea. We went around front again. I don't guess we were going to win awards for decisive action, and I was glad there were no men's magazine writers around to take it all down. We climbed the steps. The front door was a door in name only. It was the kind of door other doors make fun of for goldbricking. We gave it a mean look and it opened. I looked at Jeep. Jeep looked at me. That was about as calm as things got.

Jeep went ahead of me. The room was dark and quiet and small. There was a hallway to our left, and some doors, all closed. The bedroom was right. It smelled like someone had roasted wild animals alive in their pelts over an open flame. I didn't know what that was, but I knew I didn't like it. It burned the nose and the eyes. It made you want to tear out your hair and cry and run away into the hills. Candle-light from the bedroom cast a shape around the corner and on the wall. A big yellow square. We slowly but deliberately headed for that shape. We snuck like the Scooby Gang. Suddenly the quiet got quieter. Then there was a sound like a hard breath, and the yellow square went away. Someone had blown out the candle.

"Well, shit," Jeep said.

Something thundered toward us, out of the shadows. Sheldon Cleaves, I realized. Or a wild animal wearing a Sheldon suit. He ran at us, naked, howling across the small space with his unit flying around free like a shaved mouse. He had a sword in his hand. His pecker was out, and he was armed with a sword. Saber, I guess it was. Jeep did the sensible thing and hit the deck. The saber whistled through the air. It clipped off the brim of his ball cap and lodged in the metal flashing around the doorframe.

Sheldon grunted and tugged, but the blade was stubborn. I didn't blame it; I didn't want to work for Sheldon Cleaves, either. Jeep jumped to his feet. He hit Sheldon in the ribs and kidneys. Sheldon grunted, but kept working on the sword. It was an impressive show of single-mindedness. I left him to Jeep, turned, and started in a run to the bedroom. I didn't get far. Two shapes appeared in front of me—two big naked shapes, a couple of Sheldon's White Dragon buds, I guess. I didn't have time to ponder what all that nakedness meant. The air went hot around me. Something flashed bright in my eyes, and I fell over backward and broke a chair.

I'll never know how, but when one of the big men cut loose with what looked like an Ingram .380 machine pistol, he managed to miss everything but the sofa, the windows, and some squirrel skulls. Sheldon forgot his sword and dove through the front door like Buster Keaton doing a silent film stunt. The second big man hit the deck, too, and rolled toward the kitchen, knocking over barstools and a thicket of foot-high bongs as he went. He swept his own Ingram across the room and puckered the wood paneling with black anuses.

Jeep's .50-caliber Magnum roared. It hit the air conditioner on the wall opposite and tossed it into the yard. He fired again, and a fist-size hole appeared in the particleboard. When I uncovered my head and opened my eyes, the room had gotten emptier. The White Dragons had disappeared back into the hallway. One on either side.

"Back out," Jeep said to me.

I backed out. Sheldon was still at the top of the stairs, still gathering himself. I kicked him off the steps and to the ground. He stood back up, holding his balls. I guess he'd landed on them when he dove out of the trailer.

"You motherfucker," he said. Meaning me, I guess. He looked ridiculous, standing there cupping his balls. Then he smiled. We turned.

One of the Dragons was standing in the trailer's door-way. He aimed his gun at us. I didn't hear the shot, just its echo. It came from somewhere along the dark ridgeline, too far away to see muzzle flash. It hit the Dragon in the top of the head. His brains jumped out of his skull and landed in his open palms. What was left of him looked at them for a moment in confusion. I dove under the steps. Jeep followed.

"Who?" Jeep asked. I shook my head. I didn't know.

I didn't have the time or breath to answer anyway. The second Dragon appeared. He had some loyalty on him. I guess you had to give him that. He ran screaming into the yard after his brother-in-arms. He picked a piece of him off the ground. Another shot cracked just over our heads. The boy's right arm vanished in a red haze just beneath the shoulder joint. I think he opened his mouth to scream, but as he did, another slug knocked the top half of his head from his body, and what was left of him folded up and crumpled to the ground in a shower of blood and brain matter.

"Fucking sniper," Jeep grunted. "In the dark, no less. Night-vision scope?"

"Got to be. I can barely see five foot in front of me, and those shots came from the hill."

JASON MILLER   250

"Some of your heavy-hitting buddies," Jeep said.

"Inside."

We dove for it. Jeep dragged Sheldon with us. We made the trailer just as another shot sounded and the light fixture by our head exploded. We dove inside, ate floor. I shut the door with my foot.

"What now?" Jeep asked. Calm.

"Don't know. Suppose we could call in the cavalry."

"Wince?"

"No. I don't want his deputies' blood on my head."

Jeep grunted.

"Think they'll shoot at us if we lead Asshole out of here?" he asked after a moment.

"Fuck you, boy," Sheldon said.

"Where's your son?" I said. "Where's A. Evan?"

"Not here," Sheldon said. "And double fuck you."

Jeep said, "Or maybe we could just push him out there. Let him take his own chances."

I thought about it.

"Uh-uh," I said at last. "We still need the old bastard. To get to his son, for one thing. And as for walking him out of here, I don't think so. Pretty clear that whoever's up there wasn't gunning for us, or at least decided we're lower-priority targets, but they'll cut us down to get to him. That's for damn sure."

"I think so, too."

"I need a phone," I said.

The one on the wall had been vaporized. Probably it wasn't connected anyway. Mine was in the truck. Snug in the console. Useless. Jeep reached into his coat and brought out a pink cell. I stared at him until he blushed and looked away. A first.

"It's Opal's," he said.

Sheldon barked a mean laugh. He didn't like us and wanted to hurt our feelings. Jeep slung him across the room. He hit the wall with a sick thud and collapsed to the floor. He sat up and smirked at us.

"Who the fuck are you peckerwoods?"

I picked a card out of my wallet and started punching the tiny rubber buttons.

"I'm the guy you and your son tried to kill a week ago, old man. You should have finished the job."

"We will."

I opened my mouth to say something. But Jeep was quicker. He picked Sheldon up and threw him across the room and into the other wall. Sheldon left a hole in the paneling.

"I've learned something about myself," Jeep said. "I like beating up racists."

I had to ignore that when the other end picked up.

"Agent Carney, please."

It took them a moment to get their shit together at Command Central or wherever, moments that seemed like years. Finally, a voice crackled over the line.

"Carney."

"Hey, friend."

"Oh, goddamn. What now?"

"Nice chatting with you, too, special agent. You guys have a helicopter at your disposal?"

"What? A helicopter? Of course not."

"Dang. How about an armored car?"

"We have an SUV," Carter said.

"Roomy?"

"What the hell is this about, Slim?"

"You remember the White Dragons?"

A long silence.

"Ticktock, special agent."

Sound of Carney clearing his throat.

"Of course I remember them. What . . ."

"There's a pair of them shot dead. In the front yard of the trailer I'm holed up in."

"How . . ."

"And the person or persons who made them dead are likely still in the vicinity."

"You're trapped?"

"Like a fly in wet shit, special agent. And if you want to hear my story, you're going to have to come and get me."

"Agent Carter will . . ."

"Pee his pants, I know," I said. I wondered how long it would take the genius on the hill to start peppering the soft walls of the trailer with bullets. "Mine aren't too dry right now, either."

"Okay, I'll . . ."

"Hurry."

"Soon as we can," he said, suddenly back in control of his voice. He'd made his decision. "Where are you?"

I gave him the address and described the general location of the shooter.

"And Carney . . ."

"What?"

"The house belongs to A. Evan Cleaves."

"Sonofa—"

I hung up on him.

"Think that was smart, slick?" Jeep asked.

"Don't know. Probably not, but it was the only play we had."

Jeep didn't look convinced.

"What now?" he said.

"Carney can't find the two of you here. He does, you and I will go to jail, and shithead here will be whisked far, far away."

"True enough. How we going to do this?" Jeep asked, ignoring Sheldon's snarl. The old man writhed on the ground like a dying wasp. The impulse to crush him with my boot was almost overwhelming.

"I'll have to get the truck."

"Think they'll let you?"

"Don't know," I said. My hands were shaking, but my voice was calm. "I am willing to entertain counterproposals."

There weren't any counterproposals. I crawled to the window and peered out, but I didn't see anything but nothing. It's possible the sniper was buried, ambush style, beneath a covering of leaves and branches. It was possible he'd gotten tired and gone home. It was also possible I was in line for the British crown.

"Wish me luck." I crawled to the door.

"What's luck?" Jeep.

"Die on fire, motherfucker." Sheldon.

What a pair.

The bodies of the Dragons were where they'd fallen. The truck had taken a couple of slugs. The passenger-side window was gone, and the rear bumper had been hit, but it still looked drivable. Anyway, I don't guess I had much choice.

Morning was coming on fast now, and in the frail light the shapes of objects seemed sharp. The birds were singing in the loud, clear tone that only first light seems to inspire, and the taste of humidity was heavy in the air. The truck, parked alongside the gravel road in front of the trailer, might have been a million miles away. Getting to it was like swimming through concrete.

But there weren't any shots, no subsonic rounds to punch a hole in my belly and head. I opened the door of the truck and climbed in and turned over the engine. Just like I was going to market. I drove as close to the front door of A. Evan's trailer as I could.

"You okay?" Jeep asked from the doorway.

"I feel ten years older," I said. "But I'm alive. Think you can manage this?"

Jeep nodded at Sheldon, who lay on the floor, breathing hard and clutching his ribs. Guess Jeep had punished the old guy for the whole die-on-fire remark.

"Have to tie him up," he said. "But yeah."

I had an idea.

"Might not be necessary," I said.

Sheldon screamed like a kid, but after another moment I managed to stick him with a couple of the dog tranquilizers I'd picked up from Lew and Eve Mandamus. Before you could say *Goodnight Moon*, the old man had drifted into uneasy dreams.

"Where to?" Jeep asked, once Sheldon had been deposited not-so-ceremoniously into the bed of the truck.

"My place. And don't spare the horses."

"Good luck, slick."

"Yeah, good . . ."

A burst of shots erupted from overhead. Maybe the shooter had dozed off, or maybe he'd gone to take a piss. Whichever, he was back now. The Dodge's rear window exploded. Jeep slammed the door and hauled ass, scattering dust and river rock on his way to the road as bullets peppered my ride with small pits, blew the passenger side mirror off its post, and disappeared the little silver Ram hood ornament. I doubted my insurance would cover it.

I decided I'd had enough fresh air for the day. I went back inside. I went back in horizontal. I landed hard on the floor and kicked the door closed again. Shots came through the windows and walls. A clock turned back into random numbers. A bullet knocked the derby hat off the skinny half of a Laurel and Hardy lamp set. Now they'd gone too far.

I wanted to get away from the gun. I went into the back of the house and into Sheldon's bedroom. There was a glass pipe on a bedside table and a harness and ball gag in a pile on the floor. I was still looking at it when I heard a whimper down the hall.

I went toward it. Bathroom with a pocket door. I slid back the panel and there she was, in a ball on the floor. That sixty-five-dollar red dog.

"Thank God you're okay," I said.

She sniffed my hand and kissed my cheek. I kissed the top of her bony skull. I checked the shaved spot under her collar. The XXXs were gone and new stitches were in their place. Something had been taken out of her.

"We get to meet some FBI men now," I said. "I'm sorry. I keep introducing you to turds."

Twenty more minutes passed. A half hour. I started to think Special Agent Carney was having a joke on me. Maybe the boys and girls at Command Central were all sharing a laugh at the expense of the luckless redneck, under fire in a shithole mobile home somewhere in the hills of southern Illinois. I guess it was pretty funny, when you thought about it.

Or maybe not. About that time, the first churning of the air reached my ears from far away, and in another moment the unmistakable sound of a rumbling engine filled the air around A. Evan's trailer. The ratty curtains flapped in their windowpanes as though their interest had been piqued. I was just getting up the guts to take a peek when two big men in black suits and sunglasses came storming through what remained of the front door, scooped me up, and dropped me and Shelby Ann into the backseat of a waiting Lincoln SUV. Right next to Agent Carney.

"Drive," he said. He looked at me. At the dog.

"That your partner?" he said.

"You watch too much TV, special agent," I said.

"And you don't watch enough."

The Lincoln roared away from the trailer.

17.

COMMAND CENTRAL TURNED OUT TO BE THE BIG DAYS INN in Marion. Two rooms, too, so you know it was an important operation. Plus they had that free continental breakfast. Another guy in a dark suit sipped coffee from green Styrofoam and watched the *Today* show while boxes of Krispy Kreme donuts petrified on a table.

"This the asshole thought we had a helicopter?" Donut Guy asked, mouth full.

Carney ignored him. He stripped off his jacket. There were tea-saucer-sized sweat stains beneath his arms.

"Nervous?" I said.

"Sit down," he said. He'd been sullen during the ride over, too. Damp underarms will do that to you.

I sat on the edge of the bed.

"At the table," Carney said, not amused.

I sat at the table. Shelby Ann curled up at my feet. Carney and one of the men from the Lincoln sat opposite. A tape recorder small enough to fit up a drug dealer's rectum appeared. We were just about to get started when the door opened again and another man came in. He was an important man, you could tell. He wore his importance like a satin cape. He was sixty or in that neighborhood, dressed in a brown suit and matching fedora. Anyone else would have melted or exploded in that getup, but he was too important for the heat. His eyes were the gray of frozen cathedral stones, and his chin roughly the size and shape of a wall safe. I tried to imagine what you'd have to hit him with to put him down. Aircraft carrier, maybe.

When he saw me, he stopped in mid-stride. "Special Agent Carney, tell me, is this the slimy stack of backwoods lump meat that has been fucking up my otherwise righteous investigation?"

Carney cleared his throat. "Uh, yes, Agent Carter."

Agent Carter. At long last.

"And has he been . . . Is that a dog?"

"Yes, Agent Carter."

Carter nodded. It was a dog.

"Has this person been Mirandized?" he said.

"I wasn't clear that we were . . . that we were arresting him, sir."

Carter swept off the fedora to reveal a head full of silver hair, pomaded and furiously combed. "We weren't clear?" he repeated, tasting the words. He made a sour face.

"No, sir."

He turned on me.

"And what do you think, son? You clear?"

"On one or two things, Agent Carter."

Carter nodded.

"One or two things," he repeated. Already, I didn't like

him repeating things. "I've been doing some checking on you, son. And I must say more worthless, human beings do not often come. As near as I can tell, you're little more than a part-time bedroom snooper who has been present at more than one murder and whose known associates include all manner of shady characters, as well as a borderline psychopath named Owen Mabry, also called Jeep, himself present at several mysterious deaths."

"I also have an ACLU card," I said. Donuts chuckled quietly.

Carter nodded. Add ACLU membership to the list.

"Tell me, boy, why are you so heavily invested in shitting on my case?"

"I wasn't aware that . . ."

"Bullshit!"

Everyone in the room nearly jumped out of his seat. Donuts slopped coffee onto his suit pants, then nearly overturned his chair getting to the bathroom sink. Carter ignored him. "Where is A. Evan Cleaves?"

"No idea."

"The Harvels are missing, too. Arlis and Bundy. I don't suppose you know anything about that, either?"

"I do not."

"How are you going to make a living when I have your license revoked?"

"I'll sharpen saws."

"Play ball, Slim, or I'll put you away so long . . ."

I didn't say anything. It wasn't a moment for talking or joking. A full five minutes passed. At last, Carter sighed.

"They gave you a badge, I hear."

I showed it to him.

He said, "You realize . . ."

"Yeah, worthless, I know. Everybody keeps telling me. Let me ask you something."

"You're kidding?"

I ignored him.

"Does it make you happy? Running around threatening people's livelihoods like that? Big, tough guy like you ought to know better. I hope you're ashamed."

Carter didn't look ashamed. He stared at me. I stared at him. Carney stared at the ceiling. Donuts came back and sat in front of the TV. It was the part of the show where the news stops and the celebrity interviews take over. Donuts stared at that.

"All right. Fuck it, then." Carter sounded resolved. "What were you doing in Pyramid?"

"Looking for A. Evan Cleaves," I said.

"Why?"

"Because he tried to murder me and my daughter. And because he thinks I killed Dennis Reach."

"But you didn't?"

"Nope."

"Know who did?"

"Not exactly."

Carter nodded.

"You're still good for it, then," he said. Someone had to hang. Might as well be the unlucky bastard in nearest proximity to the crime, as Lindley had said. Less paperwork that way. "And when I'm through with you, your ticket won't be worth wiping your ass with."

Enough tough-guy talk to fill a hundred crappy novels.

"Carol Ray Reach," I said after a moment.

"Come again?" said Carney.

"She killed Dennis Reach. Least I think she did."

"And how did you come to this conclusion?"

But that answer would have taken the rest of the day, so I said, "Maybe Carol Ray was trying to bust in on Reach's dogfighting business."

Even Donuts looked at me. Carney whistled again, but cut it short when Carter gave him another of those handsome glances of his.

"Know about that, do you?" he asked, amused.

"I suspect it. Carol Ray was married to Reach, but another of her exes is a former Jackson County deputy named J.T. Black. Reach and Black have been tied up in various criminal enterprises together. I think dogfighting was one of them. Top of that, Black's old man owns a string of underground coal mines."

"Holy shit," Carney mouthed. And goddamn, even Carter looked surprised. "They're underground. They're in the mines."

"Where?" Carter demanded.

So I gave it up, the time and location of the fight, the people I'd seen there. I held back only one thing for myself: the license plate number I'd memorized the night of the dogfight. Specifically, Pimples's license plate number.

"When's the next one?" Carney asked, getting back to the fight itself.

"No idea," I said, but they were too excited to care. Carney snatched a phone and started dialing.

"And A. Evan Cleaves?" Carter asked.

"No idea about that, either," I said.

"What happened to your face?"

"Is this professional, or are we just making polite chat now?"

Carter sank back in his seat. He actually looked like a human being and not the law enforcement nightmare he'd been imitating a few moments before.

"Agent Carney tells me all this started because you were looking for a dog. Anything to that?"

"For sixty-five bucks."

"Is that the dog?"

"This? No this is a different dog. This is my dog. Not the same dog at all."

"Go home, Slim. Stay out of the way. You've helped us here today, but playtime is over now. Time to let the pros handle it."

"You've hired some pros?"

"You never quit, do you?"

"One question," I said, getting up.

"You can't seriously think . . ."

"Why the Cleaveses?"

"What?"

"The Cleaveses. From what I've seen, there are dozens

of locals actively involved in this mess. Former cops among them. What's your special interest in A. Evan and his daddy?"

Carter didn't have an answer for me. He took a phone from his jacket and dialed a number. In a moment, he was engrossed in a conversation, and I might as well have been in another time zone.

But a non-answer is still revealing. The Cleaveses must have done something none of the other doggers had done, something to attract all that attention. It all got me thinking about what Carol Ray had said before, about how her husband would take a check from anyone, and about the way that ugly sneer crossed her face. But Carol Ray had taken some pretty ugly money her own self. And I got the distinct feeling she wasn't talking about the Dragons anymore. By the time I'd made it downstairs to the parking lot and realized I didn't have a ride home, I'd pretty much worked it out.

Dennis Reach: FBI snitch.

I COULDN'T CALL HOME AND ASK FOR A RIDE, SO PHONED MY lawyer in Marion, and in a stroke of luck, either good or extraordinarily bad, he was both available and willing to play chauffeur. An hour later I'd put Command Central and the special agents behind me. For good, I hoped. My lawyer wasn't in a chatting mood. Instead, he sipped a can of Coors and listened to some pop-psychology call-in program on the radio. He appeared to have slept in his suit—more than one night, maybe—and even with those big sunglasses on his face I could see the black and purple bruises beneath his eyes. We'd made it all the way to Murphysboro before he started talking.

"My wife hits me, you know?"

"Pardon?"

"My wife." He thumbed his nose with a hand he kept on the steering wheel. "You know?"

"I'm sorry, son, but I didn't even know you were married."

"She gets drunk."

"Yeah?"

"By which I mean, she gets drunk, then gets drunk on top of that. Then things get wild."

"Ah."

"Yeah."

"You hit back?" I asked.

He took his eyes off the road long enough to look offended. "She's a woman."

"Just asking," I said. "I don't suppose you've got another of those beers?"

He pointed to the glove box, but there was only one left, and it was warm as the inside of a mitten. I put it back and closed the door.

"Have you called the cops?" I asked after another moment.

The boy shook his head.

"Still love her," he muttered. "Pretty good joke, huh?"

We were quiet the rest of the way home. I guess everybody has a problem.

★ ★ ★

EVERYBODY, THAT IS, EXCEPT JEEP MABRY. WHEN MY SAD-sack lawyer dropped me off, Jeep was sitting on my front porch, shoes off, cooler full of beer, with one of my cats sleeping in his lap.

"My name come up?" he asked as an opener.

"Now that you mention it."

"Let me guess. Murderer?"

"Close." I sat beside him and took a beer from the mini-cooler. "Borderline psychopath, I think it was. And how do you plead?"

"Define borderline."

Hell's bells.

"Where's Sheldon?" I asked, rather than pursue the top-ic further.

"Bound and gagged. In the bathtub. I hit him with a few more of those tranqs, too."

"You put him in the bathtub?"

"You rather he be in your bed?"

I didn't want him in my bed.

"Bathtub's not full, is it?"

"Now, that is an idea."

Sheldon just about ate his gag when he saw me standing in the doorway. Guess he figured the chickens were coming home to roost at long last. Guess he was right.

"Now listen up, shithead," I said. I knelt by the tub, slipped his gag down over his chin, and turned the cold water on full blast. "Since I met you and that rat's-ass kid of yours, I've been knocked every which way but loose. And now it's your turn."

"Princess phones and red-hot pussy!"

I turned off the tap. I looked at Jeep.

"Did he just say what I think he said?"

"Sounded like it."

"Exactly how many of those tranqs did you give this motherfucker, man?"

Jeep reflected.

"Don't know, exactly. Enough to make him stop kicking me in the head. Think I overdid it?"

Sheldon belched. The smell was like someone had blown up a pharmacy.

"Maybe a little. I have no idea what that shit will do to a person. Asshole's probably running from wild dogs."

Jeep nodded.

"Hope he is. What now?"

"First, breakfast," I said, trying to be practical. Really, I was wondering how many years in the pokey were lying, semiconscious, in my bathtub. Time I got out, Anci would probably be drawing Social Security. "Then Carol Ray."

"Think she'll be easier on a full belly?"

I didn't give him an answer. I didn't have one anyway.

18.

BREAKFAST WAS FINE. CAROL RAY TURNED OUT TO BE EVEN more of a pain in the ass than I'd anticipated. Her little house on Freeman Spur had been cleaned out and a hand-lettered FOR SALE sign was posted in the front yard. The kid I talked to at Shotguns & Shakes said she hadn't been in for three days.

The only other place I could think to check was Dennis Reach's, but that was another dead end. The cops had left the locks open, and most of Reach's meager possessions had been carted away, either as evidence or as booty by Dennis's erstwhile friends.

Around 5:30, I called Jeep.

"How is he?"

"Shitbird? Getting there. At least he can form complete sentences."

"Then he's better than before. What's he say?"

"It's unprintable."

"Just as I suspected."

"Any luck with Carol Ray?"

"No. She's gone."

"So what's next?" Jeep asked.

"I've got an idea, but it might take a while to work out, if it does at all." If the little rat hadn't already been hauled off, I thought. "What do you think the chances are of Sheldon's volunteering useful information?"

"Slim to none," Jeep replied. "Unless of course you're ready to play hardball."

"Which means what exactly?"

Jeep said, "We could cut off one of his legs with a chainsaw, threaten to do the other."

"Perhaps something a bit subtler."

"Hacksaw?"

"Pass. Hard pass."

"Well, that's the best I can do."

"Hold off on gassing up the Craftsman for now, son. I'm going to give my idea a try."

"You'll be back," he said. "Few more hours, you'll be begging me for my cut-off-his-leg idea."

"Maybe," I said. It didn't sound so far-fetched, really.

My call was to Merlin Coward, a Herrin cop I'd once done an under-the-table favor for. He wasn't exactly thrilled to hear my voice.

"You nuts, man?"

"Maybe, sergeant," I said. "How's tricks?"

"I paid you, Slim. Now kindly fuck off, please."

At least he was polite about it.

"I need you to run a license plate for me, Merlin, and I'm a little short on time."

"You're not listening."

I read the number into the handset, then I read it again. I had no idea whether Merlin was writing it down.

"I'll call back in twenty minutes," I said.

"Slim . . ."

I hung up on him. It felt good, I admit. Folks were always hanging up on me, and it vexed me something fierce, but I was beginning to understand the appeal of it. There was a Country Pantry across the street. I jogged over and bought a coffee and drank it in the parking lot. When next I checked my watch, twenty-five minutes had gone by.

"You're late," Merlin said without preamble.

"Bonus time, sergeant," I said. "What'd you get?"

"We're even after this," he said, not a question. I could almost feel the tension in his hand through the phone lines.

"Right. Even like Steven."

"Rig's registered to a Rhonda Lee Tipton, 409 West Valley Road, Makanda."

I asked him to repeat it while I scratched it all down on the palm of my hand. Must have misplaced my pocket notebook.

"Anyone else on the insurance?"

"Says Harold Tipton. Could be her husband."

I said, "I can't imagine anyone would marry Pimples, but I guess it could be."

"What?"

"I said thank you, sergeant."

"And we're through," he said.

"How's Sonny?"

The line went dead between us.

"He's good," the sergeant said at last.

"Still off junk?"

"Yeah."

"Glad to hear it. Give him my regards."

"I . . . I will."

So Pimples lived in Makanda. Or at least his wheels did. Assuming they weren't stolen. By the time what was left of my beautiful Dodge maxi-cab roared down into the little valley, not a quarter mile from Tipton's front door, late afternoon light was spreading slowly across the sky. I rolled past the frame house a couple of times, then parked a ways up the road, hopped down, and walked up. No reason to scare the little shit before I had a chance to wring his neck.

The street was one of those you see all the time in rural parts, half neighborhood with sidewalks, half forest. The big-limbed oak and elm trees formed a canopy over the asphalted street and blocked out the last few drops of afternoon sun. The air was heavy with the smell of oncoming rain, and the leaves twisted gently against their stems.

The yellow Ford I'd seen the night before at the Black mine was in a dirt swath on the east side of the house. Near the truck was a fat woman with dirty blond hair and a red dress strapped so tightly to her round form that parts of her seemed to be trying to escape. She was too old to be Pimples' wife; mother, I guessed. She was bent over a washtub, saying sweet, soft things to a dog she was bathing. When the dog saw me, it set to barking in a high-pitched voice and suds went everywhere. The dog jumped the lip of the tub and scurried around the house. The big woman looked up at me. She stood up and wiped her forehead with the back of a soapy hand and said, "You got some timing on you or what, son?"

"You want me to go get him?" I grabbed my lower back, hoping she'd get the hint.

She didn't get the hint.

"Her," she said, "and, yeah, I want you to go."

It took nearly a half hour. The rain came. Sweetie—that was the dog's name—had gone under the house, through the crawlspace access. Rhonda Lee Tipton—that was the lady—assured me that Sweetie would stay in there all night if someone didn't climb in after her. She said this like I should care.

"What about your son?" I asked.

"He's passed out in the shed, probably. Back property. There were some strange men here earlier looking for his worthless butt, and I guess Harold's trying to keep out of sight best he can."

"You mind if I talk to him?" I asked. She hadn't asked what I wanted and probably wasn't going to, either. She looked at me like a grocer looks at a head of cabbage.

"You don't look like one of them."

"The men from before?"

"They were in suits," she replied. "You look like one of Harold's shit-kicking buddies, no offense."

"None taken. Where's that shed?"

"My boy in some kind of trouble?"

"Maybe. Let's put it this way. It's better for Harold to sleep in the shed for the next few nights."

Rhonda Lee squeaked out a laugh.

"He sleeps out there every night. Got to where I couldn't allow him in the house no more."

"Mind my asking why?"

"It's personal." But she answered anyway, with a shrug of her fat shoulders. "I'm not crazy about his friends."

"That all?"

"You ever met his friends?"

"Some of them."

"That's all." She clucked her tongue against her false teeth, flicking them up and down with a loud, wet snap. "You going to get my dog, or we going to stand here yakkin' all day?"

I could barely tear myself away. The underside of the house was as dark and wet as a turtle's ass. Red nails, dripping rust, smiled down from rows of rotted wooden planks. Something bit me in the dark. And then Sweetie did. Twice. On the way out, my hands slipped in something foul, the exuviae of Rhonda Lee's life. I dropped flat on my chest into the muck. Sweetie tore off toward the little rectangle of daylight at the edge of the darkness. When I made it there myself, Rhonda Lee was back at the washtub, scrubbing furiously.

"She come out on her own," she said, without looking at me.

"Lucky fucking day."

She stopped scrubbing.

"I don't hold with no swearing."

"Sorry."

"You got dirt on your face."

I touched a hand to my forehead. Sure enough.

"Mind if I have that talk with Harold now?" I asked.

"Suit yourself." She was bathing the damn dog again.

"Where's he at?"

A soapy hand dribbled thick white dollops toward a hole in the tree line behind the house.

"Like I said, back there behind the house."

"Thanks."

"Stop by on your way back through," she said.

The shed was at the far edge of the property, as far away from Rhonda Lee as it could get. Harold wasn't inside, just a mattress and some blankets and a small television. I was just getting ready to give up and try Rhonda Lee again when Pimples came tromping through the tree line, zipping up with one hand, scratching his nuts with the other.

He was shirtless and shoeless, and he didn't look any smarter than he had the night I'd met him at Black #5. He saw me. He turned and bolted back into the high growth. I knelt down and took careful aim with the 9000S, and when I was good and sure I had a shot I put one in his ass. Actually, it was just below his ass, in the meat at the top of the back of his leg, but the effect was the same. The boy shrieked like a tropical bird and grabbed hold of his behind so hard he flipped completely over—ankles over bald spot—and landed in the dirt with a thud.

"I don't want to die," he said as I stood over him. I'd hit him with a rubber bullet—not the real kind—but in his panic he didn't know that. Far as he knew, he had a fancy new hole in his butt, one he could tell tales about down at his favorite watering hole or brag about to whoever was unfortunate enough to see him in a romantic way. He looked up at me now a little more closely, licking his dry lips.

"You were at the fight last night," he said, voice like a bullfrog. "The Black mine fight. I remember you."

"And I remember you," I said. I crouched down beside him and stuffed the barrel of my pistol against the underside of his chin. "But you're going to help me forget."

19.

AFTER A WHILE, I CAME BACK UP TO THE HOUSE. RHONDA Lee was sitting on the stoop with a can of beer. Sweetie was sighing contentedly in sleep at her bare feet. It was dusk, and the light was turning purple and grey in the sky.

"Heard a shot," she said. She didn't look too upset about it. "He's not dead, is he?"

"No, ma'am. He might walk with a limp, day or two, but otherwise he's fine."

She nodded, thought about it.

"I guess that's good."

I shook my head. "You got a cold heart, Rhonda Lee."

"Let me tell you something, son . . ."

"Don't bother, sister. I've heard them all."

"You're not being polite anymore. Before, you were polite at least."

She sounded depressed enough about it to curl into a ball and cry. Everything, everyone was letting her down. I thought of the boy in the field, thought of the story he'd told me.

"I ask you something?"

She shrugged. "Make you a deal?"

"Okay."

"You ask me yours, I get to tell you a thing or two."

That was maybe the worst deal ever. I glanced at the watch on my wrist. In another half hour, it would be dark. No time for sad stories or whatever she had in mind. But I still needed to ask my question.

"Deal," I said.

She looked at me until the suspicion had drained out of her face.

"Ask."

"Dumbshit back there . . ."

"Yeeeah?"

"You know about his dogging, right?"

She looked down at the ground. "Yeah."

"You ever see a guy named Dennis Reach around here?" I gave her a quick description of him.

"Maybe."

I said, "Any idea what he wanted with Harold?"

"Harold was growing a dog. Dennis come out to take a look, I think," she replied, then added quickly, "I don't hold with it myself. Sweetie . . ."

"Did he come alone?"

"What?"

"Reach. Did he come alone?"

"He was with someone."

"A woman?"

"You know everything. Why not just talk to yourself?"

That made me love her. I laughed.

"You know her name?"

"The dog or the woman's?"

"The woman's."

"I know. I was kidding."

"You ought to do the Borscht Belt."

She sucked from her can.

"People think I'm funny."

I wasn't about to go there. "Carol Ray?" I asked.

"Something like that."

"Blond?"

"Yep. That's the one. Snooty thing with a face like TV."

Okay. Shit.

I sat down beside her on the stoop. She nudged over and made room. My head was swimming. I guess I'd hoped to be wrong. I tried to imagine what I was going to tell Anci that wouldn't touch off an I-told-you-so for the ages. Rhonda Lee brought me out of it.

"Your turn to listen," she said.

"Okay."

It took me ten minutes to actually begin listening, but then listen I did. Night came. Lightning bugs sparked to life and darted around the yard and up and down the road. Rhonda Lee talked for about half an hour.

She'd led one hell of a goddamn life.

I SPENT THE NEXT DAY WITH ANCI AT PEGGY'S PLACE, HELPED her with her summer reading homework, cooked her favorite meal. Anci played with Shelby Ann. She wanted to go home, but there wasn't anywhere else to hold Sheldon Cleaves, and as long as A. Evan was still out there running around loose, taking her back to Indian Vale was out of the question.

I slept over, too. Peggy and I made love that night. Afterward we lay in bed, under a thin sheet, sweating and talking.

"Dogfighting," she said. "It's hard to believe that folks could find pleasure in something like that. Something so wicked and hurtful."

"I don't understand it, either."

"And you think these Cleaveses were working with Dennis Reach?"

"Working for him," I said. "Reach and J.T. Black were in business together, but Black was the muscle and the protection. Being a former sheriff's deputy gave him another layer of protection, too. But then Black wanted out. Reach was left in the wind, so he hired the Cleaveses to do the nasty work."

"And then they betrayed him?"

"That's sure what it looks like. Question is, who did they go to work for? They don't seem quite like criminal-mastermind types. And I don't think Leonard Black would trust those psychos with a piece of his coal mine, not the way he talked about them the other day, anyway. There's somebody else at play here."

"This Carol Ray, then?"

"I'm not sure," I said. But I must have hesitated a little too much.

"You ain't got a thing for her, have you?"

"No," I said. "Honestly. She's pretty, but you're beautiful. Plus, I'm afraid she might actually be evil."

"She comes sniffing around here," Peggy said, "she'll be evil in a body cast."

"Quite a cast of characters, isn't it?"

Peggy thought about the cast of characters for a moment. Then she said, "You know what I think, Slim?"

"Tell me."

"You know I'm not religious. I ain't been inside a church since I was a teenage prom queen, and even then it was only because my daddy died. I ain't never read the Bible, either, and as far as belief . . . well, I just don't know what I believe."

"It changes some as you get older."

She nodded.

"That and plenty of other stuff, too," she said. "Sometimes, though, I think the world really is fallen. You see things like this going on, people hurting the innocent for their own pleasure, they're more than a crime or wrong. They're a sin. And all the things we do to police ourselves—work like yours, even—well, it ain't for nothing. Fallen we are, and fallen we remain."

"It ain't a very nice thought, is it?"

"No," she said. "No, it is not."

EARLY THE NEXT MORNING, MY LAWYER AND I SET OUT looking for Agent Carter. On the way, the boy told me about a recent road trip on which he'd stuffed himself with ephedrine and driven down to Florida in search of his abusive wife.

"Didn't know she'd taken off," I said.

"A few days ago. Not the first time."

"You find her?"

He nodded, slid lower into the Lincoln's bottomless leather buckets, sucked a toothpick.

"Eventually. She'd holed up with a Bible salesman. I mean, you dig that? A fucking Bible salesman." He looked at me through the widescreen panels of his sunglasses. I nodded my head to let him know that I dug it.

"I didn't even know they still had those," I said.

"Me, neither. They do, though. So they're at this hotel, right? Not even a hotel, a motel, like this skeevy roadside thing. Gross. Anyway, the motherfucker has her tied to a bed. Handcuffed, actually . . ."

"Oh, hell."

"But like she wants to be handcuffed, you know?"

"I follow you."

"And I go in to get her."

"Armed, I take it?"

"You heard me say he's a Bible salesman, right?"

Armed.

"Any fatalities?"

He swerved through a patch of traffic so fast I thought I'd spill my coffee. The kid was a test pilot inhabiting the body of a mere mortal.

"No, but get this: I step in the room, and there's that

moment when everything freezes, right? I'm looking at them, they're looking at me, that kind of thing. They're naked. I'm in my suit. My finest suit. It's embarrassing for all of us. Stressful. So I want to break the tension. There's a book on the nightstand."

"A Bible."

"What I thought. So I lower the Python . . ."

Again, hell.

"And, you know, bang, and the book just blows up and there are bits of pages floating around like it's a parade or something. The dude—he's in his boxers, right?—the dude pisses himself and runs like hell. Truth, man, I almost did, too. I've never fired the Python in an enclosed space like that."

"Loud?" I asked.

"So loud I almost shit myself." He dug around in his right ear with his pinkie as though in memory of it all. "So anyway, assface stuffs himself out this little window in the shitter. Had to break ribs getting through it. Sherea starts screaming, and there I am, standing with this gun, like I've made this big gesture or whatever. And then I look down at what's left of the book."

"Not a Bible."

"Fucking *Dianetics*, man. I almost wasted a brother."

The idea of pursuing that line of thought made my head hurt, so instead I asked, "Cops?"

"Don't know. I got the hell out of there. Fuck it. I came home."

"When did all this take place?"

"Few hours ago."

"You dumb motherfucker!"

"What?"

"Pull your goddamn ass over."

I drove us the rest of the way. The kid huddled in the passenger seat and just shook with it all.

AGENT CARTER WE FOUND IN A COFFEE-AND-DONUTS PLACE in Marion, tucked into a corner booth, reading the local paper. He laughed when he saw us standing over him.

"I can't figure out which of you homos is supposed to be the sidekick. That Mabry?"

"My lawyer," I said.

He actually looked sorry for me. He blew his nose into a paper napkin.

"I didn't really think it was Mabry. Sit down." I sat. My lawyer started to slide in beside me. Carter raised a palm. "Not him. He can sit over there."

"You don't like lawyers?"

"I don't like lawyers. And I sure as hell don't like whatever he is. Did he really go to law school?"

Before I could answer, a kid in an apron came over. I ordered a coffee. My lawyer sat huddled in a booth opposite with his knees pulled against his chest and his face between his knees. Carter elected to ignore him.

"Talk," he said. "You're ruining my breakfast, boy."

I nodded.

"Carol Ray Reach," I said.

"We talked about her already."

"I think I know where she is."

Carter put down his coffee and stared at me.

I said, "You've already got her, right? I mean, that's really the only thing that makes sense. At first, I thought Reach was your inside man, but he wasn't, was he? It was her."

"And how'd you come to that brilliant conclusion?"

"Dunno. Leap of faith, maybe. I just can't believe that she'd be mixed up in something like this."

"As opposed to, say, moving guns and powder?"

"Even bad people have limits," I said.

"I think we're done here."

"Goddamn it, Carter."

A couple of old ladies raised their heads to look daggers at me. Carter chuckled. "They're going to throw you out of here one day, boy," he said.

"Who gives a shit? I've never even been in here."

"I mean the state."

I let that pass.

"Where is she?"

He shook his great mass of gray hair. My lawyer was asleep. His snoring filled the little room.

"You goddamn redneck idiot. You never really have figured this shit out, have you?"

"Didn't have to," I replied. "Harold Tipton knew all about it."

He didn't look shocked. He didn't spit out his coffee. He didn't jump out of his seat and spin on his head.

"You talked to Tipton?"

"I talked to whatever it is lives in Harold Tipton's brain, yeah."

Carter heaved a sigh. For a moment, he looked almost human.

"There's not much left, is there? The kid fried himself early. Not for that mother of his, he'd probably be wandering the street."

He'd probably be dead, but I didn't say so. Instead, I nodded for a coffee refill and reached for the cream and sugar.

"This game, the dogfight, it's big business?"

"Turns out. One of those weird things in the online world. Caught on somehow. Word of mouth. Dumb luck. Who can say? Something about it appealed."

"But they didn't expect it to?"

Carter replied, "Not big enough to attract our attention, no."

But it did. It had. According to Pimples, it was a trickle at first, the Black Games, as they were called. Later the trickle turned into a stream, then a rapids. Reach had set it up through the Dragons, and Carol Ray had gotten dragged into it. But she didn't know just how deep Black had gotten himself and Reach into the shit with Tibbs and his men. Without her knowledge, Reach subcontracted out to the Cleaveses. When the Cleaveses turned out to be batshit crazy and started freelancing, Dennis withheld payment, touching off a pissing match that ended with him snatching Shelby Ann. And then someone popped him.

"Meanwhile," Carter said, finishing my thought, "Tibbs

and the Dragons have taken over the games. They're pissed that the whole thing has attracted the law."

"They put out a hit on Carol Ray?"

"How'd you know?"

"Something made you pull her out."

"Yeah, on her. And on J.T. Black, who was more or less an innocent bystander."

"First time for everything."

Carter sipped his coffee. "Reach used Carol Ray to get the keys to the mine from Leonard Black. He had a thing for her from way back, and he's half nuts these days anyway. So J.T. just happened to have the wrong last name. And of course, the sad sack of shit owned the gun used to kill Reach. The funny thing is, Reach himself owned the weapon. It was right there in his house the whole time. The killer just happened upon it. Imagine, he comes in, and his target is handcuffed and helpless, and there's even a gun handy so he doesn't have to burn his own piece. He must have thought he'd forgotten his own birthday."

"Reach got the gun from Carol Ray?"

"Right. Carol Ray knew J.T. hocked it, probably to pay off his bar tab, and she collected it, maybe to piss him off, maybe hoping one day to pay back whatever bullshit he'd pulled on her by connecting him to something like this."

"A little extreme," I said.

"A little? Son, you're tougher than you look," Carter said. "Meanwhile, Tibbs put two and two together and came up with five. From his perspective, though, it's no

great loss. Black is in on it, Tibbs gets rid of a major pain in
his ass. He's not in on it, well, too bad, but . . ."

"Civilization will endure."

"Yes."

"Any idea where J.T.'s gone?"

Carter shook his head but answered with certainty, "In-
dianapolis."

"Terrible," I said. "So what now?"

Carter shrugged. "Nothing. We sit on Carol Ray while
she still has some value as an intelligence asset. She's not
virgin-clean, but she did us a good turn. She'll walk. The
Black fight will be taken down. Maybe it'll be moved somewhere else, maybe not. Whichever it is, it won't resurface
for a while."

"You'll arrest Tibbs?"

That took him a while. I already knew the answer, but
for some reason making him say it seemed important. He
sucked a tooth and frowned. He said, "We won't. Not yet."

"He didn't get his fingerprints on anything?"

"He did not. There are a few minor players who might
drop, but . . ."

Yeah. But . . .

"You'll pick up Harold Tipton?"

"Him. One or two others. And the Cleaveses, if we can
find them."

"And whoever killed Reach walks away clean."

It wasn't a question, but he answered it with his eyes
any way.

"Frankly, he's not worth burning the resources on."

"That sucks."

"These are the workings of the universe, Slim."

"So it's over?"

"All but the screaming of a thousand attorneys."

"And the bad guys win."

"No, but they abide. So do we."

"I'm leaving," I said.

"So soon?"

"Because I'm starting to like you."

"You ruined my coffee," he said simply.

"And you're a sonofabitch."

We shook hands on it. I woke my lawyer.

"I wasn't sleeping," he said. He rubbed a hand through his greasy hair.

"You were snoring," I replied.

He laughed in relief. "Thank God, man. I thought reality had gone to fucking shit."

It had. But pointing it out seemed uncharitable. The kid had enough problems.

It was nearly noon by the time we cruised past Devil's Kitchen and the wildlife preserve. We took the back way, the Lincoln screaming over the gravel roads, crunching the limestone chunks to powder. My lawyer insisted on driving, and I was too worn out from my talk with Carter to object. At least he kept it under eighty. Near Watertown, I called Jeep Mabry.

"Sheldon," I said. "Kick him."

"Done and done, boy."

"Kick him *loose*."

There was a long and disappointed silence. At last, Jeep growled, "Make a deal."

"Okay."

"I'll tie him up in a sack, drop him at police headquarters."

"Wince?"

Jeep grunted no.

"Lindley?"

Jeep grunted yes.

"Okay. Slow down some before you drop him?"

"No promises."

He broke the line. Sheldon Cleaves was in for a rough ride. I rang Anci.

"I think it's pretty much over," I said.

"Pretty much?"

"Least ways, we can go home again. Most of the bad men have gone to ground."

"That's good news, anyway. Still . . ."

"Yeah, I know. Still."

There was a burst of garble. Our connection broke up for a moment.

"Where are you?" she asked through it. "I can barely hear you."

"Near the preserve. The signal's bad out here, so if I lose you, that's why."

Another break in the connection, this time longer.

When it came back, I heard Anci's voice say, ". . . Miss Shotguns & Shakes?"

"Carol Ray? Well, it turns out she's one of the good guys. Pretty good, anyway."

"Wonders never cease. Maybe I'm not cut out for mystery solving, after all."

"What? Why not?"

"Why not? I talked you into taking the case in the first place. I thought the dog was a car. I thought Miss Shotguns & Shakes was the culprit. And the only clue I thought I'd found led me to Lew and Eun Hee Mandamus."

"What was that last thing?"

Another interruption in the connection.

". . . Wichelle. I knew I'd seen the name somewhere before."

"Bran-Wichelle?"

". . . can barely hear . . . I said Bran-Wichelle . . . metal fabricators. It was the name stamped on Lew's new security fence. I reckon I . . ."

The call dropped. I punched some buttons, hoping to bring it back up, but the signal was gone. I looked at my lawyer.

I said, "We have to get back to civilization. Fast."

"We can do fast."

He flattened the pedal. The Lincoln jumped like a gazelle. We'd just rounded onto a long and lonely gravel road when we blew a flat. It was 11:45 A.M.

"Hell," the boy said. He roared to a dusty stop, flattened his hands against the steering wheel in little slaps. "No spare, either."

Shit.

"Call a tow," I suggested.

"No phone signal, remember?"

Double shit.

He stepped out of the car, intent on inspecting the damage, I guess. I climbed out on my side, saw him walk with a crooked head toward the rear driver's side tire. A puzzled look crossed his face. He uncocked his head, opened his mouth to say something to me.

The first shot spun him around in a full circle as a little blur of blood blossomed from his left shoulder. The second shot knocked him over backward, leaving his big sunglasses floating an instant in the air. I hit the deck just as a spray of bullets spattered the Lincoln, pocking the trunk and blasting out the rear windshield. Someone was screaming. It took a moment to realize it was me.

There wasn't a shooter in sight, but the shadows of the tall growth and trees by the lake could hide a small army of snipers. I might never have seen the motherfucker if he hadn't set his dogs on me.

But he did, two of them, great burly pit bulls with necks of furiously knotted muscle and eyes ablaze with the full force of a carefully instructed hate. Right then, I knew I was going to die. And then I wanted to. Trailing the dogs was A. Evan Cleaves. And walking calmly round the bend in the road behind A. Evan, rifle in hand, was my old friend Lew Mandamus.

20.

LITTLE EGYPT. THE SHAWNEE. A PLACE NEAR THE SIMPSON Barrens.

I rehearsed my location, trying to bring myself to my senses. I needn't have bothered. The first dog jolted me back into the real world. It hit me so hard with its cinder-block skull that I doubled over and went back-of-the-head-first into the Lincoln's side-view mirror, knocking it off its post. The beast snarled from somewhere deep inside its bony chest, latched onto my right arm, and tore away a chunk of cotton and flesh. The second dog leapt atop the first and made for my throat. Lew called them off. If he hadn't, I'd have died right then on the roadside. The dogs broke away and trotted back to their master. Lew patted them on the blocky skull before returning his attention to me.

"Slim." We might have been passing each other in the grocery store.

I tried to say "Lew" back, but all that came up was a gob of blood and snot. I rolled onto my elbows and pried myself free of the road. Bits of limestone dug deeply into my palms. A. Evan chuckled and shook his funny-looking head.

"Slim," Lew said again. He looked away. "It's . . . complicated."

"Fuck you."

"I always did like you, boy."

"Double fuck-you," I said. "Eun Hee . . ."

He flashed angry. "What about my wife?"

"This is going to kill her."

He shook his head.

"She's never going to find out."

"She will."

"How's that, boy?"

"When I fucking tell her, man!" I screamed.

Lew blushed. That's something you don't see very often, a killer blushing. For a moment I thought he might relent, let me in on the joke. Instead, he crouched down and dug around in the dirt with his fingers thoughtfully, his rifle flat across the tops of his knees. "She's never going to find out," he repeated, more softly this time. "I'm your friend, boy, so I'm going to give you a head start. Turn. Run. See how long you live."

Somehow or other, I managed to stagger to my feet. God alone knows how. Standing hurt. Standing hurt bad. I was pretty sure the dogs had rebroken my ribs, and I could feel one or two of them sliding around beneath my skin. Move the wrong way, and it or they would skewer through one of my lungs and that would be the ball game. My head throbbed, and I was gasping and snapping like an angry turtle for every breath of air.

"Just one thing," I said.

"Let me guess: Why, right?"

"No," I replied. "I know why. You're a fucking insane prick. What I want to know is, what do you want me to tell her?"

I thought he'd kill me right there. Or let A. Evan do it. Sometimes, when you push it, that's the risk. Instead, he said, "Tell her what?"

"About how you died?"

"About how I died."

"When I break your fucking neck or stick your gun up your own ass."

A. Evan couldn't help laughing. Lew wasn't amused.

"Thirty seconds," he said, breathing out his rage. "And then we kill you. Or the dogs do."

The dogs were going to be a problem, no question.

I turned and started down the road, slowly at first, acclimating myself to the utter agony of it all. Faster when the utter agony of it all seemed better than what would come next.

They didn't wait thirty seconds, either. You can't even trust a murderer these days. The first shots came at around the fifteen-second mark, but they went wide right, pocking shallow craters in the asphalt road. Something hard broke free and leapt up to kiss me on the cheek. I kept moving, fast now, diving off the road to my left, into the tangled brush and up a steep grade and into the tree line. I could hear the dogs scrambling on the road behind me, their long nails clicking the rough surface. In another moment . . .

But that moment didn't come. Not yet. The dogs overran, seeking a better way up, maybe, their stubby legs unable to make the sharp climb up the embankment. The hill continued on and on, losing itself in the denser growth of oak and elm trees until it lost itself entirely in darkness.

My lungs were on fire. For some reason, I started to laugh. Something lashed me across the cheek, a bullet. Or a sapling. My feet slid around on the slick layers of leaves. Behind me, I could hear A. Evan singing, some sad old song. At the time, my frantic brain wasn't able to place it.

I climbed, heading west and trying to keep sight of the sun through the dense canopy. Once or twice, I dared to look behind me, but there wasn't anything but the sound of A. Evan's voice, seemingly quite distant, and the barking of those damned animals. I had no idea where Lew was. I'd nearly made it to the top of the hill when I remembered that I still had my phone.

Top of the hill, there was just a hint of a signal. I dialed Jeep's number with a thumb that twitched all over the little keypad, but came up empty. Voice mail. I didn't have A. Evan's number, so I dialed Lew Mandamus next.

"Where are you?" he said.

"Cute," I said. "I ask you a question?"

"You already asked me one of those, boy."

"One more. What's there to lose?"

Silence. Then, "Ask."

"What was inside Shelby Ann?"

"A chip."

"A chip?"

"A computer chip. Animals have them all the time now,

for tracking strays. Like I told you. I brought her in the shop, sewed it up inside her."

"And there's a bank account number on it, right? For the Dragons' accounts? Wasn't that an awfully dangerous way to store that information? Animals run away, after all."

"It was Tibbs's idea. He'd scan her to add money to the chip. I'd scan her to move the cash to my account. If she ran away and got picked up, all anyone would find was an ordinary tracking chip with a few extra numbers mixed in."

I said, "What do you think happened to you, Lew?"

Mandamus laughed. There wasn't anything inside that sound, no humanity, only the ice that gets left behind when everything human sluices out.

"Who the hell knows? Same thing happens to everyone. You see enough bad shit in your time, it gets inside of you, fills up your guts. Am I really any worse than Tibbs or Dennis Reach? At least I've put things back into the world. You can't erase that, Slim. Not all of it."

"I guess not."

"I can't see you, but I can hear you. Not the phone, you. The other you. You're close."

It was everything I could do not to stand and run.

"One last thing," I said. "Who took Shelby Ann from you? A. Evan or Dennis Reach?"

"It was Dennis. He saw us transfer Shelby Ann once or twice. He knew she was important but didn't guess why. I think he thought we were using her as breeding stock. He broke into the compound one night and snatched her. Stupid asshole even called me to brag about it. Dennis never could keep his mouth shut, even to save his own life."

"He didn't know that A. Evan and Sheldon had screwed him over, joined up with Tibbs."

"Not at first, no. But it didn't take him long to figure it out. The Cleaves wanted their cut. They didn't give a god-damn who gave it to them. You might say they were like dogs, loyal to whoever's feeding them."

"Tibbs got to you through the Animal Cruelty Task Force, I take it?"

"Through Leonard Black, yes. He helped Reach set it all up, but he was *persona non grata* with the Dragons because of that boy of his, so he started looking for a way to sweeten the pot, win his way back into the fold. He thought he could bring me along, an animal medicine expert, as a bargaining chip. Not everyone is ready to toss his dog in a garbage bag after one bad fight. Tibbs took a liking to me, but Black's plan for himself didn't pan out. J.T.'s former buddies were almost as shitted-off at him as they were at Reach."

"He's left the state," I said. "J.T."

"No. He tried, but Tibbs's men got to him first. Two in the back of the head. He's in the Little Grassy somewhere, I think."

"There wasn't a young woman with him, was there?"

"Was, yeah. Little cheerleader thing. Why?"

"You fuckers killed Mandy."

"So?"

"So now I'm pissed."

The line went dead. I hit my belly and snake-crawled toward the crest of the hill. I started down the other side, and then the first of the dogs appeared. He jumped on my back, and we rolled. It wasn't much, but I didn't have much. We rolled, and the dog fell off. I leapt to my feet. Something in my leg tore loose. I turned. The dog was coming on again, fast. He jumped. Just then the second dog came flying, too fast. It collided with the first dog and both went tumbling sideways and down the grade.

It was a reprieve but not much of one. They found their footing. They turned and sprinted back toward me like a pair of slobbery missiles. I caught the smaller of the two with a rock upside the head and sent it sailing into the trees. The larger came in low, then swept upward and lunged for my throat. I'd only just managed to get my hand between me and it, so its jaws passed cleanly through the ball joint on my left hand. I barely felt it.

What I did feel was that I was going to lose this fight and lose it badly. I pressed forward on the tops of my legs and the dog and I went end over end, yin-and-yang-style, down the slope. When we came up, the dog was on top and my leg pinned between us. I kicked as hard as I could, and the beast flew off me and into the tall growth, landing hard on its side.

There wasn't any stopping it, though. The creature lunged. I feigned to one side, but tripped and went over backward, only just catching myself as the dog grabbed hold of my right shoulder and tore away a sizeable piece of me. If Lew Mandamus and A. Evan hadn't known my position before, they did then. They'd never make it to me in time, though. I was going to come apart like a scarecrow, bleed to death, have a heart attack. Die badly.

There was no good way to turn. The downward slope to my left ended abruptly in a sharp drop, to where I wasn't able to see. But what the hell? One drop was as good as another. I ran for it, the dog carried along for what seemed sure to be our last ride. A bullet hit me in the back of the leg, but felt like little more than a bee sting. Over we went. I'm not sure which of us was the more surprised.

It seemed like a long way to the bottom, but it couldn't have been more than twenty or thirty feet. We hit the ground. The dog flattened beneath me with a bony deflation, its life crushed away in a sudden burst. I prized its teeth from my shoulder and stood, walked slowly, tried out the ground. There wasn't much left. Not much blood. Not much sanity.

And then A. Evan was there, cackling, crazy-eyed, scratching his damn balls.

"Slim."

"Asshole."

"First time I laid eyes on you, I knew I was going to end up killing you. Told the old man on the way home that night, too. Said, you know that I'm going to end up putting two in that boy's brain, right?"

"Shut up and try."

"Uh-huh. Just so you know, I get done with you, I'm going to do that daughter of yours, too."

I didn't have much juice left, so the kick I planted in the

boy's midsection didn't do much more than knock him back ten feet or so. When I flew up off the ground and into his grill, I think I surprised him so much that he forgot about the gun. I punched him in the throat and kicked him in the balls so hard I thought they'd come out the top of his head. Then I wrapped my fingers around the back of his head and bounced his face like a basketball three times off the nearest tree trunk. It should have killed him. But A. Evan isn't like you and me, and all I really managed to do was piss him off. When he wrenched himself free, he was trying to spit away a big yellow tooth that had stuck to the blood on his lower lip and laughing like it was the funniest joke he'd ever heard. His right arm swept up, a boot knife clutched in his hand, and I went over backward to avoid being gutted, again hitting the turf. And it was then A. Evan remembered the gun.

The first bullets from his little semiauto slapped the ground beside my head as I rolled hard to my left and down a steep embankment into a thin stream of brackish water. I'll never know how I found my footing, because there were bullets buzzing around my head and the madly repeating whipcord crack of the little machine pistol like a last devil's tattoo. I do know I was thinking of Anci.

I exploded through the tree line and back into the dark, turned hard right, and had just rounded another sandstone crop when the second dog reappeared. Appeared like an oncoming big rig. We must have taken each other by surprise, as when we collided it was like seventy pounds of fist in a twenty-five-pound sack. I shoved it away with all my

might, then kicked it fiercely in the chest when it tried to
scramble again onto all fours.

"Fucking stay down!" I screamed, as though it could
somehow do anything but what it was programmed to. I
must have hollered louder than I thought. For an instant,
the beast hesitated. But only an instant. It lunged, crashed
into my forearms, and over and over we went, back down
the slope and back into the water, where the dog snapped at
my throat with a sound like two slabs of wet plaster slapping
together.

So. Fuck it. Whatever. I'd finally bitten off more than I
could chew. No pun intended. This was it: the last roundup,
my last case. The long, wet good-bye.

I could sense A. Evan coming out of the tree line. I
could feel him raise his gun, train in on both of us like the
killer he was bred to be. But that was a mistake—and it was
the boy's last. When the first shots went wild, slapping the
surface of the water like flat, heavy stones, the dog took one
to its shoulder. It yelped and in a flash bounded away from
me and charged, unknowing and insane, at this new threat.
A. Evan shouted a command. But it was too late.

Sometimes, late at night, I still hear the sound, the
high-pitch squeal of the boy's scream of pain and confusion as the dog lunged and found the soft underside of his
scrawny throat with its jaws. The little semiauto popped,
injecting lead into the dog's chest and belly, but even in its
death throes it was a true killer. A. Evan's head snapped back
and lolled sideways with a sound like the wet snap of fresh
corn husks and a cloud of blood. The boy collapsed to the

ground, dead before his head sank into the cool banks of the stream, his throat ripped out and his head hanging by a few gory threads. The last sound I heard was the dying dog's passing sigh.

And then it was quiet again.

It took me almost an hour to circle back through the high stands of pine and black oaks and elms down the hill to the road. The day was another scorcher, and there wasn't even a breeze in the high hills to stir the humid soup. Amazingly, I found myself about two hundred yards behind my lawyer's car. I'd walked a big, hellish circle. I looked, but the boy's body was gone. So was his pistol. Lew had apparently dragged them both away.

I'd nearly made it to the car, hoping against hope that the keys were still in the ignition, when I heard the rifle hammer kick behind me. An irrational part of me thought maybe he'd have run.

"You're good, boy. I'll give you that."

I turned. Best to face it. See it coming. Be a man about it. Whatever. I kept telling myself that. You tell yourself all sorts of things when you think you're about to die.

"You look like bloody shit on a stick, but you're good. I really didn't expect you to make it off the road." He looked me a question. "A. Evan?"

"Back with your dogs."

"Dead, I assume."

"Unless he can live in two pieces."

"Then that's another problem off my plate. I found them useful for a while, of course, but things have changed now, and you understand these are people you can't fire."

"Cold, motherfucker. Course, I imagine you're also the one who shot up Sheldon's Woodrat Road playdate."

He nodded. "That was me. I've been following you around for days. Your daughter put one of those apps on your phone. A tracker. When you were in Jackson County lockup, I talked her into letting me log into the same account. That's how I found you here today, and that's how I followed you to Pyramid."

"That was some fancy shooting."

"My time in service. I always was good with a long gun. You might consider thanking me for not killing you that day. I wasn't sure whether I should."

I ignored him.

"Dennis Reach was an easier target for you, I guess."

"Took you long enough to figure it out."

"You followed me to his place that afternoon."

"Followed you and found that you'd gift-wrapped him for me. I was honestly grateful about that."

"You killed him with his own gun," I said. "Then you ordered the Cleaveses to pay me off."

"I did. And they did. Then they double-crossed me and tried to kill you. I didn't have anything to do with that. You'd done me a favor, whether you knew it or not, and I still have a conscience."

"Oh, I can tell by the way you kill off your allies."

"They're less allies than a convenience to me. Their little

stunt put us at odds for a while. That's when they grabbed you, by the way. But I finally managed to bring them back on board."

"To kill them?"

"Get them close, stick the knife in. Besides, is there any doubt they'd have turned on me eventually? You've seen them. You've seen what they're capable of."

"Plus, it's more slices of the pie for you."

"That too."

"And how big is that pie, precisely?"

"What?"

"How much is in the account?"

Lew laughed and shook his head.

"My God. You never quit."

"We have to walk to the car anyway. Might as well talk."

He lifted an eyebrow.

I explained, "You shoot me here, you'll have to move me and my lawyer's body both. Let's walk back to his car, I'll help you load him in. Or did you plan to use your own car?"

"His. You're not getting blood all over mine, boy." A real humanitarian.

Lew waved his rifle. I walked in front of him. He talked.

"Three point five million."

"Seriously?"

"Surprised?"

"I guess so. That's a lot of white sales."

Lew sniffed at the dummy making jokes with his last few breaths.

He said, "It's enough to give my Eun Hee the life she's always deserved."

"I think Eun Hee probably likes her life just fine."

"Well, I don't."

"God, you're worse than them."

We stopped again. We'd nearly reached the car. I turned to find Lew staring at me in a fury.

"Them?"

"The assholes you spent all those years cleaning up after. Like the abusers. The boy who set the cat on fire. You're worse because you think you're better, because you think that having lived a certain way for a certain amount of time gives you license now to throw a cosmic shit fit. Goddamn, man, do you have any inkling of just how many people have died because of you?"

"Just . . . just one more."

I could tell by the look on his face that I'd finally managed to piss him off for real. He was going to enjoy it now. In a way, I was grateful. I hated the idea of being offed by someone who didn't give a rat's ass. He raised his rifle and jerked the trigger.

The first shot was so loud it was like it tore through the middle of my skull in a screaming stream of molten silver. It ripped away most of Lew Mandamus's scalp and sent him whirling like a corkscrew into the ground, rifle sailing, his shot going wide. The second blew away most of his left shoulder, lifting him, howling, from the ground and into the side of my lawyer's Lincoln.

"Motherfucker shot up my car and finest suit, man," the boy said, miraculously alive, appearing from the brush.

I sank to the ground, never having known exhaustion.

Lew Mandamus was smeared across the driver's side door, gulping for breath. Amazement and terror misshaped his face. The lawyer approached, staring at him like a half-squashed insect. He raised the Python. Its smoking barrel wavered inches from Lew's face.

"You're killing . . . you're *murdering* a good man," Lew gasped. "A good man."

The kid said, "Shit's unfair, brother, all over the god-damn world," and blew Lew Mandamus's brains all over the Shawnee.

21.

WELL, THAT WAS ANOTHER WEEK IN A RECOVERY ROOM, THIS time at the hospital in Carbondale. I'd been shot and dog bit a half dozen times. What really hurt, though, was my insurance premium. Jeep and Opal sat by my bedside for days on end, until finally I ordered them away and back to their own lives. Peggy was with me nearly the entire time, but even Peggy eventually had to get back to work. Nothing I said would move Anci, though.

"I solved it," she kept saying. "I actually solved it."

"Sort of."

"Sort of, hell. I led you to Lew Mandamus, right?"

"Kinda accidentally."

She ignored me.

"And Lew Mandamus ended up being the perpetrator, right?"

"He did. But you thought he was innocent. And technically, he found me."

"Don't sit on my top hat, man."

"Sorry."

It was like the last part of a movie, end of the third reel or whatever. Everybody was dropping in one last time.

Lindley came by with frowns.

"You're innocent," he said. "I can't believe it."

"Can't or don't want to?"

"I can do both."

"You're good."

"And you're an asshole."

"I guess we're square then."

"I guess," he said. He thought a moment. "Stay out of my county, man."

Ammons came to collect his badge. The Illinois State Police had lost out on the larger bust, but they'd arrested Leonard Black.

"It's a big story," he said. He was gleeful. "You should have seen the cameras. And the icing is that all of Black's friends in high places are scurrying back into their holes. The score settling is not going to be pretty."

"I don't get you, man. Are you a cop or a politician?"

Ammons laughed himself right out of my room.

Ben Wince dropped by with cookies and Cokes. We watched some conservative booger on the tube and laughed at all the craziness in the world until the nurse appeared to shush us.

Even Agent Carter stopped for a visit, bearing flowers.

"You destroyed my case," he said.

"Sorry."

"Saved Uncle Sam some money, too."

"These are patriotic days," I said. "I just want to do what I can."

"Take." He shoved the flowers at me.

I took.

"Did you use taxpayer dollars to buy these?"

"Go to hell," he said, and walked out.

"My new best friend," I said to Anci.

ONLY EUN HEE MANDAMUS STAYED AWAY. BUT THAT WAS probably for the best. Maybe she'd been in on her husband's wickedness, maybe she hadn't. Wince didn't know, and I never asked, afraid of what I might learn. Last I heard, she was still alive, still surviving, still tending the menagerie at Shinshi. Somehow, life goes on, despite everything.

CAROL RAY APPEARED A DAY LATER. I WAS HALF ASLEEP, AND when I awoke into a world of haze she was leaning over my bed, lipstick smiling. Her floral perfume was sharp against the antiseptic neutral of the hospital. Anci stepped out quietly into the hallway. This time, she didn't offer to shake Carol Ray's hand.

"Hey, Slim."

It took me a moment longer to shake off the pain meds and prop myself slowly onto my elbows. A wall of cops filled my open door with their backs. Carol Ray had come with company.

"I insisted they bring me, before . . ."

"Before you're whisked away," I said.

"Shit has hit the fan in full, darlin'," she said, and chuckled. "Time to make a bow, kiss a few asses, and race for the sun."

"Guess it is," I returned. "Ask you something?"

"Why not?"

"Why the hell'd you get involved with this evil bullshit in the first place?"

"Boredom," she returned.

I raised my eyebrows in surprise. Carol Ray laughed a sad little laugh.

"I'm too old for bullshit, sugar. The self-deceptive kind most of all."

"Cut the shit," I said. "No one ever gets too old for that."

"I guess."

"So it was thrills. And I'm guessing something in the neighborhood of revenge."

She nodded. "Something like that. Remember when I told you about stumbling into that coke buy gone bad? Well, I didn't talk the guy holding the gun on me into letting me out. I talked him into letting me *in*. As soon as I touched down, I started collecting evidence on the whole operation. Guns, blow, booze, and theft. You name it."

"Freelance? That was pretty risky."

"Oh, from time to time I questioned my sanity, sugar. I won't deny it. But these are bad men, and someone needed to do something about them."

"But then they got into blood sport."

"J.T. and his brothers were into it from way back. They'd given it up, but Dennis grabbed the idea and ran with it. He talked me into getting Leonard Black to let us use the mine. They wouldn't tell me for what, and when I tried to make them tell me, they threatened to kill me. Twice."

"Reach was the front man?"

"He supplied the face. Least he was supposed to. But Dennis was chicken shit, so when the Dragons muscled in on his trade he brought in Sheldon and that boy of his." She shuddered. "I knew at five hundred yards they were going to be chaos and mayhem, but Dennis wouldn't listen."

"I don't guess he could have told the Dragons to butt out?"

"The White Dragons own dogfighting in southern Illinois, Slim. It's their territory. So it was either bring them in on the front end or deal with their bullshit later. That was Dennis's idea, too. No surprise."

"Fair enough. So what now?"

"I don't know, but I don't think I'm done going after bad men," she said. "I don't like assholes and I don't like liars. I don't like people who abuse the helpless. That's what made me go to the Feds, when I found out what they were really doing down there. I just couldn't take it. I still can't. So maybe I'll go into business for myself, see about putting a few more losers on notice."

I raised my eyebrows.

"Competition for me?"

She leaned over my bed. She smelled like strawberry soda and cigarettes.

"Not for you, trouble," she said. "My days in Little Egypt are done. For now, anyway. But maybe I'll see you in the funny pages."

"Or the obits."

"Hope not."

She kissed me on the cheek, and she was gone.

OH, AND ABOUT THAT RED DOG. JEEP ENDED UP COTTONING to her. And she to him. She liked me good enough, but she loved Jeep. She lives with him and Opal now. They're all in love. Not every ending is a sad one.

THE BLACK GAMES PACKED UP AND LEFT TOWN. WHEN I asked Carter to where, he only smiled mysteriously and patted me fondly on the shoulder. I really was beginning to like the sonofabitch, so I told him to get the fuck out of my room. At least the web broadcast was interrupted, if only temporarily. My lawyer made a fairly quick recovery, considering his wounds. Last I heard, he was heading south again for a final showdown with the Scientologist who'd run away with his wife.

Two weeks after my release, a pair of hikers stumbled upon the bodies of J.T. Black and Mandy in a shallow grave near the Little Grassy. Without a suspect in hand, the investigation remains open.

★ ★ ★

"So what's next?" Anci.

"What's next? How about a long stay in Bedlam? Or a vacation."

Anci snorted. "Vacation? I can just see it. You'd go crazy inside of three hours at some fancy resort. Besides, dead bodies follow you like Jessica Fletcher."

"Thanks."

She gave me a hug.

"I'm glad you're home, stupid."

"Me, too. You finished your paper."

She picked it up off the sofa. She'd written an essay about *The Hound of the Baskervilles*.

"Yeah."

"And what'd you think?"

"It was okay," she said. "In the end, anyway. I still think Holmes is full of crap, though, and the hound doesn't seem nearly so scary as the real thing."

"Amen to that, anyway."

"Uh-huh," she said. She flopped down in the light and opened her new book, Vachss's *Hard Candy*.

"Anci?"

She didn't look up. "Yeah?"

"Anci, for God's sake, don't take that one with you to school."

OTHER MATTERS NEEDED CLOSING. I TOOK A COUPLE OF weeks time to heal, time to think about everything that had happened, everything that had almost happened. I didn't expect him to answer my call, but he did, and on a hot night in July I once again found myself standing behind the hulking form of Bran-Wichelle Industrial, surrounded this time by a host of armed men. When Tibbs appeared, he seemed to have aged. Touches of gray frost spread at his temples, and worry lines traced wide swaths around his lips. He didn't look the least bit happy to see me.

"You got what you wanted," was what he said. He used his prosthetic hand to smooth down his hair, an anxious gesture, I realized.

I shrugged. "I got tortured and beaten up. I got shot. I got dog bit more times than I can count. I nearly died. A lot of other people didn't get the *nearly*."

"And we lost three million dollars of our money."

"Three point five. In Uncle Sam's pockets."

"Yes."

"Small carrots, I guess."

A thin smile broke his face, but there wasn't anything in it but rue.

"The days are changing. The black socialist boosted our recruitment somewhat, but . . ."

"But all good things."

"Something like that," he said. "You didn't come here to chat."

"No, I did not. Came to gloat."

He stared at me. The armed men shuffled, suddenly on edge.

"To . . . gloat?"

"That's right. Your fucking stupid plan backfired. When you figured out how much money Reach's games were bringing in, you tried to take them from him, all the way. You tried to take his cut for yourself. If you'd left well enough alone, Reach might never have gotten the Cleaveses involved, everything might have been fine. As it was, Reach paid a visit to your boy Lew Mandamus and decided to grab one of Lew's dogs, the one he was using to hold a certain key bank account number."

He was a frozen statue of hate, but for a change I wasn't worried.

"*Your* bank account number, as it happens. When your pals find out that it was your personal horseshit that touched off a war between the Cleaveses and Reach, they're going to ask you to join J.T. Black in a shallow grave. If they find out you tried to use me to shut the games down when the Cleaveses started to win that war, they're going to make you take your time doing it. I'm thinking . . . blowtorches."

"It's time for you to go."

I laughed. The sound of it shot around the courtyard. I said, "All those lectures about the honor of the Dragons, the quotes from Scripture, and you're nothing but a small-time crook."

"Leave."

"Seriously, brother, three weeks from now, you're a missing person. I've got a bottle of bubbly in the fridge. I want you to know, it's for the occasion."

"Leave *now*."

I tipped my hand at him and left, escorted to the parking lot and to my truck and away.

It would happen just a few hours later. And I wondered what it would be like, Tibbs quitting the warehouse as dusk spread purple and orange across a Little Egypt sky. I wondered what he would be thinking, if he honestly thought I'd let him run, even after all that bloodshed and horror and murder. I knew he wouldn't see Jeep Mabry, hiding a quarter mile away, on his belly in the high growth. I wondered whether he'd hear the shot, or feel it, if his hand would slide away from his car's door handle as the supersonic round punched a hole through the organ that functioned as his heart.

I wondered whether he'd see the sky one last time, hear the gutter-growl of the world as it tore apart around him. I wondered if he'd know the dogs had got him, too.

A BONUS STORY ABOUT THOSE DANG CHICKENS

HARDBOILED EGGS

A Slim & Anci Ruckus

"Come again?"

"Chickens, Slim. You know? Like yardbirds."

"I know what chickens are, Foghat. I thought I'd misheard you is all."

We were at Indian Vale. My daughter, Anci, was reading a book for school and sipping one of those orange sodas. Her favorites. The chicken man, and prospective client, was my old work buddy Foghat. He didn't have an orange soda. He wasn't allowed. I was barely allowed, and I paid the bills and bought the sodas. I tell you, it was a raw deal. Other than that, it was a fine fall evening. The cool breeze sighed through the grasses and the leaves of the shingle oaks. The skies were clear and freckled with stars, and the moon was out and smiling.

Foghat wasn't smiling. He was about my age, early forties, with a long face and the disposition of a nervous house cat. He said, "All kinds of chickens, too. Got into the exotic game couple years back. Belgian d'Uccle, Araucana, Welsummer, Cochin, salmon Faverolle, cuckoo Marans, modern BB red game. You name it. Even got me some of those white Sultans brand-new. Amazing birds."

"What do you do with them all?"

"Well, they're pets, mostly. I don't know. I favor them," he said. "Course, I also sell the eggs. Folks like that these days. Exotic bird eggs. They're more flavorful than store-bought and got better nutrition."

Anci looked up from her book. She said, "You don't say?"

"Oh, yeah. There's science about it and everything."

Anci looked back at her book. She said, "Well, as long as there's science."

I said, "Okay. So you got yourself some fancy chickens. Pets and egg-layers both. What's any of it have to do with me?"

Foghat frowned a little more. Back when we'd worked together, his kip was an on-site safety inspector, so frowning was basically his job. It showed, too, I tell you what. His frowns were professional frowns. They spanked your frowns on the hiney and sent them to bed early.

He scratched his nose with one of his bony fingers. He said, "I was kind of hoping you'd get them back for me."

"You lost your chickens?"

"Manner of speaking." His throat cleared a couple times. Anci smiled a little behind her book. She knew and I knew what this was. Sometimes clients hold back the real story of a case on you. It's a little dance they do. You let them dance, because you want their wallet and the dance is part of the deal, but you always know what it is. They'll give you the sugar first, so you get to hear a little about the exciting world of exotic chickens and whatnot, and then you finally get down to the bad stuff. That's what we were doing here now with Foghat.

Finally, he said, "Another manner of speaking, they were taken from me."

"Taken? Taken by who?"

Anci said, "Whom."

"Taken by whom?" I corrected. We nodded at each other. I looked at Foghat again. "Some kind of outlaw chicken enthusiast?"

Foghat said, "No, no kind of chicken outlaw, Slim. What happened was, a couple years back, well, I got divorced again. Not another wife, understand. I mean from the same one. Me and Cheryl been hitched and unhitched three times now."

"Sounds a little rocky."

He shrugged. "Can be. Some good times mixed in, too, though, so you want to maybe give it another go. I don't know. Anyway, this time she says we're bust, for keeps. I think maybe at first I didn't believe her, but then there was another fella. So that was that. We were bust. I guess I took it kinda hard."

"Easy to do."

"Or not so easy," he said. "I got to where I was slacking at work. Just couldn't focus. Missed time I couldn't afford missing and ended up getting fired by the old man. Fell behind on my bills some. You know how it is. Eventually, I reached out to some folks for a little help. You know, financial."

"Family?"

Foghat said, "No. Ain't got no family to speak of. What I mean is loan people. Like, private loan people."

"Oh, hell."

"I know. But I was fixing to lose my house, and I guess I got desperate. Anyway, I went to a guy and ended up making a deal with the devil. You remember when we were up to that PelCo mine together?"

"Sure."

"You recall a guy back then went by the name of Bandit?"

I said, "Big Bandit or Little Bandit?"

"Little Bandit."

"Oh, hell," I said again.

Anci said, "You'd be happier it was Big Bandit?"

I nodded. "Little Bandit is bigger than Big Bandit. A lot bigger. They came from different mines, and at the one Little Bandit was littler than the other Bandit they had, I guess. That other Big Bandit must have been a damn mountain. Anyway, eventually Little Bandit and

Big Bandit ended up working the same boodle, but by that time their names were set in stone, even if they didn't make sense anymore."

Anci shook her head and said, "You guys and those damn nicknames. Need a computer to keep track of it all."

Foghat said, "Big Bandit ain't never let that go, either. He's still as mad as a wet hen over it, you'll pardon the expression."

"Well, I can see that," I said. "I mean, what if there were another Slim?"

"Two times the headaches, for starters," Anci said.

Foghat pressed on. "Anyway, that's what happened. I got in with Little Bandit and, of course, right away I fell behind. Way these guys got it rigged, you almost can't help but fall behind."

"That's kind of what it's all about."

"Hell, I know. Know it now, anyway. Know it now all personal," he said. "One night, few weeks into this thing, Little Bandit and some boys showed up at my place. Things got a little rough. No lasting scars or anything, but it weren't a dance at the VFW, I tell you that. In the end, they used me to mop my kitchen floor and then they run off with my birds. I could hardly believe it. But that's what they done. Said I'd get them back soon as I paid."

"Damnation, Foghat. I hate it for you. I do. I hate it for your birds. But I can't really get involved between you and Little Bandit, you owe him legitimate money."

"That's the thing though, Slim. I don't owe him. Not anymore. I paid him. Every penny plus interest. Took me a little while and hurt like hell, but I did it. Sold my truck. Sold off a little piece of land I'd been holding back, Dad's old hunting spot up there to Olney. Cleared the ledger. But no chickens were returned to me. Little Bandit says he's keeping them. Some kind of lesson, he says. Warning to others. Says he might . . ." He looked away suddenly at the wall. His throat got thick. "Says he might butcher them, fry 'em up in a skillet. Little butter. Tarragon. Maybe a squeeze of lemon juice."

"That's pretty specific."

"You should have seen him," Foghat said. "He enjoyed it. Watching me twist like that. Suffer. Plus, way I hear he really does know his way around a kitchen."

"Kinda unusual for a thug."

Foghat said, "Slim, I'm begging you. Maybe just run out there to his place, have a word. Way I hear tell, you got a knack for this kind of thing."

"Finding lost chickens?"

"Helping folks in need. Getting things done need doing."

Anci hopped down from the couch and closed her book with a thump. She had that look about her makes me want to climb under a bed.

She said, "He'll do it."

Foghat and I said, "He will?"

"We will, I mean. I don't like bullies and I don't like assholes, and this Bandit . . ."

I said, "Little Bandit."

Foghat said, "Big Bandit is just as sweet a little old thing as you'll ever meet."

Anci said, "I don't like bullies, and I don't like assholes or bad men run off with people's pets. And this Little Bandit sounds like all three."

Foghat smiled at her. I think there was a tear in his eye. I admit, I was kinda proud, too. It was quite a speech and this was quite a kid. Foghat seized my hand and shook it.

"Thank you. Thank you both."

"All respect to your current situation, though, we can't do it for free." I said.

Foghat showed us his frown. It was a frown to beat all frowns. He looked at the floor some. He said something I didn't quite catch.

"Well, I missed that," I said.

Anci said, "He said he thought he might pay us in eggs."

LITTLE BANDIT LIVED IN THE SPRAWLING WOODLANDS south of the Vale, off Hicks Branch near Goose Creek and the Kaskaskia Experimental Forest. You might imagine, there's not much in the way of human development out that way. Few small farms. A rural school or two and a white water tower peeking over the tree line. If nothing else, it makes for a pretty drive. We were in the truck. Lovely day like that, we'd ordinarily have taken my bike, but there were chickens to rescue maybe, and I didn't have that many little helmets at my disposal.

Along the way, Anci turned to me and said, "So . . . Luke Skywalker."

"What?"

"I said Luke Skywalker."

"I heard you," I said.

"Then why did you say what?"

I said, "Why are you asking about Luke Skywalker?"

"On account of I watched *Star Wars* for the first time the other day, and now I want to discuss it."

"I was kinda hoping we'd watch that together one day."

"Well, you've been pretty busy lately, what with playing consulting detective and all, and I just felt it was time."

"Oh."

"So this galaxy he's in."

"Uh-huh?"

"You'd say it's pretty big?"

I said, "I don't know. I guess that's the idea. It is a *galaxy*."

She nodded. "That's what I think, too. Big old galaxy with more planets than you can shake a ray gun at . . ."

"Blaster."

Anci ignored me. "Shake a ray gun at, and every kind of alien race you can think of. And yet, somehow, the bad guy is his dad?"

"That's how it goes, yeah."

"And the princess . . . the one he kisses . . . she's his sister?"

I said, "You said you watched *Star Wars*. Those other things happen in the other movies. The sister thing and the dad thing."

"I know," she said. "I watched the one, looked the others up on Wikipedia."

"That's cheating."

"How you figure?"

"Reading ahead of the next movie. It's cheating."

She said, "So someone just wrote it all up online as a cheat? That what you're saying?"

"Well . . ."

"You know what? I was reading about World War Two for history class the other night. Found out who won and everything. I reckon I might get expelled now, not having gone back to fight the Hitlers myself."

I sighed. There was some things you'd just never get across to the younger set.

I said, "Okay, fine. It's not cheating. It's a personal life choice I've made when it comes to movies. So what about Luke and Vader and Leia?"

"Kind of a coincidence, don't you think?" she said. "Them all being in one place at one time, big old galaxy like that? I guess we're just lucky Chewbacca didn't turn out to be the long-lost family dog."

"I think it's the Force brought them together, like with magic."

"You mean the midi-chlorians."

"And *that's* in the dang prequels. How much Wiki-pedia did you do?"

"I did it all." She was pleased with herself. She looked out the window, all satisfied. "I am now done with the *Star Wars*."

"No, you're not," I said. I was smarting and determined to be cussed about it. "Okay, not the Force or midi-chlorians or whatever, then. How about fate? That's a thing happens in stories. Fate brought them together."

"Like us and the chickens."

"No, not like that."

"More like it was shoddy screenwriting."

I was grumpy. Damn kids and their damn *Hunger Games* and whatever. I said, "You know, that movie was a big deal when I was a boy. People lined up around the block to see it. I lined up around the block, too. Few times, in fact. Spent eight hours in the blazing heat one summer to see the rerelease and didn't even get a ticket."

"Waited long enough, you coulda just watched it at home on your couch."

"Well, we didn't have that then. Home movies, I mean. We had couches. And where the heck did you get a copy, anyway? We don't own one."

"Found one on the Internet," she said.

"Found one or swiped one?"

She looked at me. I looked at her. She leaned forward and turned on the radio and that was the last we talked about the *Star Wars* for a while.

FINALLY, WE ARRIVED AT LITTLE BANDIT'S PLACE. WAY it was, you had to leave the main road and trace a gravel path up a gentle slope and into the woods where the green ash were as big as hot-air balloons and the reed grass had put on its golden spikelets and now looked like nothing so much as a gathering of foreign kings. There weren't any chickens in evidence.

I stopped the truck and got out and said, "Wait here with your phone, will you? I don't think Little Bandit will want any trouble over this thing, but there's no reason for you to go up there just yet."

Anci seemed skeptical. Truth was, I was skeptical, too. Wanting trouble and getting trouble were two different things. She knew it and I knew it. But finally she nodded and said, "Fair enough. Try not to get your thumb pecked, though. Chickens can be pretty mean, you get in their way."

"Okay."

"And you'll get in their way."

"Unkind."

"And try not to get into a fight."

"I'll try."

"Text me the poopy emoticon, you get into a jam."

I said, "Do I have that one?"

"Just watch yourself, man."

I promised to watch myself. I promised to text the poopy emoticon. I closed the door and climbed the rest of the drive on foot and walked up to the house. It was a modest little frame house, probably built in the 1920s, painted white but dulled some by time and patches of moss from the encroaching woodland. There was a pot-bellied stove rusting in the yard. The door of the stove was open and a cat curled up inside asleep. There was a brown El Camino in the drive, but it was on blocks and it was the only vehicle in sight, so I thanked the midi-chlorians and walked around back of the house hoping to steal some chickens all easylike.

The back property was more woodland, spotted with young persimmon trees and sloping further upward until maybe two hundred yards on it was braced by a hogback of red sandstone. But no chickens or chicken houses. Not even a feather. I went to the back door and took out my tools but you could tell just by looking I wasn't going to need them. I hesitated a moment. This was getting into a whole other thing here. Breaking and entering. Plus, there might be someone inside. It didn't look like there was, but you never knew. Regardless, I'd promised to get those birds, and Anci wanted to try the eggs. Truth was, I wanted them too. They had nutrition and there was science to back it up. I stole myself for the rough work ahead. I pushed gently against the knob with one hand and the bolt pressed against its strike plate and loosed its screws from rotten wood. The door receded with a sigh. I went inside and closed the door behind me and my eyes began to adjust to the dimmer light. When they did, I froze and my mouth dropped open and I think I might have even said a bad word.

The kitchen was gorgeous. The stove probably cost more than my car; it was one of those restaurant-grade things, with eight burner-things and the separate warmer pad and a ventilation hood the size of a coffin. The counters were poured concrete, and a steel-frame island was topped with what must have been a half ton of butcher block and a brace of professional-looking knives. What at first I took to be an oddly placed gun cabinet instead held maybe two dozen glass jars filled with dried spices and a mad scientist's collection of salts and seasonings.

"Day-yum."

I turned. Anci, of course, standing in the doorway and gawking like I was gawking.

I said, "Dang it all, I told you to wait in the car."

"You ran off without your phone, genius," she said. I had. She handed it to me and lifted her nose toward the room. "This is quite a sight. How come our kitchen isn't this nice?"

"How come our anything isn't this nice?" I said. "Besides, I wouldn't have any idea what to do with half of this stuff. This thing, for instance."

"Ravioli maker," Anci said.

"Really?"

"There's a bread maker over there, too. But more to the point, I think I hear chickens."

I did, too. A muffled clucking, somewhere near-by. We walked through the rest of the house—which looked more like a regular house—and to a doorway beneath a set of stairs leading upward to what I took to be a small loft. We opened the door and walked down some steps into a cellar where Foghat's chickens were clucking away inside their cages: Belgian d'Uccle, Araucana, Welsummer, Cochin, salmon Faverolle, cuckoo Marans, modern BB red game. You name it. Even some of them white Sultans. Their feathers were all colors, or else they were spotted or striped, and sometimes they were both. They were kind of beautiful, I'll be honest.

Anci said, "You think this is them?"

"Funny," I said. "Let's get them and get out of here before the chef comes home."

East wall, there were double cellar doors such that you could walk up and out onto that side of the property, you wanted, but when we tried them they were locked from the other side.

"Guess we'll have to carry them through the house," I said.

"Everything has to be the hard way," Anci said.

I brought down a cage from the top of the stack. Best to get started. A brilliant green bird looked at me with those dark eyes that are so much like a doll's eyes.

"Don't worry, little lady," I said. "I'm going to get you out of here."

A voice said, "That's a rooster, dumbshit."

And with that, a shadow draped itself over the room.

It was like the light bulb had sparked out and the little cellar windows had blinked their lids.

Behind me, Anci's voice was impressed. "That's no moon. It's a space station," she said.

I turned and looked. It wasn't a space station. It wasn't even a moon. It was bigger than that.

It was Little Bandit.

HE SAID, "WELL, WELL, LOOKS LIKE WE GOT US A COUple chicken thieves here."

I tell you, this was a glacier of a man. He was so wide he filled the cellar door stop to stop and so tall he had to tilt his neck slightly to avoid notching his clean-shaved head on the top of the frame. His eyes were too small for his face and his mouth and lips too wide for it, like they couldn't figure out how to manage that enormous head. His arms and hands looked like two industrial Shop-Vac hoses were trying, unsuccessfully, to suck up a pair of giant uncooked hams.

I reached back and pressed Anci a little further behind me. I was cussing myself for bringing her along and I was cussing myself again for forgetting my phone in the truck. I was cussing myself for taking this ridiculous job in the first place, and cussing chickens and other birds of all kinds everywhere and at any altitude. Mostly, though, I was cussing Little Bandit.

I said, "I was about to say the same thing. Except there's just one of you."

"How do you figure?"

"Figure the first thing or figure the second thing?"

"The first one."

I said, "Well, you did take them, didn't you?"

Little Bandit shrugged.

I said, "Took them and refused to return them, once the terms of your agreement with Foghat were met?"

Little Bandit shrugged.

I said, "That true? 'Cause if it's not—if Foghat still owes you, I mean—we will walk out of here right now without fuss."

Little Bandit said, "It's true. As far as you walking out of here, though, that is another story entirely. Foghat eventually gave me what he owed me, sure, but he made me work double for it. Had to chase him, on the phone, on the computer, on foot. Even had to hire out a little help."

"Yeah, we heard some about that, too," I said. "Goons aren't cheap these days, are they?"

He took that with another shrug. "Cousins of mine, actually. Plus one buddy of the cousins. Nice fella. Lost his job recently and needed some work."

"I don't care."

He said, "So, yeah, I got my money, but I got it and I'm not too happy, you understand? Usually, I get paid back with a little cinnamon sprinkled on top, I'm happy. But the way this thing went down, way Foghat made me wait and work and sweat, I ain't exactly throwing a party. So I decided to keep his birds. Teach him a little lesson. Plus maybe the next guy hears the word and doesn't make me sweat so much."

"Tell you what," I said. "Let me take this kid out of here, drive her home, then I'll come back and you and I can talk some more or dance or whatever it is you want to do."

Anci said, "Over my dead body."

"Hush."

Little Bandit said, "Sorry, Slim. Like to help you. Really would. But you pretty much fucked the monkey coming out here like this, breaking into my house, and trying to make off with my things."

"That last business is still under dispute."

He nodded. "Okay, you can have that one. That last one. The other things, though, there ain't no dispute about it. Unless you just somehow materialized down here in my basement."

Anci said, "Could have been the midi-chlorians."

"I don't exactly follow that," said Little Bandit. "Though having that business thrown in my face don't make this any more pleasant. The midi-chlorians. They damn near ruined the franchise with that nonsense."

"That's how I feel about it," Anci said.

"What was the matter with just the Force?" said Little Bandit. He threw up his hands. "It was a perfectly elegant explanation for the universe's supernatural cosmology. I just don't get it."

Anci shook her head. "Shoddy screenwriting."

Little Bandit looked at Anci. Anci looked at Little

Bandit. Both of them nodded. Agreement had been reached.

"Little miss," he said, "I like you. Like your handle on things. Might even like to get your thoughts on the expanded universe one day, this latest movie. But right now I got to take care of business with your dad. You ain't got nothing to worry about. I'd never hurt a kid, and I ain't even gonna hurt your daddy too bad. Just shove him around a little, put a foot up his ass to teach him a lesson about sticking his nose in."

"We could call the police," Anci said.

Little Bandit nodded. "Could at that. Can't even say I'd blame you, really. Course, it'll take them an hour or more to get out here, and once they do I'll just have you arrested for breaking in. Man's got a right to protect his home, disputed chickens or no."

I said, "That's the way it is, let's stop talking and start punching."

Little Bandit came down the stairs. He came down like a locomotive. Anci leapt out of the way and hugged the wall. The chickens clucked in alarm. Somewhere, a bolt of lightning knocked a bald eagle out of the sky.

For a big man, Little Bandit was surprisingly fast. He came in low and grabbed me around the waist and tossed me backward hard and to the ground. I rolled out of the way of the aforementioned foot-in-ass and sprang upright just as one of those giant paws of his cut the air mere inches from my head. I rolled left, stopped, and pivoted back into him with the full force of my elbow, but

I might as well have been trying to knock down a school-house. He grinned and thumbed a loop of blood from the end of his nose and came in again, circling right this time. I circled left, put my right foot back, and assumed the fighting stance. Then we stopped, the both of us.

Anci had stepped between us with her phone to her ear.

Little Bandit said, "Little miss, please."

I said, "Darlin', get out of the way."

Anci ignored us. She was making a call.

Little Bandit looked at me. He said, "She's calling the cops. I told you what'll happen."

Anci shook her head. She said, "Not the cops. Animal Control and the Illinois Department of Public Health."

"Come again?"

"You got yourself a mess of exotic animals stored down here in your basement without any of the proper permits, inspection stamps, or immunization records."

Little Bandit looked at me, confused.

"What the hell she talking about, Slim?"

"She's talking about these just aren't regular yard-birds. You can't just keep them in your private residence like this without the proper paperwork and an inspector's okay."

Anci looked up. "Time the IDPH and the Animal Control people climb out of your asshole, you'll wish I'd just called the cops. You'll wish I'd called the cops, SWAT, and the dang Avengers."

Little Bandit took a step back. He raised his hands and opened his palms and showed us his lifeline. "Okay, okay. I don't want any truck with any of that."

Anci said, "That's assuming they crawl out of your asshole in the first place. They might want to quarantine your entire property, keep you under observation for a week or two. Maybe longer. Maybe a lot longer. Never know what kind of germs these birds are carrying around. You heard about this business in China? It's horrible."

Little Bandit had started to sweat now. His upper lip winked at us from across the room. He said, "I'm sure Foghat had all that looked after."

"Foghat? The guy who's divorced the same woman three times? The guy who made you sweat and dance and work for your lousy vig? The guy who had to sell his truck to pay you off? That Foghat?"

Little Bandit was practically quaking now. His eyes went this way and that. His tongue came out of his mouth with a dry sound.

Anci said into her phone, "Oh, hey, Janet. It's me, Anci . . ."

Little Bandit looked at me. He croaked, "She knows the Department of Health people?"

"Oh, Anci knows everybody."

Little Bandit lurched forward and snatched the phone from Anci's hand. He said, "Sorry, Janet," into the mic and used his big thumb to cancel the call. He handed Anci back the cell with an apologetic face.

"Guess what?"

"Chicken butt."

He ignored Anci. "Guess what? I've changed my mind about this whole thing. Got an idea. Why don't y'all take those birds and move on along? Right now. This instant. Hell, I'll even help you load them up, you give me a minute to tie something over my mouth."

Anci thought about it a little. She appeared dubious at first, but then she warmed some to the idea. Finally, she nodded seriously and said, "Well . . . okay. I guess that's okay. I was you, I'd still see a doctor, though, quick as you can."

"Thanks. I will. Frankly, though, I just want them and their germs out of here. And you. Both of you. No offense."

"None taken," she said. She smiled suddenly. "Hey, by the way, that is one hell of a damn kitchen you got up there."

'NOTHER LITTLE WHILE, WE WERE ON OUR WAY BACK north past the Experimental Forest and the long curve of Goose Creek. The light had gone down and the day had gone cool. The chickens were in their cages in the bed of the truck, neatly secured under a new tarp, courtesy of Little Bandit. Anci had phoned Foghat, who was one his way from Olney to meet us, recover his pets.

After a while, I said, "Can't say I'm precisely happy about what happened back there, but I have to admit, you did good, kiddo."

"Well, I just figured someone needed to rescue us."

"I think I could have taken him, darlin'."

"Uh-huh," she said. "Hey, why do you keep making that face?"

"What face? What do you mean?"

"Face like you swallowed a mouse. You're hurting and I can tell. What is it? I didn't think Little Bandit laid much of a glove on you."

"He didn't," I said. "It's just . . ."

"Just what?"

I said, "It's just, while we were loading up the birds, one of them pecked me pretty good on the thumb. Through its cage. Salmon Faverolle, I think it was. Real sassy little bastard."

Anci stared at me.

I said, "Hey, it hurts."

Anci stared at me.

"Bled a little, even. Might have to have it cut off maybe. Amputated. You never know. I reckon I should get us to an emergency room."

Anci stopped staring at me. She shook her head. She reached forward and switched on the radio.

ACKNOWLEDGMENTS

Special thanks are owed to a bunch of folks who helped me see this book through to completion. As ever, much gratitude and love to my agents, Anthony Mattero and Yfat Gendell. Eric Meyers is a dream editor, and his guidance on the manuscript was just invaluable. Thanks also to my friends and early readers Julie Kedzie, Steve Huff, Jeff Zentner, and Keith Buckley. You people are damn good people.

And finally, but mostly and continuously, to Laura.

ABOUT THE AUTHOR

JASON MILLER is the author of the Slim in Little Egypt mystery series. A much-followed comic voice on Twitter, Jason (@longwall26) has had tweets featured on national talk shows such as *The Ellen DeGeneres Show*, and he has been named among the funniest people on Twitter by *Playboy*, *BuzzFeed*, and the *Chicago Tribune*, among others. A RiffTrax contributor, Jason has had his jokes heard in movie theaters throughout the United States and Canada. He lives in Nashville, Tennessee.

ALSO BY JASON MILLER
DOWN DON'T BOTHER ME
A NOVEL

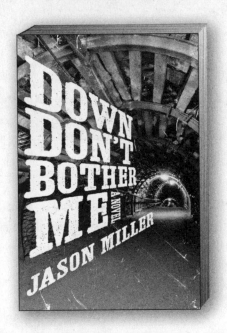

Read the first book in the
Slim in Little Egypt mystery series

"Long stretches of this unusual first novel would seem to require guitar
accompaniment. The genre conventions—treacherous women, double-crossing
friends, greedy moneymen—seem fresh in Miller's sensory-rich language....
Here's a strong talent just getting under way." —*Booklist*